Sleep No More

By Guy Hale

Act IV in the
Shakespeare Murders series

"Sleep no more! Macbeth does murder sleep."
(Macbeth: Act I, Scene II)

A Bullington Press publication
Copyright © Guy Hale, 2025

ISBN 978-1-0683633-8-2 (paperback)
ISBN 978-1-0683633-9-9 (e-book)

For permission requests, please email: info@bullingtonpress.co.uk

Interior layout by Textual Eyes
Design for Print Services

Cover by Peter Adlington

Printed and bound by CPI Group (UK) Ltd, Croydon, CR0 4YY

www.bullingtonpress.co.uk

Praise for the Shakespeare Murders series

Absolutely superb. I loved the darkness of it.
Chris Lloyd (winner of the HWA Gold Crown)

Deeply satisfying, great writing. A dark tale and a cracking read.
David Penny (author of The Thomas Berrington Historical Mysteries)

Dark, twisted and hilarious. Hale's characters are so well drawn. A brilliant read. Get thee to a bookshop.
Heather Critchlow (author of the Cal Lovett Series)

Superb writing, a masterpiece. Crime, Shakespeare and humour. What more could you ask from a book?
Aimee Louise (@whataimeereads_)

This was a book I fell in love with from the opening pages and was totally hooked right up to the unexpected ending. Can't wait for the next in this highly original series.
Andy Wormald (@amwbooks)

Wildly entertaining, darkly funny. Hamlet as you've never seen it. Had me gripped and gasping. Outstanding!
Rob Parker (author of the Thirty Miles Trilogy)

Dexter meets Shakespeare in this dark and twisted tale of revenge.
Christie J. Newport (Joffe Books prize winner)

Masterful plotting, a dark and funny take on Hamlet.
Blair Kessler (The Birmingham Film Company)

I loved this book. Very atmospheric. This Hamlet is extremely good but also very bad!
Imran Mahmood (author of I Know What I Saw)

Fresh, funny and fiendishly clever. The Croaking Raven is an absolute triumph!
A.A. Chaudhuri (Amazon bestselling author)

By Guy Hale

The Comeback Trail Trilogy

Killing Me Softly
Blood on the Tracks
All the World's a Stage

The Shakespeare Murders

The Croaking Raven
All Our Yesterdays
Put Out The Light
Sleep No More

This book is dedicated to the memory of my best friend, Clinton King. We surfed the waves and rode the roads, and life will never be as good again without you.

Chapter 1
Then Fall, Caesar

Felix Richards sat motionless, rooted to his seat. Before him on the stage lay Sir Morris Oxford; like a giant felled oak, its majesty lost.

The stage was raked. Two rivulets of blood ran down its slope towards him; he watched in horrified fascination. It was the blood of someone he had once considered a friend; it seemed inconceivable that this scene had been partly his doing. The two daggers that Oliver Lawrence had tampered with were mixed in with the others, strewn across the stage. The blades had failed to retract and the stabbing of Caesar had been real.

Sir Morris had stopped moaning now. He was lying between two doctors from the audience that were fighting desperately to save him. His skin had taken on a deathly pallor. The rivulets of blood had worked their way to the edge of the stage and now began to pool at Felix's feet, as though Sir Morris was pointing accusing fingers at him. Was this finally the end; would Oliver now be satisfied?

He didn't know, but for Felix the mission had reached its conclusion. How much blood could one man bathe in before it drowned his soul, destroyed his mind? He was done. He turned and hurried away from the awful tableau.

Caesar lay upon the steps of the Senate, his life force flowing like the River Styx. Charon, the ferryman, would be waiting to carry his soul to Hades, and he was certain that he and Oliver would be joining him there before too long.

Outside the theatre there was total chaos. Shocked audience members were milling around, chatting, crying, disbelief etched across their faces:

'A terrible accident … right in front of me!'
'There must have been a mix-up with the props.'
'Sir Morris was bleeding, howling – how could this happen?'

Felix knew. Oliver had doctored two of the knives so they wouldn't retract; it wouldn't take long for the police to work out that this was no accident. He needed to get away from the theatre. As he walked down the steps onto Waterside, two ambulances came screaming towards him, sirens blazing. Sir Morris was a big chap, but two ambulances? That was overkill.

Back inside the theatre, Fred, Toby and Whomper stood behind the doctors as they fought to stem the bleeding. Sir Morris had become very pale and his skin looked like wax. Fred followed the twin trickles of blood that ran down the stage and fell like a waterfall of death to the front of the stalls. No man could lose this much blood and survive.

Fred felt a nudge in his side. He turned and Whomper leaned in close to whisper.

'He's going to live.'

'What makes you think that?'

'The bleeding's stopped.'

'Maybe he's empty.'

Whomper shook his head. 'Look at the size of the container. There's plenty more left in that particular tank.'

Fred and Toby looked at the corpulent form lying on the stage before them.

'Whomper's not wrong, boss,' said Toby. 'That would take a lot of filling.'

One of the doctors tutted. 'Do you think you could keep your clinical observations to yourselves. We are trying to save a life here.'

'And, in our opinion, you are succeeding,' said Whomper.

'Yes, keep up the good work,' added Toby encouragingly.

The second doctor glared at them. 'What are you halfwits doing on the stage?'

'We're the police,' said Fred, using as much *gravitas* as he could muster.

The first doctor looked at his colleague and shook his head. 'Great job stopping the stabbing.'

'How were we to know? It's in the bloody script!'

Toby put a hand on Fred's shoulder and gently drew him away from the scene.

'Maybe it's best if we leave them to get on with trying to save Sir Morris.'

Fred nodded. 'Probably for the best. One more comment like that and he'd have been the one needing medical attention.'

The three of them edged silently from the stage and backed slowly from the auditorium, nodding to the doctors as they went like a group of retreating butlers from their master's study.

Once they were out in the foyer, Toby broke the silence. 'Why didn't we see that coming?'

'Don't blame yourself, Toby. How did the RSC allow someone to get in and tamper with the props … That's the question you should be asking.'

Toby nodded. 'I need to find Big Al Morris.'

Without deferring to Fred, Toby turned and headed out of the theatre, making his way towards stage door.

'He's taking this bad,' said Whomper.

Fred raised an eyebrow. 'Not as badly as Sir Morris.'

Chapter 2
Brutus Makes Tea

As Felix made his way down the river path to Holy Trinity, the sound of the chaos that reverberated around the theatre receded. It felt like walking away from madness. He could hear it in the distance but it no longer possessed him; neither did Sir Morris. A calm slowly descended as he walked through the graveyard. It was over. With the death of Sir Morris, it had to be. Didn't it?

When he reached the house on Trinity Street the door was on the latch. He pushed it open, entered and locked it behind him.

Oliver had wasted no time. He moved around the kitchen cheerfully. 'Well, that went better than I expected.' He offered Felix the biscuit tin. 'Some of your favourites in there.'

Felix opened it and took two. He bit into the first one without speaking. It felt familiar, reassuring. As he munched he stared at Oliver, which seemed to amuse him.

'Watching the old boy flap about given you an appetite?'

Felix nodded and shoved the other half of the biscuit into his mouth, preventing any reply.

Oliver reached into the cupboard, pulled out another pack and put them next to the tin. 'Just in case one packet isn't enough.' He laughed and turned back to making the tea.

It took five biscuits before Felix had clarified his thoughts. By this time there was a mug of tea steaming beside him on the table. He took a sip and looked up at Oliver. 'Is that it then, are we done?'

'Not sure.'

'But you've got him. What else is there?'

Oliver looked doubtful. 'We don't actually know if Sir Morris is dead, do we?'

'He looked pretty close to it when I left.' Felix stared at the strawberry jam filling the Jammie Dodger he was holding. 'I didn't realise how much blood was inside a body. It ran down the stage and over the edge. A person can't lose that much blood and survive, can they?'

'Morris isn't a normal human being though, is he. He has an ego the size of a small English county. That on its own should guarantee another couple of hours before the blood loss takes him.'

Felix said nothing.

'What's on your mind,' asked Oliver.

'Wiltshire. I was thinking about Wiltshire.'

'I think you'll find that's a large English county, that's why the army drive their tanks all over it.'

Felix nodded. 'Bad example. Let's assume he's going to die, what then? Are we done?'

Oliver shrugged. 'If it is fatal, we may be. Just depends. There are loose ends to attend to.'

'Such as?'

Oliver leaned back in his chair. 'Well, Clarissa Pidgeon for starters. Let's not forget I accidentally strangled Chief Wilson's wife in her place.'

'How could I forget,' sighed Felix.

'That was Clarissa's fault. If she wasn't bisexual it would never have happened.'

'Maybe if you hadn't tried to strangle her it would never have happened,' snapped Felix.

'Let's not play the blame game, dead is dead. Clarissa's immoral behaviour caused the problem. I am blameless in this unfortunate incident.'

Oliver's rationale was not that of a sane individual, and yet there was a weird logic to it. The death of poor Heather Wilson was an unfortunate case of wrong lesbian in the right place. They weren't to know that Clarissa swung both ways, or that the naked form lying before them in that darkened room, her face covered with the strawberry-patterned handkerchief, was not the victim they sought.

'You still want to kill Clarissa then, even after Sir Morris is dead?'

Oliver considered this for a moment. 'It's a question of unfinished business. I can't envisage a future where I have to share the same stage as her. She is bound to botch a scene and leave me regretting not having killed her. I want a completely fresh start, clear the slate.'

Felix couldn't believe that Oliver still thought a return to the stage at Stratford was possible. 'Let's assume Sir Morris dies and you kill Clarissa, will that be it?'

Oliver grinned. 'My, my, Felix, you sound like you're not enjoying this.'

'I'm not. Maybe to start with but it's become—'

'Real?'

'Nasty. Vindictive.'

Oliver shrugged. 'Collateral damage. I wanted revenge but then I thought of all the other hangers-on that fed off the monster. When I cut his head off, I don't want them attaching themselves to me. I want them gone.'

'You didn't answer my question.'

'No, Felix. I didn't, did I.' Oliver was silent for a moment and then, without looking up, whispered, 'It may be time to kill my mother!'

Chapter 3
Hanging By A Thread

'Can't help thinking we should have seen that coming,' said Fred. 'A whole bunch of people queuing up to stab Sir Morris and we never even considered it.'

'Maybe, but who'd have thought he would be able to get in there and tamper with the knives,' said Toby.

'Who said they were tampered with? It could have been a malfunction.'

'In one knife, maybe, but not in two. We'll soon know, SOCO are going over the scene now.'

'OK, we need to interview Caesar's assassins. Who drew the short straws?'

Toby looked at his notes and winced. 'Theo Cumberbatch and ...'

Fred sighed. 'Spit it out, Toby.'

'Hugh Pitt.'

'*The* Hugh Pitt?'

'The very same.'

'I'd heard he was coming back this season but what the hell was he doing mixed up in that stab-fest?'

'I don't know, boss. Given their history, and the fact he wasn't even supposed to be there, it's a question we'll have to ask.'

Fred rubbed his hands together. 'This is getting very interesting. I've never thrown a Hollywood star down the stairs before.'

'First time for everything, boss.'

'Have either of them been brought in yet?'

'I'm not sure but I'll check. Who would you want first?'

'Who do you think?' said Fred, a wide grin spreading across

his face.

Five minutes later they were sitting opposite Hugh Pitt in Interview Room One.

'This is DS Fred Williams and I'm DC Toby Marlowe. We'd like to ask you some questions.'

Hugh Pitt did not look happy. 'Questions? I'd have thought what happened was bloody obvious.'

'It is, Mr Pitt, but we still need to ascertain certain things,' said Toby.

Hugh jumped up, knocking over his chair. It crashed onto the stone floor. 'Look, do you know who I am?'

Fred smiled. 'Would you like us to call you a doctor, Mr Pitt?'

For a moment, Hugh looked confused. 'What the hell would I want a doctor for. I'm not the one who's been stabbed.'

'Well, if you don't know who you are, sir, maybe you need a doctor.'

Toby suppressed a smile; Hugh didn't have to try.

'Look here, Williams. You may think you're funny but you're not. I would advise you not to mess me around or I will have my lawyers ream you a new arse.'

'That's appreciated, Mr Pitt, but it doesn't alter the fact that we would like a statement from you.'

Sensing Hugh was about to launch into another outburst, Fred pushed on. 'We can do it informally or under caution. Your choice.'

His words acted like a punch to the head; Hugh's jaw slackened. 'Are you going to charge me?'

'That's up to you, Mr Pitt. Sir Morris Oxford has been stabbed and you were brandishing one of the daggers. We need your version of events.'

'You can get lost, Williams.'

'If you won't cooperate, sir, DS Williams and I will have to assume you're trying to hide something.'

'Look here, I want my manager. Now.'

'This isn't a press interview, Mr Pitt. We can lock you up if you obstruct a police inquiry.'

Hugh folded his arms, grinding his teeth as he stewed.

Toby dropped a hand grenade under him. 'Could you explain why you were on the stage tonight when you're not even in the cast?'

Hugh's mouth opened but nothing came out. For several seconds he resembled a carp stranded on the bank of a river.

'Well?'

It was all Fred needed to say. Hugh Pitt was now well and truly off balance; his Hollywood swagger gone.

'Look, do you mind if I get my chair?' Gone was the surly bully, replaced by the charming young man he had portrayed in *Four Dates and a Christening*.

'Help yourself,' said Fred. He leaned back on his chair, looking like a bird of prey contemplating its next meal.

Hugh pulled the chair up to the desk, ran his fingers through his foppish locks and turned on his hundred-kilowatt smile. It was wasted on Fred; he preferred the shade where he could be miserable in peace.

'I think I need to clarify a few things.'

'I agree, you do.' After a short silence, Fred turned to Toby. 'Would you like to start?'

Toby nodded. 'Why were you on-stage tonight, Mr Pitt?'

Hugh laughed nervously. 'You're not going to believe this.'

'You're right,' said Fred menacingly.

Toby continued. 'Why don't you try us, Mr Pitt.'

'Call me Hugh. The mister thing's a bit formal.'

'Why not,' said Fred. 'We can be informal until we charge you.' He finished his sentence with a wink.

'It was all a bit of a jape really.'

'What, the stabbing,' said Toby.

'No, no, not that. Me being on-stage. Old Morris has never really liked me, especially since I went off to Hollywood and became a star. He's pretty miffed that I'm back in Stratford this season. Theo thought it would be a bit of fun if I played one of the Senators that stab Caesar and Sir Morris saw me as I lunged towards him.'

'And was it fun?'

Hugh shook his head sadly. 'No, DC Marlowe, it wasn't. Theo had already stabbed him and, when my turn came, he seemed in real pain. I gave him a huge grin as I stuck it into him, but if he recognised me he never showed it. I thought he was lost in the part. He looked like a man who had really been stabbed.'

'He had,' said Toby.

'I know that now.'

'Don't you find it a bit strange that the person who helped you play this little joke was also the only other person whose knife didn't retract. More than a coincidence?'

'Theo would never hurt Sir Morris.'

'You sure of that, Mr Pitt? Your actions are looking very suspect.'

'Look, I'm not a killer. Ask anyone.' There was mild panic in Hugh's voice now.

'We intend to, Mr Pitt, have no fear on that score.' Fred pushed a blank statement across the desk. 'Would you like to sign a confession now, save us all this bother?'

'No, I would not. I didn't do anything.'

'Apart from attempting to stab one of England's greatest actors to death.'

Hugh slumped in his seat, all pretence gone. 'Those knives must have been tampered with.'

'OK, let me get this straight. You left here under a cloud after falling out with Sir Morris, and now you return as a star and stab him when you shouldn't even have been on-stage. Doesn't look good, does it?'

'It wasn't like that.'

'It was exactly like that,' snapped Fred, rising from his chair. 'Mr Cumberbatch is in Interview Room Two. I suggest you have a think about your real reasons for being on that stage tonight while we have a chat with him.' He turned and headed out of the room.

Toby followed, curious to see where they were headed. There was only one interview room in Guild Street Police Station.

Fred made his way to the kitchen and put the kettle on. 'Fancy a cuppa?'

'Is the Pope a Catholic?'

'I believe he is.'

'You don't really think Hugh Pitt is guilty, do you, boss?'

'Course not, he was just having a bit of fun. Wanted to see the look on Morris' face when he stabbed him. If the knives hadn't been doctored it would have been quite funny.'

'If you say so, boss.'

'I do. Imagine he's on-stage, Senators all over the place. He looks up and sees an actor he sacked two years ago coming at him with a dagger.' He shook his head and laughed. 'Priceless!'

'Probably,' said Toby.

Fred nodded. 'Yeah, those boys were just unlucky.'

'Shall I get his statement and kick him free?'

'No.' Fred pulled down the biscuit tin and leaned back against the kitchen table. 'Let's leave him to stew for a bit.'

'What's the point if he's not guilty?'

'He may not be guilty of attempted murder, Toby, but he's certainly guilty of being up himself. I think a little time to contemplate the fact that being famous doesn't give you a free pass everywhere will do him good.'

Toby nodded. 'I see your point, boss, but it seems a little mean when we know he's innocent.'

'We don't actually know that though, do we? We think he's innocent but he did stab Sir Morris, can't argue with that.'

'No, don't suppose we can.'

'Kettle's boiled,' said Fred.

Toby started to make the tea as DC Ginger Dalton entered the kitchen.

'Two sugars in mine, please.'

Toby sighed and pulled down another mug.

'How would you like to do me a favour?'

'Love to, boss,' lied Ginger.

'Pop to Interview Room One and inform Mr Hollywood that the desk sergeant will be in to do his cavity search in fifteen minutes.'

'Really?'

'No, but he doesn't know that.'

Ginger chuckled. 'You're enjoying this too much, boss.'

'Tell him the sergeant is trying to find his nail clippers first. That should conjure up a nice image.'

Ginger was still laughing as he left the room.

Toby put a mug of tea down in front of his boss. 'Was that really necessary?'

Fred took a sip. 'Course not.'

'Then why do it?'

'Happiness is like a precious butterfly, young Toby. In those rare moments in life when you see one, you have to make the most of it.'

'This is making you happy?'

'Course it is! Not often you get chance to see a Hollywood film star wetting his pants. And you're going to get the best dinner party story ever. You'll be telling it for years.'

'It doesn't seem right though.'

Fred shrugged. 'Maybe not, but it's been a bad night and I

don't like him.'

'Do you think Sir Morris will make it?'

'Only time will tell, Toby. He's hanging by a thread and judging by the size of him, it'd better be a bloody strong one.'

Chapter 4
Then Fell Caesar?

Felix's journal lay open before him. Would this be the last entry, the final act in this sorry tale? He had wanted this revenge for Oliver, and for Oliver's father, Richard. Now he had succeeded the victory felt hollow. Revenge, he was discovering, was so much finer in contemplation than actuality. The fear, the pain, the blood; all of that was behind him now. He began to write.

Entry 4 The Journey's End?

If you are reading this, I am dead. The Oliver I knew is gone and our plan is complete. The deed is done. Sir Morris lies bleeding upon the bed we made for him. Has justice been served? The question is impossible to answer, there is no real justice here. Revenge, the price seems too high. I have reached a decision: whether Sir Morris lives or dies, I am finished with it. I have no stomach for further bloodshed. Clarissa and Beatrice do not deserve to die and I will not be a part of it. I will be patient, for waiting is all any of us can do now. Sir Morris' heart still beats, the great are hard to kill.

There is a cold wind blowing where once Oliver's soul did dwell. Like the Devil's apprentice, I have waited upon the whims and desires of my master for too long. The fall from a righteous quest has been lengthy and I now walk in the shadow of an evil I created.

Forgive me. I never meant it to go this far. Evil has an energy all its own, it feeds on itself and multiplies. Becomes more powerful, consumes its creator and leaves you helpless in its wake. There is a madness inside Oliver that I can no longer reach. I see it in his eyes, hear it in his voice; a bottomless pit of hatred that can never be filled. When next we meet, I will tell him I am finished. He may not let me live but I cannot stand by and allow him to kill Clarissa and Beatrice. How I will stop him, I do not know. Our roads are parting. He will take the one less travelled and that will make all the difference. Good and evil, our final destinations.

Oliver put down his pen and read his diary entry; it was a little overblown. He knew he was sometimes guilty of prose that looked like he had swallowed a thesaurus written in the 1800s, but that was his style. He was a Shakespearian actor and the past was where he thrived. He picked up his pen and began to write again.

This has been a strange journey; some moments sublime, others truly horrific. I cannot seek to justify or explain all that has taken place. When you read this try to understand that it was about so much more than it ended up being. A beautiful revenge, a rise from the ashes. Our Phoenix burned too brightly and the fire consumed us all!

Felix closed the journal and put down his pen, hoping this would not be his last entry. For now, he stowed it in the boat's secret compartment. Tomorrow, he would seal it in a heavy-duty envelope and take it to Ting Hu, the postmistress in Bull Street. A woman of multiple talents, most of them criminal, and a keeper of secrets for the right price.

Chapter 5
Waiting Game

Given the headlines, Inspector Sidney Beeching was remarkably calm. He had summoned Fred and Toby to the incident room. 'Any news on Sir Morris?'

'Yes, sir. He was critical but, apparently, they have stabilised him. Now we will just have to wait and see.'

Beeching nodded. 'The old boy is hard to kill. How the hell did Lawrence get into the theatre and tamper with those knives?'

Fred held up a report. 'SOCO reckon someone jammed in parts of a saxophone reed and glued them in place.'

'So, are we looking for a carpenter who plays jazz?'

'No, sir, I don't think we are. It's Lawrence but he's like a ghost, flitting in and out of places unseen.'

'He's an actor,' said Toby. A master of disguise. He's been trained to appear as someone he isn't. We need to be out there, stopping everyone in Stratford.'

'Be nice if we could, Toby, but we don't live in a police state. That action isn't open to us.'

'What about a curfew, sir,' asked Toby.

'That would have to come from a higher power. Curtailing civil liberties would not go down well.'

'It's better than murder,' said Fred.

Beeching nodded. 'It is. Look, I'll suggest a curfew to the higher-ups and let's see what happens. In the meantime, I suggest you focus on the theatre. He got in there somehow and tampered with the knives; someone must have seen him.'

Fred wasn't so sure. 'How do we know they weren't tampered with before they were taken to the theatre?'

It was a fair point.

'I might be able to help with that, sir.'

Beeching turned to Toby. 'How?'

'Alan Morris is in charge of the sets at the theatre. He's coming in this afternoon. Hopefully he can shed some light on it.'

Fred nodded. 'Makes sense.'

'What about our other potential victims,' asked Beeching.

'We've put a twenty-four-hour bodyguard with them. Where they go, our men go. We might not know where he is but we've secured his potential victims.'

'Good idea, Fred. Who knows, he may get desperate when he sees there is no way of getting at them.'

'I wish I believed that, sir, but Lawrence ...' Fred looked at the board filled with the faces of the dead. 'He's not like any killer I've ever come up against. He's clever, invisible. We don't even know what he really looks like.'

'I know, Fred. This case is a real career killer. At least poor old Wilson can carry the blame for now, but at some stage it's going to sit at our door.'

Fred said nothing. He didn't like Beeching. Hated the way he had subtly placed the blame for their failure to stop the killer on a dead man who could not defend himself. Beeching was a career officer; political expediency was his god. He had bought them some time but the clock was ticking.

Chapter 6
The Old Post Office

Ting Hu ran a tight ship. She had been in charge of the little Post Office in Old Town for nearly twenty years. To most it seemed like a typical small-town affair but, to those in the know, it was a place to fence stolen goods. Ting was a one-woman crime wave; beneath the calm veneer of homely efficiency beat the heart of a criminal mastermind.

Whomper pulled up outside Ting's. He needed something that couldn't be found in Woolworths, and he knew if Ting didn't have it, she would soon find it.

The bell rang as he pushed the door open. As if by magic, Ting appeared behind the counter.

'How do you do that?'

'I move in mysterious ways, Whomper. What do you want?'

'I'm after a store item.'

Ting nodded. 'Store item' was code amongst her regulars for non-Post Office business. 'Buying or selling?'

'Buying.'

Ting gave an approximation of what could have been a smile. She had never been given to overt displays of emotion in all the years he had known her.

She opened the side door and ushered him through. 'You go into the store and I will get Claude.'

Whomper nodded. Claude was Stratford's resident Frenchman. He had arrived with Ting after one of her European journeys and never gone home. They were a great team and almost impossible to categorise.

The place never failed to amaze Whomper. He walked from

the small Post Office into the back room and was greeted by a huge Aladdin's cave of stolen goods. Ting was the biggest fence in Warwickshire. Anything that didn't require a receipt and could be paid for in cash was there.

'So, what are you after, Whomper?'

'A gun.'

Ting didn't flinch. 'You plan on killing someone?'

'Only if they try to kill me first.'

'The Shakespeare Killer only goes after attractive actor types. You'll be fine.'

Whomper ignored the insult. 'I do act and many ladies have found me attractive.'

'There is a lot of mental illness around these days,' sighed Ting. 'That and poor eyesight.'

Ting's words were matter-of-fact, without malice. He didn't take offence.

'What kind do you want?'

'Something compact. A handgun I can keep in my pocket.'

'You sure you're not going to kill anyone?'

Whomper smiled. 'How long have you known me, Ting.'

'Too long.'

'Harsh. Have you ever known me be violent without provocation?'

Ting thought about it for a moment. 'Depends how you define provocation.'

This wasn't getting Whomper anywhere. 'You going to sell me a gun, or what?'

Ting shrugged. 'You got cash?'

'Of course.'

'Then you know the answer.' She moved towards the back of her warehouse. 'You want one with bullets?'

'Not much point without them,' said Whomper.

'Still work as a deterrent.'

'And what do I do if it doesn't? Shout, "bang"?'

Ting sighed. 'You could always pistol-whip them to death.'

'If I was going to do that, I'd be buying a baseball bat.'

'I've got some of those. Just got to get the blood off them first.'

'New stock?'

'Fresh in last night. You want to look?'

Whomper shook his head. 'Nah. I'll stick with the gun, thanks. I like my violence at a distance.'

Ting looked disappointedly at Whomper. 'I thought you were a bit butcher than that.'

'I used to be but I prefer my contact sports with women these days.'

Ting's face broke out in a genuine smile, a rare sight. 'You're funny, Whomper.'

'I do my best.'

Ting leaned into a shadowy corner and pulled out a handgun. 'How about this one?' She held up a pistol.

'Luger. Semi-automatic.'

'Very good, Whomper. What else do you know?'

'Holds eight bullets. This looks like a World War Two variant.'

'It is.'

'Does it work?'

Ting raised the gun. 'You want me to shoot you to find out?'

'That won't be necessary. Where did it come from?'

'You can't ask questions like that. I didn't.'

'Got any bullets?'

Ting nodded. 'Two boxes with forty-eight rounds in each. You could start a war with that.'

'And it works?'

'Course it does. I have my reputation to think about. The firing mechanism works perfectly. It's been looked after.'

'Any form of guarantee?'

'Yeah. If it doesn't work and someone kills you, you can bring it back.'

Whomper smiled. 'Seems fair. How much?'

'Twenty-five pounds.'

'That's a bit steep!' Whomper hefted the gun in his hand. 'Mind you, with two boxes of ammo I suppose it's not too bad.'

'Ammo not included,' snapped Ting.

'What's the point of a gun without ammo!'

'Not my problem. You want bullets or not?'

'Of course, how much?'

'For you, Whomper, a tenner.'

'Ten pounds!'

'Per box.'

'You drive a hard bargain, Ting. Any discount for an old customer?'

'This look like a registered charity?'

It didn't. Whomper pulled a roll of notes from his pocket. He peeled off four tenners and a fiver, which promptly disappeared into a leather pouch around her waist. 'Thanks, Ting.'

'You want it wrapped?'

'Nah, I've got plenty of room in this jacket.' He filled his pockets. 'Lovely doing business with you, Ting.'

'No problem. Just don't mention my name if you get arrested.'

'I wouldn't dream of it. I know the rules.'

Ting walked around Whomper and blocked the doorway. She looked serious. 'You sure you're not planning to kill anyone, Whomper.'

'I'm not planning to … I like to be spontaneous with my killing.' He smiled and slipped past her with a litheness that belied his size.

Ting watched him climb onto his BSA Rocket. With one thrust on the kick-starter the engine burst to life, rattling the windows.

He roared off towards the centre of town.

Claude stood beside Ting and watched him go. 'You really think he's going to kill someone?'

'Hope not, I've got a motorbike with his name on somewhere in the back.'

Claude smiled. 'You never stop, do you.'

'Capitalism never sleeps.' Ting turned and headed back inside.

The little Post Office in Old Town, where most bought stamps and posted parcels but, for those in the know, there was another world waiting for anyone with lots of cash and no conscience.

As Whomper rode down Church Street the weight of the Luger in his pocket comforted him. The dream he had last night was too vivid, the hands around his throat too strong. Insurance: that's what he needed. Even he was beginning to feel nervous. Stratford was a town on edge.

Chapter 7
Critical Condition

Lady Beatrice Oxford sat at her husband's bedside. He was barely recognisable. An oxygen mask covered his face, and tubes and wires protruded from all parts of his body. His usually ruddy cheeks were deathly pale, only the beeping of his heart monitor confirmed that he was still alive.

She had feared that it would come to this. From the moment Desmond Tharpe had been stabbed by the river she had known Oliver was back. Sins of the past always came back to haunt you.

If Morris died, would she be next? Would her own son kill her? She wouldn't blame him. She had made her choice; traded her child for fame and security. How could she ever look him in the eye and explain? If that day ever came, she couldn't foresee a way out.

The door to Sir Morris' room swung open and Fred Williams stood in the doorway. 'How is he?'

'It was touch and go,' Beatrice sighed. 'But apparently he's over the worst of it. The doctors actually think he's improving.'

'Can we talk?'

Beatrice looked sullenly at Fred Williams; she didn't like him much, but she knew she needed him. If the police didn't catch Oliver soon … She let the thought die; there was nothing to be gained from going down that route. She gestured towards a chair. 'We can talk here if you're quiet.'

Fred nodded. 'Of course.' He pulled up the chair and sat down next to her. 'Oliver nearly pulled it off.'

Beatrice nodded. 'Yes, he's clever. Who'd have thought? Alan Morris will be beside himself.'

'You don't think it's his fault, do you,' said Fred.

'No. Alan wouldn't have missed that. He checks everything. Oliver must have crept into the theatre and doctored the knives himself.'

'You think it's him, then?'

'It's him. I wouldn't be surprised if he was in the audience watching. This is just a play to him, he's lost touch with reality. He's a monster.'

Fred nodded slowly. 'You agree with us.'

'Hard not to, given the evidence.' Beatrice seemed calm; resigned to her fate.

'An officer will be with you twenty-four hours a day, Lady Oxford. Oliver won't be able to get to you. And there's one stationed just outside this room to protect Sir Morris.'

'What's the point? Oliver will wait for as long as it takes. He wants all of us dead and Morris and I are the last two.'

'He wouldn't kill his own mother, would he?'

Beatrice looked sadly at Fred. 'The truth is, I wasn't much of a mother. Not when he needed it. I made my choice and it wasn't him. I'm reaping the whirlwind that I sowed, sergeant.'

Fred put his hand on her knee. 'You don't know that. He's been away for a long time, anything could have caused it.'

Beatrice smiled. 'Nice of you to say so but I think we both know better. People don't commit mass murder if there isn't a motive. We didn't treat Oliver well and now he wants to make us pay. Look what he's done … Can you imagine what's going on inside his head? I think I have to take some responsibility for that.'

This was not the Beatrice Oxford Fred had dealt with before. There was a sadness, a resignation. An acceptance that she was no longer in control of her destiny.

'We will catch him, I promise you.'

Beatrice scoffed. 'You don't even know what he looks like, sergeant. How will you do that?'

'I don't really know, if I'm honest, but we won't give up. The odds are stacked against him. If you and Sir Morris are indeed his last intended victims, how is he going to pull it off? We've given you twenty-four-hour protection. He'll have to go through us to get at you.'

'You think he won't?'

'Well, he hasn't killed anyone outside of the RSC, has he,' said Fred.

'What about Chief Wilson's wife?'

'That was mistaken identity. She was just unlucky.'

Beatrice sighed. 'I think you're fooling yourself, sergeant. Oliver will stop at nothing to finish the job ... and anyone who gets in the way will be fair game. My son is mad. Any sense of reason has long gone.'

Fred had never seen someone so defeated. 'We will catch him, Lady Oxford.'

She smiled weakly. 'I'm sure you will, sergeant, but it won't come in time for me. My life was about to change. I've been offered the part of my dreams, so I was finally coming back to the stage after all these years.'

'You still could,' suggested Fred, with a lightness he didn't feel.

'No,' she waved her hand towards Sir Morris' inert form. 'My dream has ended there. He's not a young man. If he lives, I will be his carer. He can never return to the theatre with those injuries. And I could never be so cruel as to leave him behind, make him watch me rebuild my career while he is robbed of his. If Oliver only knew how sweet and complete his revenge has become. In failing to kill Sir Morris he has put an end to both of us.'

Fred excused himself; there was nothing he could say to that. Beatrice Oxford seemed broken, crushed more by the fact that her return to the theatre had been thwarted than the plight of her wounded husband.

Stress does peculiar things to people and, right here in this moment, Fred felt something for Beatrice Oxford he had never thought he would: pity.

Chapter 8
The Witches' Promise

Toby jumped as the phone on his desk rang. He had been miles away; lost in the twists and turns the terrible summer had taken. The streets and parks of Stratford now resembled a charnel house, with the town becoming the playground of a killer who always seemed to be one step ahead of them.

'DC Marlowe.'

'Toby, it's Whomper. We need to speak.'

'We are speaking.'

'Face to face. I've got something you need to see. Can you come to my house in Shottery?'

'You have a house in Shottery? That's a bit up-market for you, isn't it.'

'I could take offence at that, Toby. I inherited it from my uncle. It's detached and has a big garage where I keep my motorbikes.'

'So why do you need to see me?'

'I had a dream last night and my sisters were there.'

'That's weird.'

'Not in the dream, they were stopping at the house. I knew there was something strange in the air, so I set up the camera in the bedroom and let it roll.'

Toby winced. 'I don't want to see that sort of film, Whomper. That's more up Kinky's street, he was on vice.'

'Not that kind of film. Trust me, Toby, you'll want to see this.'

Toby was pretty sure he didn't, but Whomper sounded desperate and that wasn't like him. 'OK, I'm on my way. What's the address?'

'It's the last cottage on the left before the Bell on Shottery

Lane.'

'OK. I'll be there in ten minutes.'

'Great. That'll give me time to set the projector up.'

'Whomper ...'

'Yeah?'

'It's nothing ... adult, is it,' asked Toby nervously.

'No, Toby, it's not. I wish it was.'

The phone line went dead and Toby, not feeling reassured, headed for his car.

Toby had always found Whomper's sisters on the disturbing side of strange; sitting on a settee squeezed between them didn't improve things.

'Whomper's made a film,' said Denise.

'And we're in it,' added Valerie.

'That's, er, nice,' said Toby.

Whomper turned towards them, having finished the final adjustments to the projector. 'Technically, you're not actually in it. I'm talking about you and, in my dream, I'm talking with you ... but you're not there. You do understand that?'

Valerie and Denise blinked at him in unison, their expressions blank.

'OK, let's roll the film.'

As the flickering image came into focus, Toby's fears seemed as if they were about to be realised. The bedsheets writhed like storm-filled sea waters breaking on a harbour wall. There were sounds coming from beneath the moving sheets. Guttural, animalistic.

'What the hell have you got under there, Whomper?' cried Toby.

'Relax, it's not what you think.'

'You don't know what I'm thinking.'

'Well, whatever you're thinking, it's not that,' replied

Whomper emphatically. 'Just shut up and watch.'

Toby did as instructed. The writhing stopped and the under-blanket grunting ceased. Silence fell. Toby looked at the sisters on either side of him; they held his thighs with a grip that a drowning man would envy.

'Exciting, innit,' sighed Denise.

'It is,' agreed Valerie. 'I haven't seen one of Whomper's home movies since the milking parlour episode.'

Toby decided not to ask.

On the screen, Whomper appeared from beneath the sheets. He sat bolt upright, his eyes wide open and fixated on something way beyond the lens of the camera. He spoke in a distant voice, unrelated to his normal speech pattern.

'An armed head, a bloody child.' He stared desperately into the distance, trying to focus on something only he could see. 'A child crowned, with a tree in his hand.'

Toby looked from the screen to Whomper, as Denise and Valerie rose from the settee and began to speak.

'By the pricking of my thumbs, something wicked this way comes. Open, locks, whoever knocks.'

On the screen, Whomper appeared to answer them. 'How now, you secret, black, and midnight hags? What is't you do?'

Back in the room, the sisters replied. 'A deed without a name.'

Whomper seemed to be in a trance as he watched himself. The Whomper on-screen, in a film that had been recorded the previous night, was reacting to his sisters in real time. Toby didn't understand what was happening but he knew it wasn't good.

Without warning, there was thunder and a flash of lightning on the screen in Whomper's bedroom, and Whomper was looking up at a terrible apparition whose shadow fell across his face.

'Tell me, thou unknown power—' demanded Whomper.

'He knows thy thought,' said Denise. 'Hear his speech but say thou naught.'

It all suddenly became clear to Toby. This was Act 4, Scene 1 from *Macbeth*.

'Macbeth! Macbeth! Macbeth! Beware Macduff! Beware the Thane of Fife! Dismiss me. Enough.' Valerie finished the speech and fell back onto the settee, seemingly unconscious.

Whomper continued. 'Whatever thou art, for thy good caution, thanks. Thou has harped my fear aright. But one word more—'

Denise held up her hand. 'Valerie will not be commanded. Here's another. More potent than the first.'

But Valerie *was* commanded. She sprang to her feet, fully awake and looking totally different; filled with a mad energy. 'Be bloody, bold, and resolute. Laugh to scorn. The power of man, for none of woman born shall harm Macbeth.' She collapsed again.

On-screen, Whomper smiled triumphantly. 'Then live, Macduff; what need I fear of thee? But yet I'll make assurance double sure and take a bond of fate. Thou shalt not live, that I may tell pale-hearted fear it lies, and sleep in spite of thunder.'

Toby looked down at Valerie but she did not rise, she didn't need to. Denise was back on her feet and he heard the end of a very familiar speech.

'Macbeth shall never vanquished be until great Bernard Wood to high Dunroamin shall come against him.'

That bit didn't sound right, thought Toby, but only for a split-second.

On the screen, Whomper spoke. 'That will never be. Who can impress the forest, bid the tree. Bernard Wood shall never rise against Macbeth.'

And then it was over. Whomper's sisters had collapsed on the floor in the deepest of sleep. The screen went blank and the image of Whomper's Macbeth faded. Like a light being switched on, as the screen went blank, the real Whomper sprang to life. 'Did you see that, Toby? What does it mean?'

'You've been eating cheese at bedtime again?'

Whomper nodded. 'Yes, yes I have, but it's more than that.'

'Go on.'

'Bernard Wood was Oliver Lawrence's agent.'

Toby nodded. 'Yeah, I wondered what happened to Birnam Wood. And Dunsinane, for that matter.'

'You mean Dunroamin.'

Toby laughed. 'Do I?'

'Yes, you do. Dunroamin is the bungalow on Sanctus Road that Bernard Wood's mum used to live in.'

'She still there?'

'No. She died last year.' Whomper grabbed his head in his hands. 'It's all in here, I've seen it before. There's a hidden message in the dream.'

'What message?'

'Bernard Wood is coming back to Dunroamin. Don't you see, Toby? If Oliver is our Macbeth, then the fates are conspiring against him.'

Toby didn't see; he looked around the room and all he saw was crazy. 'So how does that help us catch him?'

'We don't,' said Whomper. 'We kill him.'

Toby was confused. 'Who kills him. Macduff?' He laughed and shook his head. He liked Whomper but this was descending into complete madness.

Whomper grabbed his arm. 'None of woman born shall harm Macbeth. Don't you see … our Macduff will kill Oliver. That's what the dream is trying to tell us. All we need to do is find out who our Macduff is.'

Toby shook his head and stood up. 'Thanks, Whomper. That was … weird. I'll check if this Bernard Wood is back but, as for the rest of it, well. It's a bit much, isn't it.'

'Our visions never lie, Toby. You know that.'

Toby smiled. 'Maybe, but I think they got a bit confused last night.' He patted Whomper on the shoulder. 'Did he say anything else?'

'One thing, but it made no sense.'

'What was it?'

'Remember Sorrento.'

Toby shook his head; the only Sorrento he had heard of was in Italy.

If he had thought harder, he would have remembered Sorrento Maternity Hospital in Birmingham. The place he was born.

Chapter 9
Big Al

Big Al Morris did not look happy. He was a man who liked things to be right and he worked hard to make sure they always were. When somebody messed with his props it was personal.

Fred could see the anger in Alan's eyes as he sat opposite him in Interview Room One at Guild Street nick. 'It was definitely sabotage then, not a malfunction?'

'Of course it's sabotage. Those knives were working perfectly when I checked them. Somebody's jammed a broken saxophone reed into the side of the blade and added super glue to make sure.'

'You're certain about that?'

Alan glared at Fred. 'Yes. I inspected them myself down at your lab.'

'OK. That confirms it was definitely an attempt to kill Sir Morris.'

'Does it give you any clues?'

Fred shrugged. 'Unless there's a sax-playing carpenter who's missing a reed, not really.'

'Are you taking this seriously, DS Williams? The star of the RSC was stabbed on-stage with two of my props. To say I'm unhappy is an understatement.'

'I'll be honest with you, Mr Morris. We think it's Oliver Lawrence but we can't prove it yet.'

Alan nodded. 'I knew him when he was a fine, young actor.' He smiled wistfully. 'He was amazing, such a talent. Just like his father but without the crazy drinking. He was such a lovely guy … I can't believe he's responsible for these murders.'

'We believe he's here for revenge, thinks his career was sabotaged by Sir Morris and some of his group.'

'It was. I saw it happen. He was definitely given the cold shoulder. The lot of them turned their backs on him; it wasn't pretty.'

Fred nodded. 'It was that obvious?'

'Yes, poor lad was beside himself. He could see it all slipping away.'

'What about his mother?'

'Beatrice?' Alan sighed, sadness crossing his features. 'Poor Beatrice. She was trapped between a rock and a hard place. Oliver was her son but Sir Morris gave her the roles, paid the bills. She needed him and his support. How could she turn against Sir Morris when he held all the cards.'

'But Oliver is her son. Isn't blood thicker than everything?'

'If she could play tragedy, maybe. But she couldn't. Beatrice was born to play comedy but Sir Morris always miscast her. She didn't have the *gravitas* for the heavy roles.'

'Why would he do that,' asked Fred, genuinely surprised.

'Because when she plays comedy, she is sublime. Sir Morris doesn't want that. There can only be one star at Stratford and it has to be him.'

'But doesn't he love her?'

'He loves only himself,' snapped Alan.

Fred scribbled something in the margin of his notepad. Big Al Morris was clearly no fan of his namesake. 'OK, Mr Morris, I think that's all we need for now. You've been very helpful.'

Alan rose wearily from his chair. He turned to leave but stopped and looked at Fred. 'You going to catch him soon?'

'I hope so,' said Fred.

'You better had because if I find him first there won't be anything left worth catching.' Alan spoke slowly, chose his words carefully. There was no doubting he meant every word.

'I know how you feel, Mr Morris, but you can't go taking the law into your own hands.'

'Watch me.'

The hairs rose on the back of Fred's neck. Big Al wasn't playing around. Oliver had messed with his domain, tampered with his props. This was personal, a matter of professional pride. He would not rest until Oliver had been punished one way or another.

'Don't do anything stupid, Mr Morris.'

Alan gave him a rueful smile. 'Define stupid,' he said in a voice so quiet it was barely audible. He turned and walked out of the room without a backwards glance.

Fred watched him go, knowing that if Big Al found Oliver before them there would be another body added to the growing pile.

Chapter 10
Not To Be

Oliver Lawrence and Beatrice Oxford sat alone; he in the kitchen at Trinity Street and she in her room at the White Swan Hotel. Both were thinking about Sir Morris and his battle to cling to life. Neither wanted him to make it.

Oliver knew that once Sir Morris was dead, his quest would be over. Revenge would have been served ice cold and in full. This didn't satisfy him the way it should and he couldn't put his finger on the reason why. That wasn't true; he knew but didn't want to admit it.

If it was over there would be no more killing and, the truth was, he enjoyed it. Every last bit of blood drawn, every bit of life throttled out and every scream and look of terror his revenge had elicited ... he had loved it all. He had become a monster and he didn't care.

Maybe Felix was right, the character he had created was now playing him. Was this a form of madness? It troubled him not; Sir Morris had to die, as did Clarissa Pidgeon.

And what of Felix? He seemed to have lost the zeal required for the task; could he rely on his silence? It was a question he didn't want to ask because he knew the answer. His old friend had lost the taste for their adventure, didn't have the stomach for any more blood.

Oliver did not feel the same. He wanted to bathe in the blood, swim in a river of it, kill everyone ... and then? He could restart his career, make it back to the stage he so loved and missed. It was a crazy dream, an ambition wreathed in madness, and yet it all seemed so logical. Kill everyone, remove the obstacles that blocked the path of his return to greatness. It could be done, couldn't it?

Beatrice sat alone, lost in thoughts her conscience could not reconcile. Would her life be better if Morris died? It was a hard thought to bear, but it was there and no force of will could remove it from her mind. With Morris gone she could play the parts she wanted, build a career again, be the actor she always knew she could be.

Only one thing lay in her way: Sir Morris. His life had hung by a thread but he was strong, with a huge appetite for life. He was stable, had been for the last eight hours. The thread by which his life had hung was now a rope. A thick rope. It needed to be cut.

Beatrice stood and walked over to the sink. She began to wash her hands over and over again but they never seemed to be clean. She looked at her face in the mirror; still beautiful but gaunt through lack of sleep, troubled by dark thoughts she could not shake. She looked closely at the mirror and saw her features harden; a dark resolve forming within her. The words came, unbidden, to her lips.

'Come, you spirits, that tend on mortal thoughts, unsex me here, and fill me from the crown to toe top-full of direst cruelty.'

Her mind was made up. She dried her hands, pulled on her coat and headed for the hospital.

As she reached for the door handle, she paused. Outside in the corridor was her police protection officer. She didn't want to be followed where she was planning to go.

She shook her head, stepped towards the window and opened it as quietly as she could. There was a fire escape leading to the rear of the White Swan Hotel. She paused and looked out across the car park to make sure there were no witnesses to her escape. She flicked off the lights of her room, quietly slipped out onto the fire escape and disappeared into the night unseen. Back in the corridor her police guard sat quietly on his chair, unaware that his ward had slipped out into the night and was headed for an appointment with destiny.

In Trinity Street, Oliver, too was resolved. Sir Morris must die tonight. Now was the moment. He was weak, the merest touch would shove him from this world into the next. He felt the power of destiny within him. The king lay upon his deathbed and Oliver must make sure he never rose. There wasn't room for two kings. His time had come.

He pulled on his coat and made for the door, pausing to appraise his reflection before departing; he looked every inch the heir apparent. He reached for the handle but hesitated. There was something he needed, to forget it would render his mission fruitless.

He turned back to the kitchen and saw what he sought: the knife block by the bread bin. He went over to it and gazed at the six handles proffered towards him. 'Pick me, pick me,' they called, like sirens luring him to the rocks of fate.

He ran his fingers across their smooth wooden handles and pulled out the bread knife. He chuckled. He could slice him up with this one but, no, this was not the weapon that would take the life of the king.

He pulled out another and this was much more to his liking. The handle felt secure in his hand and the blade, all Sheffield steel and uncompromising, had the lethal feel he sought. The blade was only six inches long. Would it be long enough to penetrate the protective blubber that years of indulgence had wrapped around Sir Morris' once lithe frame? He hefted it in his hand. It would if he pushed it hard enough.

'Is this a dagger which I see before me?' He held it aloft. 'Yes, it is.'

He pulled it back towards him and thrust it out. 'The handle toward my hand? Come, let me clutch thee. I have thee not and yet.' Oliver grinned insanely at his reflection in the kitchen window. 'I see thee still. I have thee. A dagger of the mind, a false creation.' He threw the knife in the air. It spun a lazy rotation before he caught it by the handle and slipped it into his pocket.

A bell rang from Holy Trinity.

'I go, and it is done; the bell invites me. Hear it or not, Morris; for it is a knell, that summons thee to heaven or to hell.'

The die was cast. Both Oliver and Beatrice made their way towards the hospital where the wounded king of the RSC lay.

Chapter 11
A Gathering Storm

Fred put down the phone. 'That was Sir Morris' surgeon.'

Toby and Ginger looked up.

'He going to make it,' asked Toby.

'He's stable.'

'About the only one,' said Kinky, before rendering himself speechless by putting a whole chocolate digestive in his mouth.

'You have a great bedside manner, Kinky. Anybody ever told you that?'

Kinky shook his head.

'Can we interview him, boss?'

'Yeah but not yet. It's going to be a while before that happens, Toby.'

'Is there any point? We know who it was and we know how he did it. We were there, we saw it happen.'

'I know but we always seem to be one step behind. He's playing with us, having fun.' Fred seemed genuinely depressed. 'I just wish I could find something to hit.'

Right then, Kinky started to choke on his biscuit. Fred's eyes lit up with delight. In three strides he was at his side. He raised his arm in the air and swung it down with huge force onto his convulsing back.

The remains of the digestive came flying out of Kinky's throat, along with half a lung. He pitched forward onto Toby's desk, letting out a howl of appreciation. That's what it sounded like to Fred. The blow seemed to have cleared Fred's mind as well as Kinky's windpipe. 'So, where does Sir Morris' stabbing leave us?'

Ginger tried to answer but his reply was drowned out by groans.

Fred leaned over and pulled Kinky up by his shirt. 'Don't milk it, Kinky. Stick to eating half a biscuit in future, maybe even consider a third.'

'He needs to eat half his body weight every day to maintain his figure,' said Ginger.

Kinky looked at him reproachfully.

'Come on, guys, we need to focus,' said Fred. 'Oliver Lawrence is out there somewhere and he must know that Sir Morris is still alive.'

'You think he might have another go while he's in hospital,' asked Toby.

'Course I do. He wants him dead.'

'We have an officer on the door of his room and two at the entrance to the ward. We'll be ready if Lawrence decides to put in an appearance.'

'But they don't know what they are looking for, none of us do,' said Toby.

'We know he is forty-two and over six-foot tall. We can start with that and nick anyone over six foot for starters.'

It wasn't much of a plan but it would have to do. At least it would keep him away.

'You get down there, Toby. Make sure the guys don't let him through.'

It was already too late. Oliver had been walking down Rother Street on his way to the hospital when he saw a familiar figure leave the White Swan Hotel: his mother.

He paused in the shadow of the American Memorial Fountain and watched her head towards Alcester Road. She was going to see Sir Morris. He fell in step behind her, staying fifty yards back.

They hadn't spoken in years. There had been a time when he wanted to kill her but perspective and the passing years had softened that desire. It still remained though, lurking in his subconscious, ready to be activated at a moment's notice.

There was a nice driveway leading up to the entrance of the hospital; maybe he could catch her there, have a little chat. He increased his pace and soon caught up. It was evening now. The traffic had thinned, visiting time had ended and the driveway was deserted. They were alone.

'Hello Mother.'

Beatrice froze. He saw the tension in her shoulders as her body stiffened. She turned slowly to face him.

She hardly recognised the man that stood before her. Gone was the fresh-faced, willowy young man she had known, replaced by this square-jawed athlete. 'Oliver, is that you?'

'You know it is.' He smiled without warmth. 'I've changed, haven't I.'

She nodded. 'We all have.'

He looked her up and down. 'You, not so much. Morris must be looking after you better than my father ever did.'

His words were like an accusation and she flinched as he said them.

'Look, Oliver, it's not that simple. You were young, you didn't understand.'

'Don't try to justify your tawdry actions. I'm really not interested.'

'Are you going to kill me?'

Oliver looked at his mother, assessing her. She still looked good and, what was it he felt? … Nothing. 'You know, Mother, right now, I don't think I am. I pity you more than hate you.'

'I don't want your pity. I don't even want your forgiveness.'

'That's lucky, because you're never going to get it.' He inched closer until he could feel her breath on his face. 'But blood is blood and family ties will out. For now, Mother, you are safe. Though I make no guarantees. The few bedtime stories you read me and that lovely lemon drizzle cake you used to make are hardly a free pass into a safe future now, are they?'

Beatrice looked into the eyes of her son – the child she had betrayed – and saw only madness. She should have felt guilty but another sensation was stirring within her: opportunity. 'Why are you here?'

Oliver let out a mirthless laugh. 'You know why I'm here.'

'To kill Morris?'

'I think so.'

'You think so? I thought this was all about his death.'

'It is, but …'

'You have doubts?'

He looked into his mother's eyes. 'Not until now. Looking at you I'm beginning to wonder if it might be best to let him live. He will never make a full recovery, never return to the stage. Imagine how grumpy and impossible he'll be. Unable to act, his stomach in a bag, robbed of his fame. He will be a living nightmare, your nightmare. Maybe I should leave you to live out your lives together. You deserve each other.'

'You're not really thinking this through, Oliver. Morris is a fighter. He's driven by an ego that is so big it could turn the tides. He may recover … and what then?'

'But he won't.'

'Are you sure? Can you take that risk?'

Oliver looked at his mother. All traces of fear were gone from her face, replaced by an intensity he had never seen her display before. He smiled.

'Let's get this straight, Mother. Are you suggesting I should kill your husband?'

Beatrice looked at him long and hard, assessing whether she could get away with what she was about to propose. She took a deep, slow breath and launched into a place from which there could be no return, no forgiveness.

'I want you to kill him. Kill him for both of us.'

Oliver had not expected this. He took a step back. 'Why?'

'Because …' She knew the words but she could not say them.

Oliver stepped back towards her, his surprise now turned to anger. 'Why?'

'Because he's your father!'

Oliver froze; he'd heard the words but they did not make sense.

Beatrice reached out and took his hand.

'Liar!' He shook her off and stepped away.

'It's not a lie.'

'You're a liar,' he spat the words out like a shot from a gun. 'Richard was my father.'

Beatrice shook her head. 'No, he wasn't. I'm sorry.'

'Whore!' Oliver raised his arm to slap her.

'He raped me!'

Oliver swayed, his arm suspended in mid-air. For a moment it seemed like he was going to fall. Everything he knew, everything he had ever thought … The very foundations of his life were crumbling before his eyes. 'Why would you say that? Richard was my father.'

'He loved you like a son … thought you were his son.' Beatrice could see the pain, the disbelief, in her son's eyes. She looked away. This was good, it was what she wanted. She looked up at him again, tears in her eyes, giving the performance of her life.

'Morris raped me. He is your father.'

'Why didn't you tell me?'

Beatrice sighed. 'He was our boss. Your father was ill. What was I supposed to do?'

'But if he raped you …'

'It was 1931. Do you think the police would have supported me against the great Sir Morris Oxford? We would have lost our jobs, everything.'

Oliver stood there in disbelief. Richard Jenkins wasn't his

father; he couldn't bear the thought. 'My acting came from Richard, everybody said so.'

'That was from being around him, watching, listening as he read to you. You absorbed his greatness but it was never in your blood.'

'But after father died, why did you marry Morris?'

'To protect you. Without Morris' support, how would I have cared for you? Put food on the table, a roof over your head.'

'But …'

They stood silently facing each other. Oliver was stunned by the enormity of what his mother had just told him. Beatrice watched the emotions playing across her son's face. The strong, athletic features now resembled a small boy, a sadness in his eyes that almost made her regret her lie. Almost.

'A mother's love for her child is sometimes full of compromise. Morris was my compromise. I did it to protect you.'

A sob broke from Oliver's mouth and he hugged her to him. 'I'm so sorry, Mother.'

Beatrice melted into her son's embrace. Her lies had woven the web she desired. Oliver was her weapon to point, her dagger to thrust into the king. She would get him to kill Morris so she would be free to be the queen. Play the parts she desired. And Oliver? She would stay close to him for as long as he was useful. All the love in her heart was reserved for one person: herself.

Chapter 12
The Fruits Of A Poisonous Tree

DI Mel Townsend swept into the incident room like royalty; well, that's how it seemed to Fred. 'Mel. What are you doing here?'

'I thought I'd make sure you weren't trying to fit my brother up for stabbing Sir Morris.'

Fred laughed. 'Sir Morris was stabbed at the theatre. Your Phil's idea of a cultured evening is a game of darts, six pints and a pie.'

Mel nodded. 'True but that still doesn't make him guilty.'

'Come on. You know that was Chief Wilson's doing, God rest his soul.'

'True, poor sod.'

'I felt sorry for the chief. His new wife murdered and his career in tatters. You can almost sympathise with why he did what he did. He'd lost everything.'

'I know but Phil's my brother, Fred. I have limited sympathy.'

'I guess Beeching's going to be your new boss then?'

Mel flinched. 'Afraid so. Can't say I'm looking forward to it.'

'Oh, he's not so bad.'

'Really?'

Fred laughed. 'No, he's bloody awful. What really brings you here, Mel?'

'I heard about Sir Morris. Sounds terrible ... right on the stage.'

'Yeah, I was there. At first I thought he was just overacting but when I saw the blood, well …'

Mel flinched. 'Ouch, nasty.'

'Lucky for the old boy he'd stopped at two. If they were all done, he'd have been like a pincushion.'

'Is he going to die?'

Fred leaned back in his chair. 'Fifty, fifty at the moment. As long as there are no more secondary bleeds, he should be all right.'

'You think Lawrence will be back to finish the job?'

'Hard to tell. If it was me, I would wait and see if the old boy carked it before taking the risk of trying again.'

'You've put some protection in the hospital though, haven't you.'

'Course I have, Mel. One on the door to his room and two in the main entrances. Can't take any chances.'

'Anything I can do?'

'Tell me where he lives.'

They both laughed but it was hollow, empty. So many dead bodies, lives ended, families ruined. It was their job to stop it and they felt so damned helpless.

'You going to stay here, Fred?'

'At Guild Street?'

'Yes. There's a promotion to be filled, it could be you.'

'No, flying a desk wouldn't suit me. I like to get my hands dirty. Preferably around some criminal's throat.'

'Aw, come on. You need to move up at some point.'

'Even if I could, I wouldn't. I came in to this job to nail wrong 'uns. I'm not interested in playing politics. Beeching spends more time ironing his uniform than he does catching criminals.'

'You're too cynical, Fred.'

'I've always been cynical.'

'You should try hope. It's good for your soul.'

'Hope is just postponed disappointment. Once you realise that, the world's a happier place.'

'Where's Toby?'

'I sent him to the hospital to make sure Sir Morris is secure.'

Over at the hospital, Toby had arrived. He hurried up the drive, skirting past an emotional couple cuddling at the side of the path. *Maybe they had been given bad news.* It was the closest he had been to Oliver Lawrence.

Oliver looked up as Toby entered the hospital. The moment had passed; it was now too late to get to Sir Morris.

'Shall we grab a drink?'

Beatrice looked up at him. 'What about Morris?'

'DC Marlowe's just dashed through the front door. We won't get near Morris tonight.'

'So, when? He needs to die, Oliver.' There was desperation in her voice.

'Don't worry, I have an idea. Let's go for a coffee and talk about it.'

Beatrice nodded, unable to hide her disappointment. 'Where? You can't come to my hotel, someone may recognise you.'

'Did you?'

'I suppose not.' She looked him up and down. 'To be honest, if you hadn't spoken, hadn't told me who you were, I would have struggled to recognise you. You've changed so much.'

'Come on then.'

The reunited mother and son turned and walked away from the hospital, leaving a husband and father hovering between life and death in their wake.

Beatrice needed Oliver to return and finish the job; clear a path to her new life.

And Oliver? His mind was blown, everything he had thought was real had been shattered in a few seconds. It was a lot to take in. If Morris was his father, could he kill him despite everything he had done? He would talk to his mother and try to form a new plan. He was pleasantly surprised by how keen she was to kill Morris. The day had been full of surprises.

Chapter 13
An Unexpected Liaison

Toby had returned to Guild Street to find Fred and Mel talking
over a cup of tea in the incident room.

'All OK at the hospital,' asked Fred.

Toby nodded, trying to hide the irrational pang of jealousy he
felt at seeing them together. 'Yeah, looks like the old boy is going
to make it.'

'You a doctor now?'

'No. I saw his consultant, he told me.'

'When can we question him?'

Fred looked at Mel. 'Question him about what?'

'The attack.'

'We saw the attack, we were in the audience. We probably
know more about it than him.'

Mel nodded. 'Yeah, I suppose so. Doesn't seem right, though,
does it?'

'What do you mean?'

'Seeing the attack, knowing who it is, and yet not knowing
anything.'

'Great, that makes us feel so much better. Did you come over
here to cheer us up because it's not working.'

Mel put her mug down; she looked a little awkward. 'No, that's
not why I'm here. Beeching asked me to come over.'

'Beeching already giving orders at Coventry,' asked Fred
warily.

'Yeah, moved his new desk into Wilson's old office. He's
probably being measured for his chief's uniform as we speak.'

'So, what did he ask you to do, ma'am? Come and see if Fred
and I are capable of catching our killer?'

Mel didn't shirk Toby's question. 'More or less. He thinks you're on the right lines but he wants me to go over everything, make sure nothing's slipped through.'

'Covering his arse, more like,' snapped Fred.

'We can't really blame him for that, boss. With one murder he'd be getting nervous. This many bodies, it's a real career killer. Any tea left in the pot?'

'Yeah, help yourself.'

Toby poured himself a mug and went over to the whiteboard. He picked up a marker and turned to Mel and Fred. 'I have a theory.'

'He has a theory. Looks like everything's going to be fine after all, Mel.'

They both laughed but Toby continued.

'I think we're approaching the end.'

'I hope so, there's no bugger left to kill,' said Fred.

'There is. Sir Morris, the king himself.'

'Which king? I don't know if you've noticed but Shakespeare had a few.'

'Shut up, Fred, hear him out.' Mel nodded at Toby. 'Go on.'

'I think, in Lawrence's mind, Sir Morris has become Duncan.'

'*Macbeth*,' scoffed Fred. 'But that would make him dead at the end of the play.'

'Not necessarily. He didn't die in *Hamlet* or *Othello*. He writes his own scripts, takes what he wants from the Bard's texts. Bends them to his own twisted needs. This is the endgame, this is where it finishes. We need to catch him before his final curtain or he will slip away forever.'

'I'm sorry, Mel,' said Fred. 'He went to art school. I'm trying to knock it out of him but he keeps reverting to his theory.'

'But you agree?'

Fred looked pained. 'Sort of, but he's making the facts fit his theory. It works if we assume the killer is Oliver Lawrence and he is back for revenge. A twisted luvvie could maybe think like this. Could play the roles of Hamlet, Othello, Macbeth. Justify his killing by becoming those characters. I've met killers who were just as deluded, just as crazy. But if we said that to the press, can you imagine their reaction?'

Mel could. 'You can never repeat it outside this room, Toby.'

'I know.'

Mel sat back. 'Let's assume you're right. Play out the scenario for us.'

Toby wrote "Duncan" on the board. 'If Sir Morris is Duncan, who is Macbeth?'

'Lawrence,' said Mel.

'Yes.' Toby wrote Macbeth on the board, below and to the right of Duncan. He turned back to his colleagues. 'OK. If that's the case, who is Lady Macbeth?'

The room fell silent as they all thought about the question.

Fred was the first to answer. 'This is going to sound crazy, but I've always thought Beatrice Oxford has a touch of Lady Macbeth about her.'

'What makes you say that,' asked Mel.

'I went to see her at the hospital after Sir Morris had come out of surgery. She seemed broken. Not by the attack on her husband but by the fact that it would prevent her returning to the stage. I just thought it was a strange reaction.'

'I know what you mean, boss. That time I went to see her at Woodstock there was definitely something of the night about her. Gave me the creeps.'

Mel looked confused. 'But she's Lawrence's mother, so … how can she be his wife?'

'Think about it.' Toby turned back to the whiteboard and began scribbling. 'We think Lawrence was following the plot of *Hamlet* at first. In that, Hamlet's mother marries his uncle after his father is murdered. Beatrice married Sir Morris after her first husband, Richard Jenkins, died.'

'Talk about life imitating art,' said Mel. 'But how does that link to her being Lady Macbeth?'

'Maybe it does in Lawrence's mind. He sees himself inside the plays but he's writing his own scenarios to suit his will. What does Lady Macbeth want?'

'Macbeth to become king,' said Fred.

'Exactly. And who is the king?'

'Duncan.'

'In Lawrence's mind?'

Fred nodded thoughtfully. 'Sir Morris.'

'And who wants him out of the way so she can continue her career?'

Fred looked at Mel and they both looked back to Toby.

'Have you gone stark staring mad? Beatrice Oxford is in danger from her son, not in league with him.'

Toby wanted to reply but he really didn't have any facts to support his theory. He turned and studied the whiteboard. When he looked at what he had written it seemed crazy, the work of someone who had been eating the wrong kind of mushrooms. And yet …

'Fred's right, Toby. It's an entertaining theory but there's nothing to support it.'

Toby shrugged. 'When you put it like that, maybe I've been paying too much attention to Whomper's dreams.'

'Whomper dreamed this,' asked Fred.

'Listen, Toby, we all want to catch our killer but we have to stay rooted in reality. If Whomper has suggestions take them on board, just don't let them take the place of facts.'

'I know, ma'am, but Whomper's dreams and visions have a nasty habit of coming true.'

'Whomper doesn't know anything for sure. Nobody has even seen Lawrence for fifteen years.' Fred got up and squeezed Toby's shoulder. Mel and I are going to grab something to eat, tomorrow is going to be a busy day. You want to join us?'

'No thanks, boss. I've got a few things to do.'

'Night, Toby.'

Toby smiled at Mel. She looked good beside Fred as they stood in the doorway, they made a nice couple. 'Night.' He watched them go and turned back to the board. None of it made any real sense and yet he was sure there was something in his theory. The events in Stratford were not normal. They were being enacted by a madman intent on revenge, lost in the tragedies of Shakespeare and descending into a web of madness that was spinning out of control.

What was it Whomper had said? *Macbeth, Macbeth, Macbeth. Beware Macduff.* But who was Macduff? He wrote Macduff on the board, below and to the left of King Duncan's name.

He knew that Sir Morris was Duncan and Oliver Lawrence was Macbeth, but who was Macduff? *None of woman born shall harm Macbeth.* What else had Whomper said? *Sorrento!* What the hell did that mean? He wrote it beside Macduff and stood back. There was someone missing, he scribbled the name "Banquo" beneath Macduff. Banquo had been Macbeth's friend, surely Oliver had to have someone helping him. But who?

Duncan (Sir Morris)

Macduff (Sorrento)   Macbeth (Oliver)

Banquo (?   )   Lady Macbeth (Beatrice)

Mauldvina (?   )

He had written one other name on the board: Mauldvina. Banquo's wife, murdered by Macbeth. Was this where Clarissa

Pidgeon fitted into the twisted script? She should have died but Chief Wilson's wife had been murdered in her place. If Clarissa was Mauldvina, who was her Banquo? If only Toby had known that Clarissa had once been Felix Richards' girlfriend everything would have started to make sense. Not knowing this only left him with more unanswered questions. Would Lawrence come back for her?

Which females die in Macbeth? Lady Macbeth, obviously, but who else? His A levels were some years behind him and all he could think was that Banquo held the key. He put a question mark next to Banquo's name.

Toby stepped back and looked at what he had written. It appeared to be the scribblings of a madman. If anyone apart from Fred or Mel saw this he would be sectioned and led off by men in white coats. There were more questions than answers and none of the answers made sense.

He took one last look at the board, trying to memorise what he had written, then he picked up the rag and slowly began to rub it clean.

Removing the closest theory to the truth that there had been during the whole investigation.

Chapter 14
Clarissa's Secret

For someone who had dodged death, Clarissa Pidgeon seemed surprisingly calm. She felt sorry for Heather Wilson but she was more relieved that it hadn't been her. It had been a sad case of mistaken identity. Regret did not figure in her life; it stopped you moving forward and she was always running towards the horizon, looking for the next thing. In her forty-three years of life she had not found it and these days she had given up looking. When you don't know what you are looking for it's hard to find.

She was sitting at the bar in the Dirty Duck. Tonight's show had been cancelled, even though there was an understudy. The police and RSC management had decided to cancel all performances for the foreseeable future. She had time on her hands and it made her uncomfortable. Time to think and with those thoughts the memories she would like to forget returned. But how do you forget a child?

Felix walked along the riverbank from his mooring. He needed a drink, but not alone. He sought the comfort of strangers, meaningless conversation. A chance to lose himself, to forget the events he had witnessed ... and his role in them. The Dirty Duck would be his remedy.

As he entered the bar he saw a familiar face. 'Clarissa, how are you?'

She smiled. 'Felix, I haven't seen you for a while.'

'I've been busy.'

'Doing what?'

He shifted awkwardly from foot to foot. 'Oh, this and that.'

'Sounds mysterious. Are you a criminal!'

'No, no, just busy.'

'Would you like to join me?'

He smiled. 'Yes, I'd like that very much. Been a tough week.' He sat down wearily.

'I thought I might see you at the theatre. Are you still reviewing for *The Herald*?'

'No. I'm taking a break at the moment. I was at the theatre last night though. Had a ringside seat to Sir Morris' stabbing.'

'Ghastly, wasn't it. I was in the wings waiting to come on when it happened. I heard this terrible cry. I remember thinking that Morris' acting had really improved.'

'That's harsh, Clarissa. Poor Morris didn't deserve that.'

'You think not? You're about the only one that does. When I remember some of the stunts he's pulled over the years, I'm surprised someone hasn't done it before. Loathsome man.'

'But you're one of his regular players.'

'I am but only because I need the work.' Clarissa chuckled. 'But you know what he's like, you worked with him for years. You remember how he treated us when we were doing *As You Like It*?'

Felix did remember; it was a happy memory. She had played Rosalind to his Orlando and, in a fine example of life following art, they too had become lovers. 'Those were happy days. We were so young.'

'Well, I was, dear, but you were old enough to be my father,' said Clarissa, the smile on her face full of malicious intent.

'Unfair,' protested Felix. 'Elder brother at worst.'

'You fool yourself if you want to, but we both know the truth.'

Felix didn't know the whole truth, about the baby that Clarissa had carried secretly. She'd given him up for adoption without telling anyone at the theatre, not even the father of the boy. Could she ever tell Felix? She didn't think so. Too much time had passed.

She had created a well of secrets from which she could not draw. If Felix found out he had a son, he would hate her forever for not telling him. And what of her? She was not mother material, consumed only by herself and her own wellbeing.

She could never look Lance in the face and tell him the truth. He was the brightest young talent at the Old Vic and well on the way to being a star. With parents like Felix and her it was bound to happen.

She pulled herself from unwanted thoughts and turned back to Felix. 'What are your plans?'

Felix shrugged. 'I don't know. I think I'm going to leave Stratford and head north, follow the rivers and canals until I reach the Scottish Borders. I need to lose myself for a while, get away from ...' He looked across at the woodland and the river beyond it. 'This place.'

Clarissa nodded. She understood how he felt. There was a dark undercurrent running through the streets of Stratford, a fear that went unspoken for the most part. Death walked the streets, lurked in the shadows of the night and hid in doorways, always ready to fulfil its fatal obligation. They were all helpless, waiting for the hammer to fall.

'Did you ever love me, Clarissa?'

She hadn't expected that question; it took her off guard. 'That's a little out of the blue. Have you been alone on your boat for too long?'

'Don't make fun of me, it was a genuine question. Did you?'

'What, love you?'

'Yes.'

Clarissa shifted uncomfortably on her seat. 'That's hard to say, Felix.'

'Why don't you try.'

She sensed the terseness in his voice. 'Have I upset you?'

'No. Disappointed, maybe. But we were young and compassion is best suited to the old.'

'My, we are feeling philosophical today. Have you been

reading Auden again.'

Felix smiled sadly. 'No. Sonnet Eighteen.' He sat down opposite Clarissa and took her hand.

'Shall I compare thee to a summer's day?
Thou art more lovely and more temperate.
Rough winds do shake the darling buds of May,
And summers lease hath all too short a date.
Sometime too hot the eye of heaven shines,
And often is his gold complexion dimmed;'

The bar had fallen silent as, one by one, the clientele stopped to listen. Even Clarissa was stunned to silence by Felix's delivery. His voice so clear, his tone so sad; genuine emotion inhabiting every syllable. This was a shared moment and she acknowledged it with her silence.

'And every fair from fair sometime declines,
By chance or nature's changing course untrimmed.
But thy eternal summer shall not fade
Nor lose possession of that fair thou ow'st,
Nor shall Death brag thou wand'rest in his shade,
When in eternal lines to time thou grow'st.
So long as men can breathe or eyes can see,
So long lives this, and this gives life to thee.'

Felix's words had fallen gently on the ears of his audience. All were moved and then came the applause, spontaneous and unbidden. Even Dick and Julia Mayrick joined in.

Felix acknowledged the applause, almost embarrassed by the impact of his words.

Clarissa leaned towards him and kissed him gently on the cheek. 'That was beautiful, Felix, where on earth did it come from?'

'Shakespeare.'

'I know that but where did that recitation come from? That was no performance, it was straight from the heart.'

'It was, from me to you. I've always wanted to tell you but …'

'But what?'

'I never could find the words,' he sighed. 'So I let Shakespeare find them for me. I hope you don't mind.'

Clarissa didn't know what to say, it didn't stop her speaking though. 'Do you love me, Felix?'

'Weren't you listening, wasn't I clear? Thy eternal summer shall not fade. Nor lose possession of that fair thou ow'st, Nor shall Death brag thou wand'rest in his shade.' He leaned back and looked at her. 'Don't you understand?'

Clarissa shook her head. 'No, are you asking me out?'

He took her hand and squeezed it hard. She flinched. 'You're hurting me, Felix.'

'Listen,' he hissed. 'Your death does wander in his shade. Oliver wants you dead. Get out of town and don't look back. The very devil is on your scent.'

Clarissa pulled away from him. 'You're frightening me, Felix. I … I thought you loved me for a moment back there.'

'I think I do. I only realised it when I was reading the sonnet last night. There was something between us, something unspoken. We have unfinished business. I can't put it into words but it's there, like an unwanted guest at the feast. I realise now, too late, that I love you. I've always loved you. We were meant to be together.'

Clarissa sat back, she had no witty comeback. Felix had bared his heart and his words were true. There was a bond between them; a son, who was now a man. She wanted to blurt it out, to tell him he was right. She had felt it too, back then when they were young and their blood ran hot. When reason fled on passion's wings and they lost themselves in each other.

But time had cooled the boiling blood of passion and reason had distilled itself to lies and unspoken denial. She had gone too far down the wrong road to turn back, and now they stood at a crossroads. He would go one way and she another. Unless …

'Felix, there's something I have to tell you.'

He held a finger to her lips. 'There is nothing to be said, now is not the time for words. Get away from this place while you can. Oliver is here, I know it. He's tried to kill you once, he will try again.'

She looked into the eyes of the man she had loved for so long without ever acknowledging it. Casting her favours upon the wind for so many years in a vain attempt to forget, but the past will always find its way back to you. There is nowhere to hide from history. It waits, unseen, and then reveals itself.

'What about you, Felix? Will you stay?'

He shook his head. 'No, I'm going tomorrow. Please go too.'

She nodded. 'Very well … but we have tonight.'

He looked into her eyes; this was no flirtation, this was real. 'We do.' He took her hand and they stood.

'So long as men can breathe or eyes can see,
So long live this, and this gives life to thee.'

They kissed and left the Dirty Duck together for the very last time.

Chapter 15
No Milk Of Human Kindness

Beatrice sat alone in her hotel room at the White Swan. She had talked with Oliver late into the night. Her feelings were impossible to judge. A mother's delight at a son's return? Fear that he was there to kill her? Regret, for the way she had betrayed him, sold him out for a better life? And, maybe, desire? Not for him but for what he could give to her: freedom. With Sir Morris gone she would be truly free to live her life, regain her career, spend his money. Oliver could be the instrument that procured this destiny. All she had to do was load the bullets and then help him point the gun. If she could persuade him to kill Sir Morris, she could have it all.

She poured herself another drink. Had Oliver believed her story? It had been the performance of her life. To convince him that Sir Morris was his father, well, that bit was true. To tell him he had raped her … the tears had flowed, the sobs had shaken her body and he had held her in his arms. It had been a beautiful lie.

"I'm so sorry, Mother. Why didn't you tell me?"

He had believed her and, with this, his hatred for Sir Morris had grown. He was hers to command. Like Lady Macbeth, she would manipulate him to do her bidding and then … If he succeeded and wasn't caught, what would she do?

He had said he wanted to return to the stage but to do that he would have to go to a small provincial theatre, pay his dues, become someone else. Or she could betray him.

It wasn't really a question. Alive he held too many secrets and, if she was honest, of all the emotions she had felt last night there was just one missing: love. When she held him in her arms outside the hospital, she was acting; she had felt nothing.

The muscular middle-aged man bore no resemblance to the willowy son who had disappeared all those years ago. He was Oliver in name only; the child she had given birth to was gone, replaced by this murderer. She owed him nothing. Too much water had flowed under the bridge and the tide had washed away all her feelings for him. Now he was good for only one thing; to finish what he had started so she could be free. She wanted Morris gone forever and his blood on Oliver's hands.

She had always thought she could only play comedy but last night had showed her she was wrong. With the right motivation she could enter the darkest, most horrific of tragedies and be totally at home in the role. She'd heard great actors talk about motivation and never really understood what it meant ... but now she did. Her path had become clear from virtually the moment Oliver had made himself known.

His return to Stratford had hung over her like a Damoclean sword. Now she would place that sword in his hand and direct him towards Morris. The plan had a pleasing synergy; Oliver kills Sir Morris and frees her in the process. Everyone wins, apart from Sir Morris, and what of Oliver? She would cross that bridge when the deed was done.

Beatrice looked down at her hand. She could feel the dampness of the warm spot of blood that lay there but she could not see it. How could she feel guilt for a crime not yet committed, a crime she would not commit, she had no need. Oliver would be her sword, her solution, her freedom.

What had happened to her during the events of the last few days had changed everything. All she had become now meant nothing. The wealth, the position in society, it wasn't what she wanted.

Freedom to be an actor ... What price would she pay to achieve it? She knew the answer. Anything. She had become infected by Oliver's madness and she would use it to her own ends. The milk of human kindness did not run through her veins and they should all fear her nature. The king would soon be dead and she would have that crown, though it be bathed in the blood of her husband or child. Blood can be washed away but destiny is forever.

Chapter 16
Such Sweet Sorrow

As the morning mist lay gentle on the river, Felix made his way down towards Lucy's Lock. He had left Clarissa asleep in his bed. Last night had been the confirmation of a love that had lain unspoken for years. In those few hours of affirmation, he and Clarissa were consumed by a tender regret that they had discovered the truth too late. They loved each other, had always loved each other. What fools we are in love. The truth lies before us and yet we dance around it, avoiding it for fear of ... what? Commitment? Love was strange, all-encompassing and Felix knew that last night he had tasted it for the first, and probably last, time.

In an envelope under his arm, he held his journal. He was taking it to Ting at the Post Office. He would put it in her safe, no questions asked. Not if you paid the right money.

He reached the bridge and climbed the steps to cross the river. If he met Oliver here, what could he say? Oliver could read him like a book.

He paused for a moment and looked across the bridge to the pathway that led up the other side of the river towards Holy Trinity. There was no one around. He gazed back down the river towards the theatre. It was a beautiful sight but all he could see were the bodies that he and Oliver had so carelessly scattered about the landscape.

Desmond and Tabitha Tharpe in the river. Gerard Soames on the bandstand. Lizzie Birchwood by the tunnel under Southern Lane. As he watched, the green waters slowly turned blood red. He squeezed his eyes shut. When he reopened them, the blood was gone. The beauty of the scene had returned but Felix knew he could never unsee what he and Oliver had done. This beautiful place, that he loved so much, had been ruined for him by their actions.

He could not stay here and he realised he could never return. As he crossed the bridge it felt like a door was closing behind him, a door he could never reopen. This place was no longer his. Tears clouded his vision. What had he done?

He tightened his grip on the package under his arm. This was his record, his version of the events that had unfolded this terrible summer. A document not of justification – for there could be none – more an explanation akin to his last will and testament.

He walked up the pathway towards Holy Trinity. This route would take him right past his house on Trinity Street. Oliver would be there now; what if he saw him? He decided to walk through the churchyard and then turn up Old Town to avoid it. He had come too far – risked too much – to fail to get his journal safely under lock and key. When the truth was one day told, he wanted history to know that it hadn't all been bad.

Inside all the horror had been the seed of a beautiful quest, a revenge so pure that all actions seemed justified. They weren't, nothing justified what they had done but maybe, when time had dulled the pain, history would understand the reason. It was a faint hope but he needed it to be read. Not now, but one day.

Felix walked briskly down Old Town, passing Hall's Croft and remembering the night Oliver had wooed Lizzie Birchwood to her death. He shivered; this place was littered with ghosts. He upped his pace and soon found himself outside the Old Post Office on Bull Street. He glanced at his watch: seven fifteen a.m. He was much too early, or so he thought.

As he went to sit on a wall opposite, the blind on the door flipped up and Ting Hu peered out at him. The door swung open.

'I didn't think you'd be open at this hour,' said Felix.

'Why did you come then.'

Felix shrugged. 'I dunno, seemed like a good idea at the time. You open?'

'Depends, you got cash?'

'Of course.'

'Then I'm open.' She stood to one side and ushered him in.

'Thanks, Ting.'

'No need to thank me, money never sleeps.' She shut the door behind her, pulled down the blind and bolted it.

'So, you're not really open,' observed Felix.

'You look like a man that needs to spend some money, I can help you with that.'

He chuckled. 'You Chinese never stop, do you.'

Ting's eyes flashed in anger. 'I'm not Chinese. I'm from Singapore.'

'What's the difference?' It was an indelicate question but Felix had never been there.

She shook her head. 'If I was Chinese, I'd be a communist and this shop would be shut. Now, what do you want, Felix?'

He pulled the package from beneath his left arm. 'I want you to put this in your safe.'

She nodded. 'Is it stolen?'

'No, why do you ask.'

'Rent would have been higher. Folks that put stuff in my safe don't use safety deposit boxes in banks, if you know what I mean. How long do you want it for? It's fifty pence a day.'

'That's a bit steep … over fourteen quid a month. I could buy a shed for that.'

'Buy one and put it in there then.'

Felix shook his head. 'No, I need it in the safe. I don't think half inch shiplap is going to be secure enough.'

'Good, so how long do you want it in my safe for?'

Felix wasn't sure how to answer this question. 'I don't know to be honest.'

'What do you mean, you don't know?'

Felix could see Ting was getting irritated. He'd been in her shop for a couple of minutes and she hadn't relieved him of any money yet.

'Can we sit down and discuss it?'

'You think this is a cafe. It's not.'

Just then, Claude walked in with a mug of tea for Ting. 'Oh, bonjour, Felix. How are you today?'

'Fine, thanks, Claude.'

Ting sighed and pointed towards the door in the store. 'Let's go in the warehouse, Felix. I'm sure we'll find somewhere to sit in there. You want a tea?'

'Please.'

'You hear that, Claude?'

'*Ce n'est pas un problème.*' Claude flounced out of the Post Office, headed for the kitchen.

Felix had only been in the warehouse a few times and it always took his breath away. A real assortment of items that should be in somebody's house but, for some reason, had found their way into the "cash only" stock of Ting's private warehouse, entry by invitation only. The door that ran into it from the Post Office looked like any internal door but it was always locked during the hours of business. Behind it was a four-inch-thick metal door which could only be opened by punching in a six-digit code.

Ting pointed at a leather sofa which still had its protective plastic wrapper on. 'You OK sitting on plastic?'

Felix nodded. 'Yeah.'

Ting sat down opposite him. 'So, what kind of document is it?'

Felix hesitated, unsure how he should describe it. 'I suppose it's a journal of sorts.'

'About you?'

'Kind of.'

Ting grinned. 'I don't think you need to lock that up, Felix. Nobody's going to want to read that.'

'You'd be surprised, Ting. I'm more entertaining than I look.'

'You'd need to be.'

Before Felix had time to be offended, Claude appeared with his tea and put it down on a small table at the side of the Chesterfield. Ting gave him a look and he disappeared back through the door without a word.

'Make sure you don't spill any. That table used to belong to Lord Burke of Ponty.'

'Who's he?'

'A minor English Lord. He made his fortune in crime.'

'Is he dead?'

'Hard to tell. He lives in Wales.'

Felix nodded. 'It's been stolen from him, hasn't it, Ting.'

'I prefer reappropriated. His family had businesses in Hong Kong, Singapore and India. Made a huge fortune and built an estate in South Wales. Spent years furnishing it with stolen goods from all over the world. My supplier just liberated a few pieces.'

'Does he know?'

'Oh yes. He's furious but when you've stolen them yourself you don't have any receipts for the insurance, do you.'

Felix tried to take a sip of his tea but he was too busy chuckling to manage it.

'You're like Robin Hood, Ting, taking from the rich to give to the poor.'

'I don't give anything, this is a business.' She glanced down at Felix's package. 'What's wrong, Felix?'

'Why do you ask?'

'The package says, "Only to be opened in the event of my death." And that's not your usual address.'

They looked at each other and said nothing. He would never

win a staring contest with Ting.

'I'm in trouble.'

'How bad?' She nodded towards his package. 'You ill?'

'No.'

'You going to kill yourself?'

'No.'

'Someone want you dead?'

'It's too early for this, Ting.'

'OK, now we're getting somewhere. Who wants to kill you?'

'I'm not sure anyone does. I just have a feeling, you know?'

'Course I do, lots of people wanted to kill me over the years.'

'And yet, you're still here. What's your secret?'

Ting shrugged. 'Most aren't serious.'

'And those that are.'

She looked at him like he was stupid. 'I kill them first!'

'You're kidding.'

'Am I?' Ting sipped her tea. 'What's in the package, Felix? Will it get me in trouble?'

Felix thought about it for a moment. If Oliver knew the contents of his journal and its location, Ting would be in danger. 'This can only be opened in the event of my death and then you must take it straight to the police.'

Ting looked like she was about to faint. 'No police. I have my reputation to think about.'

'I think your reputation will be safe. Just make sure you give it to either DS Fred Williams or DC Toby Marlowe. You know them?'

'Every entrepreneur in Warwickshire knows Fred Williams. He's not a big fan of free enterprise.'

'But he's honest.'

'You say that like it's a good thing. The only way you can get him to look the other way is by putting a pint behind him.'

Felix smiled. Ting always made him smile. Her commitment

to crime was unwavering but somehow appealing. He leaned forward and touched her arm, something he had never dared do before.

Ting looked down at his hand as if it were the deposit of a passing bird. 'What's wrong, Felix? Nobody touches me.'

'I'm sorry but this is serious. I'm in danger, I need to leave town. If something happens to me ...'

'Like death?'

'Yeah, like that. I need this package to get to Williams or Marlowe.'

Ting nodded thoughtfully. 'How long do you think you've got?'

'Why do you ask?'

'Rent. Space in my secret safe doesn't come free.'

At fifty pence a day it would soon mount up. 'What if I give you fifty quid to be going on with?'

He watched as Ting did the maths in her head. 'So you think you'll be dead within three months. You must have done some bad stuff.'

'I have.'

'Maybe I should give you a hundred and read it myself.'

Felix snatched his package up from the table. 'You can never do that, Ting, never.'

Ting seemed a little taken aback by his reaction. 'Don't worry, I won't. But if it's that bad why not take it to the police now for your own safety?'

'Because it implicates me too. The ... person I have worked with may need to be stopped. If I'm dead, I must leave it to Williams and Marlowe. With what's in here they will be able to find ...' he paused for a moment, stopping himself from saying Oliver's name. 'This person. What's in here will link them to their crimes.'

'You talking about murder? I don't like murder, Felix. It's bad for business. I don't think I want to look after your journal.'

'A hundred quid for three months?'

'I look after the journal, but you go one day over the three months and if I haven't heard from you the book goes to the police.'

'That's fair.' He passed the package to her and opened his wallet. He peeled off one hundred pounds in fresh ten-pound notes and placed them on the table.

Ting looked at them but not with the piranha-like desire she normally reserved for cash. She was wary, unsure for a moment as to whether she should get involved. As she gazed at the money her doubts lessened. The little voice inside her said, *Easy money, take it.* There was another voice, quieter but insistent. *Don't get involved, this is blood money.* The first voice answered. *It may be blood money but it's not my blood.*

Ting got up and took the package over to the safe. 'Turn around, Felix.'

'Don't worry, it's my package.'

'You don't understand. If you don't know the number, nobody can torture it out of you. It makes you safer.'

Felix turned around. There were six beeps as the code was entered, then the door clicked open.

'I thought those things had tumblers.'

'You've been watching too many bank robbery movies. It's 1972, Felix, you gotta move with the times. Besides, anybody who got into here would already be dead.'

'How do you work that out?'

'Door locks behind you when you come in. If you don't have the codes, you aren't going anywhere. When I open up in the morning, I'm going to kill you.'

'I never know if you're telling the truth.'

'You don't ever want to find out.' The safe door clicked shut.

'You can turn around now; your secrets are safe.'

He held out his hand. 'Thanks, Ting.'

Ting winced. 'You already touched me once today, that's enough.'

'Hopefully see you again, Ting.'

'I hope so too, but I don't think so.'

Felix smiled and left Ting Hu behind in her secure empire. She was the keeper of his secrets and he hoped they would never need to be read.

Chapter 17
To Be An Orphan, Or Not

Oliver sat in the kitchen at Trinity Street. Last night had been interesting. He hadn't expected to like his mother ... and he hadn't. She was shallow, self-centred and seemingly without shame; all the attributes required to be a star.

When he finally left her at the end of the evening they had hugged. It hadn't felt real, like two actors playing a scene.

There was no love between them; too much had happened. Two strangers linked by what should have been an unbreakable bond but was in reality just a genetic fact. It was strange meeting his mother again. Mother? That word didn't seem real; surely being a mother means unconditional love, giving up everything for your child.

Beatrice had given up nothing, she'd just stood back and let Morris move him to one side. Very much the same as she had done with his father. Regardless of the facts, Richard would always be his dad. He had loved him unconditionally, idolised him.

The truth had come as a nasty surprise. How could he ever accept Morris as his father ... and yet, he felt it was the truth. He had looked into Beatrice's eyes when he had questioned her and he had seen the truth; she was guilty, regretful and defiant.

There was one question that was eating away at him. Felix had been his parents' best friend; how come he didn't know that Morris was his real father? It didn't seem possible that his mother would have kept this from him. This was something he would need to ask Felix at their next meeting; it was another question mark in his trust for him.

Felix was wavering; so much killing, had he reached his personal Waterloo? There were questions to be asked but they would have to wait. The sword of Damocles swung above Morris and it seemed like it needed a nudge to complete its fall. But how could he do this with so many police guarding the hospital?

Oliver needed a plan. He grabbed a notepad and began to scribble down his thoughts. Disguises had worked for him before but, even if he could pass himself off as a doctor, no one was going to allow him anywhere near Morris unaccompanied.

He needed something more … A diversion. What kind of diversion? He tried to think of something that would totally focus the attention of the police and staff, take them away from concentrating on Morris.

Nothing came to him that seemed remotely workable. Firing a gun would cause panic and alert the police that the attacker was after Sir Morris. The guards at the hospital were probably armed, given the nature of his crimes.

He could cut the power and cause a blackout but, again, the police would think it was part of a calculated attack.

No. He needed to think outside the box, deflect attention from Sir Morris. Do something so momentous that all thoughts would be centred on averting a potential tragedy.

He sat down, his legs feeling suddenly weak beneath him. The idea had come to him fully formed and seemed unimaginable, but he had imagined it and he knew that it could work.

So far, apart from the mistaken identity of Heather Wilson, no one had been hurt; collateral damage had been kept to a minimum. But this idea put everything in peril. So evil and calculating that it would spread fear and chaos throughout the hospital, giving him the time and confusion to get Morris away from there without being seen.

He wrote it down on the paper; it didn't seem real. Could he really think this way? What if something went wrong? There was so much that couldn't be planned for, so many lives that could be lost. He looked long and hard at what he had written and realised that he didn't care. At the top of the page was one word: fire!

Chapter 18
Burn It All Down

Sir Morris' room was on the second floor of the west wing of the hospital. It sat at the very end of the corridor and could only be accessed from two places. There was a lift at the far end but it lay behind the two sets of fire doors that partitioned the intensive care ward.

Sir Morris was the only patient in residence at the moment. Oliver looked at the layout of the hospital he had drawn roughly on a piece of A4 paper. If he started the fire in the middle compartment, he would have time to finish Sir Morris off. He just needed to draw the protection officer away and get him on the other side of the fire.

There were several wards below, to the other side of the lifts and stairs, that were fully occupied by patients. This would certainly concentrate the efforts of the services on getting the innocents out of the building. If he could position himself on the west side of the fire, Sir Morris would be trapped on the wrong side of the inferno, alone. Well, almost. Oliver would be with him.

He looked at the plan again. How would he escape? There was a fire door outside Sir Morris' room. In an emergency it could only be opened from the inside. That would be his escape. The police or rescue services could not get in from the outside. Perfect!

How would he start the fire? There was a jerrycan of petrol in the garage at Trinity Street that would do the job. How would he get it into the hospital? He thought about this for a moment. He could put the can inside a suitcase and claim that it was full of clothes and toiletries for Sir Morris.

The guard would probably want to inspect it and that would

be the moment he attacked him, knocked him back into the corridor and left him stranded on the other side of the final fire doors. Then he could take his time and light the place up like a bonfire. It was an old building with plenty of wood in its design; the place was a tinderbox, an inferno in waiting.

There would be panic; a hospital fire, your worst nightmare. Many could die in the flames. He considered this for a moment and realised that, as before, he didn't care. Fate is the hunter and it will always find you. Those in the wrong place at the wrong time, well, they would be collateral damage.

Felix was right. He was beyond control, all objectivity gone. Focused on one thing: revenge, regardless of the cost.

At the hospital, DS Ken White sat outside Sir Morris Oxford's room. DS Williams had sent him there as a punishment; Fred didn't like him and the feeling was mutual. The joke, however, was on Fred.

The corridor was warm, the chair comfortable, and that nice little nurse brought him a cuppa every hour, on the hour. He'd tucked three Marathon bars into his pocket, only two left after the last cup of tea. This was an easy number. As far as he was concerned, Sir Morris could hover at death's door for as long as he liked. *Oh yes*, he thought. *The joke was very much on Fred.*

In a few minutes time he would be changing his tune and screaming to a God he didn't believe in.

There was a good seal on the top of the jerrycan but Oliver had splashed plenty of Hai Karate aftershave to mask the smell of the petrol. It hadn't worked as well as he had hoped because, in truth, there wasn't much difference between them. He was dressed in a doctor's white coat, stethoscope around his neck, and looking for all the world like he belonged. His name badge read *Dr Harvey Crippen*, his own nod to a fellow murderer. If anyone in the hospital saw it, he hoped it would make them smile.

There were two constables in the foyer and he strode past, greeting them with a confident, 'Good evening.' He was in the lift before they had chance to respond. It moved slowly to the second floor and he braced himself for what may greet him when the doors opened.

His luck held. As the doors parted there was no one waiting. He stepped into the corridor and glanced to his right. The east wing was humming with activity. Nurses bustled from patient to patient doing the drugs round. Visiting time hadn't started yet and the matron was busy making sure her ward was immaculate, as always.

Oliver smiled and turned to the west wing, amused by the fact that visiting hour would soon be the last thing on everyone's mind.

He walked briskly down the empty corridor and through the first set of fire doors. He checked the area and opened the final pair of doors. There, on a plastic chair, he was greeted by the sight of Sergeant Ken White. With tea in one hand and a Marathon bar in the other, he was failing to take his guarding duties seriously.

Ken looked up, half the chocolate bar inserted in his open mouth. This was Oliver's opportunity. Instead of beginning his cover story he simply strode over to the officer and, with the flat of his free hand, rammed the Marathon bar down his throat. Ken began to choke and fell to the floor, grasping his neck.

Satisfied that trying to breathe was keeping him occupied, Oliver opened the fire doors. Without hesitation, he opened the jerrycan and began to pour the contents all over the floor that lay between the two sets of fire doors. He threw a match into the void and closed the fire doors behind him.

There was a whoosh as the petrol ignited and, for a moment, the fire doors swung slightly apart. He felt a blast of searing heat and knew that no one would be coming through those doors. He turned back to where Ken lay retching on the floor, desperately trying to clear his airway.

He shook his head and tutted. 'Watch out for the nuts in those, they can get stuck in your throat.'

The message didn't register with Ken, who was starting to turn blue.

Oliver ignored him and opened the door to Sir Morris Oxford's room. He took a second to glance back down the corridor before he entered. The compartment between the two sets of fire doors was ablaze. Screams of alarm rang out from the far end of the corridor as the people on the east wing became aware of the fire. *That would keep them busy for a while.*

Sir Morris lay on the bed, propped up by several pillows. There were tubes coming from his stomach and arms, and an oxygen mask obscured his face. He was still Sir Morris but less so, diminished by his wounds, robbed of his power.

'All flesh is indeed mortal,' whispered Oliver.

The screams and shouts from the other side of the inferno became louder as the fire alarm began to sound. Accompanied by the choking cough of DS Ken White, the peace of the intensive care room had been well and truly shattered.

Oliver leaned over the bed. 'Wake up, Morris, the future is calling.'

Morris' eyes fluttered drowsily.

'Wakey, wakey. You're missing all the fun!'

Morris' eyes fluttered again and finally opened. He lay frozen for a moment, taking in the wail of the fire alarm, the screams of nurses and patients. He sniffed the air. His nostrils flared and his eyes filled with terror. There was a fire and he was trapped, helpless, in his bed.

He looked up at Oliver without recognition. 'Help me.'

'Don't panic, Morris, the fire won't get you.'

Morris cast a glance in his direction. His terror turned to

confusion as their eyes met. Oliver saw the slow spreading of realisation.

'Oliver?'

He held up his hands. 'Ta da! It's me, back from the dead. Are you pleased to see me?'

Sir Morris pulled off his oxygen mask. 'What are you doing here?'

'Oh, come now, Father. I'm sure you've worked that out by now. If it helps, I'm not here for a touching family reunion.'

It clearly didn't help. Morris squirmed and tried to push himself up the bed away from Oliver. 'I'm not your father ... Richard is.'

'That would have been nice if it was true but, sadly, it's you.'

Morris looked confused. 'No, no. Your mother and I weren't a couple until after your father died.'

'Spare me the lies, Daddy. Mummy told me about the two of you, even suggested that you had been ... forceful.' Oliver pulled a look of fake contrition. 'Suggested you were a bit rapey. That's not a good look for a Knight of the Realm, is it?'

Before Morris could reply, he was interrupted by DS Ken White staggering through the door, his mouth foaming like a chocolate fountain. The Marathon bar had begun to melt and, with it, small pockets of oxygen had found their way into his desperate lungs. He had dragged himself to his feet and, for once in his life, was trying to do his duty.

'Stop!' He lunged towards Oliver like a half-drowned man. Oliver stepped to the side and laughed as Ken headbutted the wall, knocking himself out in the process.

'You'll have to excuse me, Father. I need to put the trash out.'

He bent down and grabbed Ken by the ankles then dragged him out of the room and into the corridor, leaving a dark chocolate stain across the floor as he did so.

The fire was out of control now and both sets of fire doors

were ablaze. Smoke was starting to sneak under the seals at the base of the door. Oliver dragged Ken over to it and used him to plug the gap. He stood back and admired his handiwork. Ken White may not have been a good detective but he was an excellent draught excluder. All those snacks had not been in vain.

Oliver returned to find Sir Morris trying to get off the bed. He had only got as far as putting his legs over the side and sitting up. That was all he could manage; he was spent.

Oliver walked around the bed, pulled up a chair and sat down to face him. 'Anything you want to say to me?'

'Help me.'

Oliver shook his head. 'Oh, I think it's too late for that, Father, don't you.'

'I'm not ...'

Morris didn't finish his denial as a flash of flames burst out of the adjoining wall. 'Oh, my God. You have to save me, Oliver.'

Oliver leaned back, unconcerned by the roar of the inferno on the other side of the rapidly failing wall. He ignored the alarms, the screams of panicked patients and staff. He was at the epicentre of chaos and he liked it.

Sir Morris looked at him imploringly. 'Son, if I am your father, save me.'

Oliver nodded. 'Strong   move,   Dad.   Is   that   an acknowledgement of paternity?'

'For God's sake, it's whatever you want it to be. Get me out of here.'

'No, I don't think I can. Mummy wants you gone. She wouldn't like it if I saved you.'

Oliver watched the words register. He could see that Morris didn't understand them.

'Of course Beatrice would want you to help me.'

'You'd think so, wouldn't you, but ...' Oliver stood up and

shrugged his shoulders. 'Apparently not.' He backed away towards the door. 'I've so enjoyed this little chat, Father.'

'Don't go, Oliver, don't leave me here to burn.'

'Oh, I think the smoke will kill you first. But if it doesn't, just remember that you lit this fire yourself long ago. You watched Richard and I go up in flames. Now it's your turn. Good luck.'

Oliver gave Morris a deep bow and backed out of the room. The fire was now licking across the ceiling, furnishing the area above Sir Morris' bed with a crown of flames.

'Oliver!' Sir Morris' scream rang through the corridors of the burning hospital with a power he had no right to have. 'Oliver!' There was terror in those calls, but Oliver would not return and Sir Morris knew it. He slid off the bed and crawled beneath it, hiding from the flames above him like a child cowering from a nightmare. He began to cry and drew up his knees, despite the pain from his wound, and tried to curl himself up into a ball.

In the corridor, flames were licking through the fire door. Ken was beginning to smoulder nicely but he wouldn't hold back the smoke and the flames for much longer. It was time to go.

Without looking back Oliver made for the exit, pushed down hard on the bar and burst out into the night. The fire escape was empty. He ploughed on, taking the steps two at a time. He reached the bottom and sprinted for the hedgerow to make his escape. As he reached the safety of the hedge a cry from within the inferno stopped him in his tracks.

'Oliver, for God's sake, save me. OLIVER!'

The cry carried such power that it made him turn and look back at the terrible scene he had created.

'Oliver, please.'

The voice sounded hopeless, despairing, and it drew him back like a moth to a flame. Why run when no one was chasing him?

He should savour the moment; it had taken so long to create. He walked slowly round to the front of the hospital and stood back to admire his handiwork. The flames reached for the night sky, spitting and crackling, drowning the desperate screams of his father. This was it then, the end. He held up his hands in celebration and screamed triumphantly into the night. 'The king is dead, long live the king.'

Only one person saw him do this: Ginger Dalton. He had just pulled up on the road outside as, to his horror, he had seen the flames leaping out of the building. He heard a thud as a door was thrown open above him, watched as a man fled down the steps, leaving the devastation behind him … and was finally released from his shocked stance as he was faced with a man holding up his arms triumphantly as he shouted something indecipherable into the night.

There was only one man he could think of who would be sick enough to celebrate this devastating sight. He jumped from his car and gave chase but, before he had closed the gap, the man turned and spotted him running towards him. It was Oliver; he knew it. As he got closer, Oliver turned and sprinted towards the side of the hospital. Ginger was less than ten paces from him. The hedgerow Oliver was headed for was at least eight feet tall. He had him. He steadied himself, waiting for Oliver to slow as he approached what appeared to be a dead-end, but Oliver never broke stride. A couple of feet from the hedge, he launched himself into the upper part of the laurels and plunged head first through them.

Ginger expected Oliver to be stuck in the thick branches but Oliver had hit so hard and high that he had gone right through. Ginger sped up and launched himself at the same spot that Oliver had disappeared through. The branches tore at his arms and legs. The back of his arms were gashed where he had held them up in front of his head. As he hit the ground on the other side, he could feel the blood already running down his arms. This gave him hope; if he was hurt maybe Oliver was hurt too. As he dragged himself to his feet and stared into the night, something to his left caught his eye. It was Oliver, running hard and headed towards the cattle market. If he made it there, he could lose himself in the maze of buildings. He began to give chase but as he did so a terrible howl echoed across the night.

'OLIVER. OLIVER!'

There was terror in the voice and he knew at once it was Sir Morris. He looked up and saw Oliver disappearing over the fence that led to the cattle market. He gave chase once more but froze as a scream of pure terror rang out from the inferno that was now lighting up the night.

'Help me!'

He stopped. He wanted Oliver but he couldn't ignore the desperation in that voice. Ginger turned and reluctantly hurled himself back through the hedge and towards the inferno.

As he neared the fire escape, he looked up and saw the door was open. When he reached the top, he realised Oliver had crashed through the door with such force that, when it had smashed against the wall, it had broken the mechanism and failed to close. Here was his way in.

There was a deep orange glow emanating from within. It was a place Ginger didn't want to go and yet he had bounded up the steps, speeding towards a scene that normal people would be running from.

He steadied his breathing and launched himself through the opening.

The heat was almost unbearable. The whole ceiling danced with flames. At the foot of the collapsing fire doors he saw DS White. Flames sparked from Ken's jacket as he tried to crawl away from the inferno.

Without thinking, Ginger ducked down and ran to him. He grabbed Ken roughly by the arms and dragged him to the fire escape. Once they were outside, he adjusted his grip and dragged him down the stairs. Ken's legs bounced off every step. They reached the bottom and Ginger dropped Ken on the ground, turned and raced back up the stairs into a red hell.

The once protective doors were now a wall of fire. The flames engulfed the ceiling and dribbled debris like a molten river. For a moment he stood, transfixed by the beauty of the fire. It was a living, breathing thing, winding like a snake and consuming everything in its path. He dropped to the floor to get below the flames and crawled into Sir Morris' room. The bed was on fire and from beneath it he heard a whimper.

'I'm over here.'

Ginger peered through the glowing haze and located Sir Morris. His right hand stretched out towards him.

'Help me. Please … help me.'

'I'm coming.' Ginger crawled towards him and as he did so there was a roar followed by a thud as the ceiling of the corridor came crashing down behind him turning the doorway – his only route of escape – into a fireball. He looked back at Sir Morris, who had watched it happen from beneath the bed. For a moment they locked eyes and Sir Morris shook his head; they were dead men.

Ginger mouthed the word "sorry" but Sir Morris was not watching any more. The mattress above him had become a bed of flames. Like a storm-cloud releasing its first drops of rain, globules of fire fell from it, igniting Sir Morris' clothes and hair. In a moment he was covered from head-to-toe. No longer a human, just a writhing torch of fire being consumed by the flames.

Ginger turned away, he couldn't watch. His hair smouldered and emitted a bitter odour as it began to burn. Was this the end? There was so much he wanted to do with his life. He glanced around, resigned to his fate; there was no way out.

The smoke was getting thicker. He dropped to his knees and crawled towards the outer wall of the room where the fire hadn't taken hold yet. From his new vantage point he searched for something, anything, that he could use to help himself. There was nothing. The window to the right of the blazing bed blew out into the night. As the air rushed into the room, its oxygen fuelled the hungry fire. He threw himself to the floor and froze as the fire rushed above him, howling with molten anger, a wild river of flame. He watched and waited; this was a flashover. If he survived it … If …

The flames consumed the cool air and fell back from the window. Sensing it was now or never, Ginger charged towards the hole and launched himself out into the night, unaware of what awaited him in the darkness but sure it could not be worse than this inferno of death.

Chapter 19
Aftermath

Fred and Toby stood looking at the smoking ruins of the west wing of the hospital. Once again, Oliver had outsmarted them. Had done something that none of them thought him capable of. Up until this point his mission for revenge had concentrated only on those he felt had wronged him. Heather Wilson had been a mistake, but this ...

'We have to get him, Toby. He's out of control. To risk all these innocent lives. He's a total nutter.'

'I know, boss, it's a miracle all the staff and patients got out. If that nurse hadn't aimed the extinguishers at that fire door...' Toby didn't finish his sentence, the thought of what could have happened was too much to contemplate.

'Well, Sir Morris is gone. Do you think that's it?'

'I'm not sure of anything any more. I thought I knew him,' sighed Toby.

'You can't second-guess a nutter, son. Without Ginger it would have been a lot worse.'

'Is he OK?'

Fred smiled for the first time that morning. 'He dislocated his shoulder when he hit the ground. He was lucky. There was a sloping roof outside the window he dove out of. He slid down it and fell about twelve feet to the flower bed below. Reasonably soft landing. Ruined two hydrangeas, though I'm pretty sure the hospital won't be asking for damages.'

'And what about Ken?'

'Jesus,' Fred shook his head in disbelief. 'Doc said the melting Marathon stopped him inhaling too much smoke. Not quite enough to choke on but enough to filter out some of the toxic fumes. He looked like a chocolate brownie when I saw him. You couldn't write that, could you.'

'At least he's alive, thanks to Ginger. You going to put him in for a medal?'

'What, for saving Ken? I reckon I should knock him back to uniform for that.'

They both started to laugh.

'You know,' said Fred. 'I think this may be the end of it.'

Toby nodded without conviction. He didn't think it was over. He remembered the list he had written on the whiteboard. Who was Banquo and who was Mauldvina? These were questions that had to be asked, even though the answer could mean death. He should have mentioned it but Fred had already cut him a lot of slack with his theories. He needed proof. For that, he would need to look deeper ... and do it alone.

Members of the press were having a field day dissecting the fire at the hospital. The death of Sir Morris Oxford was a cause for national mourning. His passing marked the end of an era. Stratford was in shock.

The loss of Sir Morris was one thing but the lengths the killer had gone to was beyond the comprehension of any sane person. He had set fire to a hospital to get just one man? What level of madness was this?

Questions were asked by the press, and the public demanded answers.

When Fred and Toby returned to Guild Street, Inspector Beeching was waiting for them. He had been hiding himself away at HQ in Coventry. His temporary role covering Chief Wilson's death would not last long unless the Shakespeare Killer was caught.

'Where have you two been?' he demanded as Fred and Toby

strolled in.

'The hospital, sir, checking in with SOCO.'

'Anything?'

Fred shook his head. 'The fire has destroyed all potential evidence, but they confirmed it was started deliberately using petrol. It looks like our killer tried to contain the fire to the second floor of the west wing. Only Sir Morris and Ken White were on that level.'

'Suppose we should be grateful for small mercies.' Beeching held up a special edition of *The Herald*. 'Have you seen this? Doesn't make for comfortable reading, does it?'

Fred and Toby said nothing as Beeching picked up another paper; this time one of the London broadsheets. '"Sir Morris Oxford dead in Stratford Hospital Inferno." It's the bit underneath I don't like. "What is the Stratford force doing to catch the Shakespeare Killer?" It goes on to suggest we aren't capable of doing the job.' Beeching eyed the pile of newspapers on his desk. 'But this,' Beeching held up a copy of *The Daily Globe*. 'Is far worse. Our old friend Patrick Fryer has done a right hatchet job. He's suggested that my position should be part of a new round of Beeching's cuts.'

'That's actually quite funny,' said Fred.

'You think so, do you. Need I remind you that if I go down, we all go down. I promised you the chance to move up if we get this case closed. If I get Wilson's job, I can push it through. Don't you want to be a detective inspector, Fred?'

Fred shrugged. 'The money would be nice.'

'Is that all you've got to say?'

'Pretty much. You know I don't really go in for all this career progression rubbish, sir. I like catching villains and preferably knocking them about a bit in the process. Real job satisfaction, if you know what I mean.'

Beeching looked imploringly at Toby. 'Please don't copy this dinosaur, Marlowe. Times are changing and Fred's ways won't be acceptable for much longer. I'm not sure they ever were.'

Fred shrugged. 'Everyone's a critic.'

Beeching threw down the copy of *The Daily Globe* and pointed to the chairs in front of his desk. 'Sit down. We need to put together a statement which doesn't make us look totally clueless. Any ideas?'

Fred was the first to speak. 'I think with the death of Sir Morris it could be over. Lawrence's mission was revenge on Sir Morris and all those he thought ruined his career. By my reckoning he's killed everybody he wanted to, plus a mistake.'

'Chief Wilson's wife?'

'Yeah. And if you add in the chief's death as well, the body count is getting pretty hefty. I think he's probably done enough.'

Beeching looked at Toby who clearly wasn't nodding his agreement. 'You have doubts, Marlowe?'

'I do, sir. I don't think he's finished.'

'Go on.'

Toby shifted uncomfortably under the gaze of his superiors.

'Say what you think, young Toby. Nobody will criticize you for that.'

'I think he still wants to kill Clarissa Pidgeon, she was part of his plan. Killing Heather Wilson was a mistake and she can't replace Clarissa.'

Beeching nodded. 'I can see that. Anyone else?'

Toby daren't say what he really thought in front of Beeching, so he softened the edges of his theory. 'I still think Beatrice Oxford is a target.'

Beeching spluttered. 'You think he would kill his own mother?'

'Why not, he's killed everyone else.'

Toby turned to Fred. 'You think so, boss?'

'Listen, I've never been on a case like this but one thing is apparent. Lawrence, if it is Lawrence, doesn't want to get caught.'

'What makes you say that?'

'I've worked on a couple of serial killer cases but nothing like this. Three murders in the Dwayne Thor case and four in the Kelly Love case. In both of those they left messages, clues on their victims. With this lot, nothing. He doesn't want to be caught because he has unfinished business.'

'I think I know what that business is, boss.'

'Go on, Toby.'

'I think he believes he can return to the stage.'

'Are you mad,' scoffed Beeching. 'He's killed eight people and was responsible for Chief Wilson's death. How could he ever get back to the stage?'

Toby nodded. 'I know it sounds crazy, sir.'

'It bloody well does.'

'But—'

'Oh, there's a but, is there, Marlowe. There always is with you.'

'Let him finish, sir. Toby has been on the mark up till now,' said Fred.

Toby really didn't want to say what he thought. Beeching would laugh him out of the building, but what choice did he have? There were lives at stake and, if he was correct, they could save them. There comes a point when you just have to go with what you believe and damn the consequences; this was that point.

'We still don't know for sure what Lawrence looks like. We have an artist's impression that's been aged from a sixteen-year-old photo. We have no fingerprints, no verified sightings, nothing that conclusively links him to these murders. We don't even know if the real Oliver Lawrence is still alive. What's to stop him going by a different name, starting at another theatre and then working his way back here one day?'

'Are you crazy?' snapped Beeching.

'No, sir, but I think he is.'

Toby's words hit home and stopped Beeching dead. 'Do you think he's right?' He turned to Fred for support and found none.

'He has a point, sir. We have to consider everything.'

Right now it was clear that Beeching was contemplating his less-than-glittering career disappearing down the toilet. He held up a hand. 'OK, let's take a deep breath.' Beeching sat back in his chair. 'Let's assume for a moment you are correct, Marlowe. If he does want to continue acting, who would he have to kill to be safe and allow that to happen?'

'His mother, for sure. She would definitely have to go.'

Beeching scribbled it down on a notepad, shaking his head in disbelief as he did so. 'Go on.'

'Clarissa Pidgeon would still be on his list. She knew him, was involved with him. She could recognise him, it would be way too risky to let her live.'

Beeching wrote Clarissa's name down, sighing as he did so. 'Is that it?'

His question was almost pleading, in the hope that there would be no more, but Toby had no comfort for him.

'Bernard Wood.'

'Who's he?'

'He used to be Lawrence's agent. His mother lived in Stratford, on Sanctus Road. She died last year and rumour has it that he's coming back to Stratford and moving into the family bungalow.'

'And why would he be a target? Surely, as his agent, he supported him.'

'He did but if Lawrence came back there is a chance that Bernard would recognise him. They were very close.'

Beeching started to close his notebook but hesitated. 'Please tell me that's it?

Toby shook his head.

'For God's sake, Marlowe. Do you think he's planning on

killing everyone in Stratford?'

'No, sir, but I think he has an accomplice.'

This was news to both Fred and Beeching.

'How long have you been thinking this,' asked Fred.

'For some time, boss.'

'It would have been nice if you'd shared it with me. Would you like to bring me and Inspector Beeching in on this theory?'

Toby really didn't think he would like to but this was the moment. Speak now or forever … He knew the rest. If he said what he really thought and he was wrong, well, the consequences didn't bear thinking about. Beeching would laugh him out of his office.

'I think this is his finale. Lawrence is tying up all the loose ends. All those names … I believe, in his mind, they represent characters in a play.'

'Oh, for crying out loud, you're not saying this is another bloody Shakespeare play. Can you imagine what the press would say if they got hold of this theory of yours. We'd all be sectioned.'

'To be fair, sir, Toby's theory was pretty spot on regarding the similarities to *Hamlet* and *Othello*.'

'He's just making the facts fit the play, Fred.'

'Maybe … but they do. Let's hear him out.'

Beeching pursed his lips and leaned back on his chair. 'Very well but tread lightly. Anyone mentions it outside of this room and you'll be back on the beat before the week's out. Do I make myself clear?'

Toby looked at Fred, who nodded.

It was now or never. 'I think Lawrence is acting out *Macbeth*, sir. He wants to be the king – to take Sir Morris' crown – so Sir Morris had to die. He was Duncan.'

Beeching put his pen to paper, then put them both back on his desk instead. 'Write it down, Marlowe. I can't actually get involved in this nonsense.'

'Yes, sir.' Toby got up and walked over to the whiteboard in the corner of Beeching's office. He picked up a red pen and wrote *"Macbeth"* at the top. Beeching muttered an oath under his breath.

'There are direct similarities between the play and Lawrence's actual life.' Toby glanced at his two superior officers.

Beeching looked on in irritated disbelief. Fred, on the other hand, looked interested. Whether it was in Toby's theory, or he was just fascinated to watch him destroy his career in front of him, he couldn't tell.

'In the play, Macbeth is egged on to kill King Duncan by Lady Macbeth. She's ambitious for him to be king and she wants to be queen.'

'But Lawrence isn't married. Who's his Lady Macbeth,' pondered Beeching.

'Beatrice Oxford.'

'That's ridiculous.'

Fred leaned forward. 'Let's hear him out, sir.'

'We've interviewed Lady Beatrice Oxford and she *is* ambitious. She resents being sidelined by her husband and wants to be back on the stage playing roles that suit her talent. Go back to the first murders and we see other similarities with the plays.'

Beeching looked like he was about to explode.

'In *Hamlet*, his father was murdered by his uncle who then became king and married his mother. Lawrence's father, Richard Jenkins, was pushed out of the theatre by Sir Morris. He wanted his crown as the greatest actor on the British stage. Jenkins killed himself and not long after Beatrice married Sir Morris. Lawrence called him 'Uncle Morris' when he was younger. The similarities are very clear.'

'It is uncanny when you look at it like that, sir. If we assume that Lawrence is a little crazy, those are the kind of delusional mental leaps he would be taking.'

'It's just like he did with the first murders. Those were based

96

96 *Sleep No More*

on *Hamlet*.'

'You mean Desmond Tharpe?'

'Tharpe was Sir Morris' right-hand man. His Polonius, if you will. He was stabbed by Hamlet, Tharpe was stabbed by Lawrence.'

'And his daughter Tabitha. How do you account for that, Marlowe?'

'Polonius' daughter Ophelia went crazy and drowned. Tharpe's daughter drowned in the river after witnessing the mutilated body of Terry Fibbs the day before, just like in the play. Tabitha also used to be Lawrence's girlfriend.'

Beeching was still scowling but there could be no denying that Toby's theory regarding the plays represented some startling, inexplicable similarities.

'What about Fibbs. How was he related?'

'Fibbs, like Soames, was Sir Morris' tame newsman. Morris got them both to print doctored reviews to make Lawrence look bad.'

'And who would they be,' asked Beeching firmly.

'Rosencrantz and Guildenstern.'

Beeching didn't say anything to that. He knew his Shakespeare and, slowly, everything that his young DC was saying was making horrible sense.

'When Chief Wilson's wife was strangled, she had a black handkerchief across her face with crocheted strawberries on it. Just like—'

'Desdemona.' Fred finished the sentence for him.

Beeching leaned forward, elbows on his desk, and massaged his temples, trying to ease the throbbing headache that was building. 'Write it up, Marlowe, I want to see how this,' he struggled to get the words out. 'Theory of yours finishes.'

Toby scribbled the names and connections onto the whiteboard, adding the names of Lizzie Birchwood and Chief Wilson. He turned to face Fred and Beeching, both of whom were now listening intently.

'If I'm right, Lawrence now thinks he's Macbeth, that he needed to kill the king, Sir Morris. He's done that. In the play he then kills Banquo's family.'

'And who would our Banquo be, DC Marlowe?'

'That's the million-dollar question, sir. I think it's his accomplice.'

'Oh, the mysterious accomplice that nobody's ever mentioned. You want to explain that.'

Toby didn't, but he had no choice. 'I don't believe he could have done this alone, someone's got to be helping him. He's clearly not staying in a hotel or B&B, we've checked them all.'

'You think he's being sheltered by a local.'

'I can't think of any other reason that we haven't found him.'

'What are you suggesting, questioning local residents on the streets and poking around their flowerbeds?' Beeching sounded dismissive. 'Can you imagine how that would go down with the locals, all those trendy lefties having their personal freedoms compromised.'

'Better than being murdered or burned to death in a hospital fire though, sir,' observed Fred.

'There is that,' agreed Beeching.

'After the hospital fire I think the citizens of Stratford would go along with virtually anything that brings these murders to an end.'

Beeching leaned back in his chair and considered Toby's words. 'You could be right. After the hospital fire there will never be a better time to do it.'

'If we announce a house by house it may flush him out,' said Fred.

Beeching looked alarmed. 'Search the houses? We can't do that, it's Stalinesque!'

'If we don't there's not much point though, is there. If he has an accomplice, he or she will just cover for him. We need to search the buildings.'

'No, Fred, that's too much. If we don't find him, I will be demonized. Not only as a useless copper but also a fascist. We have to be more softly, softly.'

Fred smiled. 'We have eight victims including Chief Wilson. It's a bit late for softly, softly.'

'No, we're not doing that. You can knock on doors and make general enquiries. If we come across anything that doesn't feel right, then we can follow up.'

Fred went to protest but Beeching shook his head. 'This isn't up for debate, Williams. You can start tomorrow after I announce it at the press conference this afternoon. At least we'll look like we are doing something.'

Toby and Fred glanced at each other; it wasn't lost on Beeching. 'You have something to add, Marlowe?'

'I think I should identify any likely suspects who could be helping Lawrence as a priority, sir.'

'Very well, get on with it and report back in twenty-four hours.'

Unfortunately, the suspect they were looking for didn't have twenty-four hours.

Chapter 20
Falling Into Place

Beatrice Oxford had been expecting the knock on the door since she heard the news about the fire at Stratford Hospital on the radio that morning. Oliver, it appeared, had decided that his biological father was surplus to requirements. This pleased Beatrice; her son had indeed done the dirty work for her. All she had to do now was find a way of getting rid of him too.

One by one she would remove the obstacles that stood in her way. It felt strange to want something so badly, having dismissed its possibility for years. She'd held back the yearning, ignored the call. This time nothing and no one would stop her. There was no amount she would not pay; her husband, her child. All would be sacrificed for her destiny; to get back on that stage where she belonged.

A knock rattled the door and she realised that, lost in her own thoughts and fantasies, she had ignored the first knock. She hurried to the door, set her face in the concerned look she felt appropriate, and then opened it. DC Marlowe and DS Williams stood outside her room.

'Oh, it's you. Bit early for visitors.'

Toby smiled weakly. 'Can we come in, please, Lady Oxford.'

Beatrice stood aside and ushered them in. She pointed towards the sofa. 'You might as well sit down.'

'I'd rather not if that's all right. I'm afraid we have some bad news for you.'

Beatrice allowed a look of mild alarm to play upon the corners of her mouth, she knew she had to play this perfectly. 'I don't like the sound of this.'

'Have you had the news on this morning, ma'am?'

'No. I never listen to the news, far too depressing. Why do you ask?'

Toby glanced at Fred, who gave an almost imperceptible nod for him to continue.

'I'm afraid there has been a fire at the hospital.'

Beatrice allowed her mouth to fall slightly open and a momentary expression of confusion to pass across her features. It was beautifully done. 'Fire … at the hospital?'

'I'm afraid so.'

'Is everyone safe?'

Toby shook his head. 'No, not everyone.'

Beatrice grabbed Toby's arm. 'What about Morris, is he safe?'

'I'm very sorry to say, no. Sir Morris perished in the flames.'

For a few seconds the grip on Toby's arm became vice-like and then Beatrice Oxford looked up at the ceiling and let out the wail of a wild animal. It came from somewhere deep inside her, another country where your deepest fears and sorrows walk untethered. It was raw and untamed and could not be reasoned with.

'Morris. Morris!' She held her head in her hands and began to scream.

Not her husband's name this time, nothing intelligible. Just the expression of raw pain that knew there was no remedy; a deep, long river that led to despair.

Toby reached towards her trying to hold her hand but she flinched, crouching back as if in fear, looking up at him like a cornered animal.

And then the accusations came. Harsh, venomous and accusatory. 'You killed him, you let Oliver kill him.'

Toby tried to calm her. 'Lady Oxford, I promise you we did everything we could.'

'Promise? Your promises have no currency. You failed him

and you failed me.' Beatrice saw the shock written on both Toby's and Fred's faces; they hadn't been expecting this. She pressed her advantage and took her performance up another gear. She was enjoying herself.

She ran at Toby and beat him with her fists, hammering against his chest and clawing at his face. She was like a force possessed; it was all Toby could do to hold her off.

Fred moved swiftly behind her and tried to ease her away from Toby. She turned on him like a hunting wolf and launched herself, howling like something from a nightmare. Her sharp nails dug into Fred's cheeks and she pulled down hard until there was blood dripping down his face.

He pushed her away but she launched herself at him once more. With a deftness that defied his girth, Fred stepped aside and Beatrice – in full-on venomous attack mode – charged straight past him and into the wall. A moment later, she was lying unconscious on the floor.

'What the hell did you do that for,' demanded Toby.

'Do what?' said Fred. 'I just stepped aside and let physics decide the outcome.'

Fred leaned over Beatrice Oxford's prostrate form. 'She's much nicer when she's sleeping.'

'How are we going to explain this?'

Fred shrugged. 'It appears to me she fainted and clipped her head on the arm of the sofa as she went down.'

Before Toby could react, Fred had picked her up and laid her on the sofa. 'I think you'd better put the kettle on. She'll need some hot, sweet tea for the shock.'

Toby stood there stunned. 'You let her run into the wall.'

'No, that never happened, Toby. You didn't have a clear view. Lady Oxford fainted and grabbed at me as she fell. She drew blood, accidentally, with her fingertips in passing.'

It was a version of the event that had just occurred. Not the one Toby had witnessed, but a version nonetheless. He made his way to the kettle that stood on a tray on the dressing table. There were two cups, milk and tea. This being the Swan, there was also a nice china teapot and a plate of shortbread that had clearly been made in the hotel's kitchen. The kettle was full and Toby pressed on the switch before turning back to his boss. He was bent over Lady Oxford.

'She's coming round.' Fred pressed his handkerchief to the livid scratches on his cheek. There hadn't been much blood and the flow had already stopped.

'Lady Oxford,' whispered Fred, more tenderly than Toby had expected from the man whose actions, or lack thereof, had placed her there. 'Are you OK? You fainted.'

Her eyes flickered open and she looked up at Fred in confusion. 'Morris?'

'No, Lady Oxford. It's DS Williams.'

She blinked at him. 'There's blood on your cheek.'

Fred smiled. 'Just a little. I tried to catch you as you fell.'

'Oh.' She forced a smile. 'That was kind.' She looked across at Toby then back to Fred. Beatrice couldn't remember fainting but she remembered why they were here. 'It was about Morris, wasn't it?'

Her words were pitch perfect; the uncertainty in her voice, the slight edge of fear that danced around the edges of her question. Beatrice Oxford was giving the performance of a lifetime, despite being slightly concussed.

Fred knelt down and took her hands gently in his. 'I'm afraid you've had a bit of a shock.'

'I have?'

'Yes. It's Sir Morris.'

Slowly the look of confusion on Beatrice's face was replaced by a memory. 'The fire ... at the hospital?' Fred nodded.

She looked over to Toby for confirmation. The look on his

face confirmed her darkest fears. Well, that's how she made it look. She stared back at Fred who was still holding her hands. 'Morris is dead, isn't he?'

'I'm very sorry, Lady Oxford.'

There were no screams this time, just gentle sobs of acceptance as poor Beatrice Oxford realised, through the shards of grief and mists of mild concussion, that her husband had indeed perished.

It was a moment she would look back on with awe; never had she known she was capable of acting a scene of such raw, uncontrolled emotion. She was a far better serious actress than she had dared hope. Such was her skill that she had even managed to faint without being aware of it. This was next level duplicity and wasn't that what the real art of acting was? Telling a lie so convincingly that all who saw it believed it to be true.

Toby held out a cup of tea. 'There you are, Lady Oxford. Four sugars for the shock.

She took it from him gratefully. 'Thank you, you've been so kind.'

'We try to be empathetic, Lady Oxford,' said Fred.

She sipped her tea and nodded. 'I'm sorry about the scratch.'

Fred stroked his cheek. 'Think nothing of it, Lady Oxford. Occupational hazard.'

Fred had left Toby with Lady Oxford and made a call to Mel Townsend from the reception of the White Swan.

'Hi Mel, it's Fred.'

'What a mess.'

'Me or the fire?'

She chuckled. 'Both. Where are you?'

'At the Swan, just had to break the news to Lady Oxford about Sir Morris.'

'Jesus. How'd she take it?'

'Not well. Went a bit crazy then fainted. I tried to grab her as she went down and got clawed across the face for my trouble.'

'Is she OK?'

'Yeah. Caught her chin on the arm of the sofa as she went down, bit stunned but seems fine now. Toby's made her a cup of sweet tea.'

'Does she need checking over at the hospital?'

'What hospital,' asked Fred.

Mel laughed, she couldn't help it. 'Fred Williams, sometimes I wonder if you're wired right.'

'You know I am, Mel. Anyway, I'm after a favour.'

'Anything, if I can.'

'Would you come over and have a chat with Lady Oxford? I want your opinion, we didn't get the reaction I expected from her.'

'How do you mean?'

'Well, at first, before she fainted, she was angry, accusing us of failing Sir Morris, but now,' he paused for a moment. 'It's like she's a different person.'

'Shock can do that to someone, Fred. You've been on the job long enough to know that.'

'I know,' Fred paused again, trying to distil his thoughts. 'There was an almost resigned acceptance after she came round. It was like she was playing a different scene. Same situation but a totally different reaction.' He shook his head. 'I just need a second opinion.'

'You think she's lying.'

'If she is, she's the best liar I've ever seen.'

'Then what?'

'I dunno, Mel, something just feels off. Would you talk to her, see what you think?'

'Course I will, Fred. Is WPC Kettles there?'

Fred brightened at the sound of her name. 'Yeah, she's at Guild Street.'

'Good, she'll have a good bedside manner. Get her to sit in with Lady Oxford until I get there.'

Fred didn't reply. He was too busy thinking about WPC Kettles and imagining what her bedside manner would be like.

'Fred?' Mel's voice snapped him out of his daydream.

'Sorry, got distracted. It's been one hell of a day and it's only just getting started. I'll get Kettles over here now.'

'OK, I'll be there within the hour.'

The line went dead. Fred pressed for another outside line and summoned WPC Kettles from Guild Street.

Chapter 21
Agent Provocateur

Toby walked into the foyer of Stratford Hospital. The west wing was cordoned off and the smell of burned timber lingered in the air like a bad memory. He shuddered; the fire could have been a catastrophe. Only the quick thinking of a nurse with a fire extinguisher had prevented the spread until the fire brigade arrived.

Lawrence could have killed dozens of innocent people. Any residual sympathy Toby had harboured for him was now gone. He was a madman and needed locking up.

He stopped at the reception desk. 'Could you tell me which ward DC Dalton is on, please?'

The receptionist looked at her book. 'Ward four, first room on the right.'

'Thanks.' Toby braced himself, unsure what he was going to find. He'd seen burns before, and he prayed Ginger had escaped the worst of it.

As he opened the door to Ginger's room, his worst fears were allayed. Ginger was looking a bit redder in the face than usual and his ginger hair was now just singed, darkened stubble on his head, but he looked good, considering ...

'Hi Dave, how you feeling?'

'Like a piece of bacon.'

'Yeah, you do look a bit crispy around the edges.'

They both smiled but behind those smiles was the knowledge of what could have been. Toby could see it in Ginger's eyes, a fear he had never seen before.

'You want to talk about it, mate?'

'No.'

'I'm afraid I have to ask you some questions. I need to know what you saw. I don't like having to ask, but you know how it goes.'

'I know. I was hoping I wouldn't have to think about it for a while. Trouble is, it's all I can think about. Just keeps replaying again and again in my head. A bloody nightmare on repeat.'

Toby pulled up a chair and sat beside his friend's bed. He pulled out his notebook. 'Tell me what you saw when you first arrived.'

Ginger's eyes glazed over as he thought back on the events of the night before.

'I didn't intend to go to the hospital but I saw the blaze as I was driving past. Soon as I saw it, I knew it was Lawrence's doing.'

'What made you think that,' asked Toby as he scribbled away.

'I knew that Sir Morris was in the west wing. I was there in the morning when we were setting up the police protection. When I saw that wing was ablaze, I didn't think it was a coincidence.'

'Did you see anything suspicious?'

Ginger fixed Toby with an amused stare. 'What, apart from flames leaping out of the roof?'

'Yeah, apart from that,' said Toby. 'Did you see anyone?'

Ginger nodded. 'A man hurtled down the fire escape, really moving. Which seemed fair enough in the circumstances, but then …'

'Then, what?'

'He stopped running. That's when I realised who he was.'

'OK. Let's be clear about this. What exactly did you see?'

'Oliver Lawrence was standing in front of the hospital watching the fire. His arms were aloft, like he was celebrating. It was sick. I went after him but he saw me and ran into the grounds. Before I could catch him, he dove through the top of the laurel hedge and made for the cattle market. I followed him through but

I couldn't just ignore the screams from inside. Sir Morris', as it happens.'

Ginger fell silent and it was clear to Toby that he was remembering everything he had seen and heard last night.

He shook his head slowly, almost in disbelief. 'It was terrible, Toby. I've never heard screams like that before. He knew he was dying. I looked up at the roof and the fire was really taking hold. I knew if I didn't get in there straight away it would be too late. I had to let Lawrence go.'

'You did the right thing. Without you, Ken would be dead too.'

Ginger nodded slowly. 'I just wish I could have got Sir Morris out.'

'We all do but you did everything you could, mate. There's talk of a commendation.'

Ginger sighed. 'That won't bring Sir Morris back, will it?'

'No … but it will acknowledge your bravery.'

'I was just doing my job. You would have done exactly the same if you were in my shoes.'

Toby shook his head. 'I'm not so sure I would have. I've looked into a blazing building before, not a place I think I could go.'

Ginger's face was a mask of shock and sadness. 'Yeah, you could. When I heard those screams, I just knew I had to try. He sounded like a terrified animal.'

Ginger was struggling but Toby knew he had to get the description of what happened before he left.

'I'm sorry, mate, but I need it all.'

Ginger nodded. 'OK.' He took a deep breath and tried to let the tension out of his body. 'I'll try.'

'Good man.'

'As I ran towards the building the fire escape door was still open. It looked like the gates of hell. Before I realised what I was doing, I had run up the stairs and thrown myself into the corridor.'

Ginger shook his head slowly. 'You can't imagine the heat, Toby. It was starting to lick across the ceiling, tongues of flame seeping through the fire door, even the smoke was catching fire. Ken was lying at the foot of the door and tried to scramble towards me. He looked like he was coughing up blood.'

'That was a melting Marathon bar,' said Toby. 'Apparently, nearly choking to death on that stopped him inhaling too much smoke. A melted-chocolate filter, if you will.'

A momentary smile crossed Ginger's face. 'Is that what it was! I didn't have time to check. I just dragged him out of there, down the fire escape and onto the lawn, far enough away to be safe.'

'What did you do then,' asked Toby.

'I went back in for Sir Morris.'

Toby scribbled a few more notes and then looked at Ginger. 'I think we can leave it there. We all know what happened next.'

'No, I want to tell you,' insisted Ginger. 'I can't ever unsee it but maybe talking about it will help.'

Toby shrugged. 'Up to you, Ginger. It's your call.'

'I want to,' he said, and then to himself, 'I think I have to.'

Toby reopened his notebook and raised his pen. Ginger's face bore the haunted look of a man who had seen the other side of darkness. His eyes, sunken in deep recesses, stared out from his blackened head, framed by what appeared to be a smouldering mass of stubble.

Toby had seen that thousand-mile stare before in photos of shell-shocked troops in the two Great Wars. He didn't want to push Ginger too far but he had to know. 'Did you manage to get close enough to Sir Morris to speak to him?'

'Yes, I crawled into his room. The fire was spreading across the ceiling. I had to stay low or else I would have caught fire. Sir Morris was under his bed, trying to shelter from the heat.'

'Was he still conscious?'

Ginger nodded. 'Afraid so. He asked me to help him, but I

couldn't get to him. I didn't know what to do, Toby. I was just crouching there, every fibre in my body telling me to get out but … the look in his eyes. He was begging me to save him and I think we both knew I couldn't.'

Toby didn't say anything; he had stopped writing now. It didn't seem right to put Ginger's words down on paper; it was too painful, too real.

'I was caught up in indecision. I wanted to save him, Toby, I really did. But the heat was unbearable and part of the ceiling had fallen down between us. It had set fire to the mattress.

'I remembered there was a fire extinguisher in the hallway. I thought, if I could get to it, maybe I could beat the flames back enough to get to Sir Morris. Before I could turn back another part of the ceiling and partition collapsed behind me, cutting off my escape to the extinguisher and the fire escape. I was trapped.

'I turned back to Sir Morris. The hand he had held out towards me was slowly withdrawn. We looked at each other and we knew we were dead men. I'll never forget the look on his face. I told him I was sorry and then he just curled up in a ball, like a frightened child, and waited to die.'

For a few moments Ginger stopped talking as he replayed the terrible scene in his mind. 'I couldn't go back and I couldn't go forward. I realised I was going to die. You ever felt like that, Toby? Believing that this was it?'

Toby shook his head. He'd had his moments but nothing like this.

'I hope you never do, mate. Everything I have ever done and everything I want to do flashed across my mind. I saw it all. Felt the memories, the regret for things I would never get to do. It was surreal. The roof was beginning to come down on me and my mind was replaying events from my past.'

Ginger looked at Toby and smiled weakly. 'It's true what they say. When you're dying your life really does pass before your eyes.'

'But you didn't die, did you,' said Toby.

'No, I didn't.' Ginger shifted painfully in his bed. 'I saw Sir Morris die though, poor bugger. He had balled himself up into a foetal position but the mattress caught and within seconds, as it began to melt, globules of molten fire began to drip down on him.

'He screamed as the first drops hit him, squirming like a trapped wild animal, but he couldn't escape it. It was dripping down in huge lumps now like the lava flow from a volcano. It was terrible.' Ginger fixed Toby with an unblinking stare. 'I saw his face catch fire, Toby. His face!'

Toby reached out and laid his hand on Ginger's. 'It's all right, mate. You got out.'

'But he didn't. A person shouldn't burst into flames, should they.'

'You can't dwell on it, Ginger. You did everything you could.'

'Wasn't enough though, was it.' There were tears in Ginger's bloodshot eyes. Toby gently urged him to finish his story. 'How did you get out?'

Ginger shook his head in disbelief. 'It was a miracle. The window to the right of Sir Morris' bed blew out.

'I hit the deck because I knew when that cold fresh air hit the flames it would cause a flashover. I've seen videos about a fire like that. I lay on the floor and watched it shoot past me like it had been spat from the mouth of a dragon. I think I screamed but I couldn't hear my own voice, nothing prepares you for that roar as it tries to devour everything in its path.

'Never realised it before but fire, when it's out of control, is a living breathing thing. It was beautiful and yet terrible. I took one last look for Sir Morris before I ran for it. The mattress was starting to collapse on him. I saw him reach up, trying to hold it off him but his arms just disappeared into it. He didn't scream after that, he just seemed to be absorbed by the flames. The flashover had finished and I jumped out of the window.'

'Did you know what was on the other side,' asked Toby.

'No. I just knew it had to be better than where I was.'

Toby had put his notebook away. He couldn't imagine what Ginger had been through. There were demons haunting Ginger and they would take a long time to fade, if they ever did. 'I'll see you tomorrow, mate.'

Ginger nodded but it was obvious he wasn't really listening. His thoughts were lost in a place where only fire could survive. A burning molten hell which he could never unsee.

Toby hoped Ginger would take some time off and get some help. He had seen other officers come back too soon before and it had never ended well.

Chapter 22
The Witches' Prophesy

As Toby walked out of the grounds of the hospital a feeling of helplessness came over him. It seemed that whatever he and Fred did they just couldn't get near to Lawrence. He was like a shadow, always just out of reach. For the first time since the murders had started, he realised they really were nowhere near to catching Oliver Lawrence.

As he walked past the American Memorial Fountain, he became aware of a motorcycle roaring up from the town centre towards him. The rider nodded and screeched to a halt beside him.

'Toby.'

'You do realise there's a thirty miles per hour limit on this road, don't you, Whomper.'

Whomper waved such frivolous matters away with a raised hand. 'Never mind that. I have news.'

'Go on then, let's hear it.'

Whomper climbed off his motorbike and signalled Toby to come close. 'Bernard Wood is back in Stratford.'

For a moment the meaning didn't register with Toby. He took in Whomper's excited expression. 'And that's news because?'

Whomper couldn't hide the exasperation in his voice. 'Bernard Wood shall come to Dunroamin. The prophesy, don't you remember?'

Toby did remember but he didn't want to think about it. 'So, Oliver's agent is returning to Stratford?'

'Think, Toby. Bernard Wood shall come to Dunroamin. What does it mean?'

'*Macbeth*?'

'Exactly, the prophesy is coming true. Macbeth shall never vanquished be until Great Birnam Wood to high Dunsinane Hill shall come against him. Oliver Lawrence is about to fall.'

Despite his theory about Lawrence following the plot of *Macbeth*, Toby was struggling to join the dots on this one. The only problem was Whomper and his sisters had been correct before. 'How does Bernard Wood coming back to Stratford affect Lawrence?'

'He knew him better than anyone.'

'What, even his mother?'

'Maybe. He spent a lot of time with Lawrence in his last two years at Stratford. He was headed for greatness and Bernard was looking to get him film and TV deals. He invested a lot of his time in him, and then he just disappeared. He never got over such a wasted talent and he blamed Sir Morris and Lady Oxford for Lawrence's disappearance.'

'OK. I hear what you're saying but what does it mean?'

'When we prophesied Bernard's return it was symbolic. It means something. These things aren't just random.'

'They seem pretty random to me, Whomper.'

'That's because you're thinking like a policeman.'

'I am a policeman.'

'No. You're better than that, Toby. You have an open, enquiring mind. Think.'

Toby did think. If he divorced the facts from the prophesy, what did it mean? 'You think that Bernard Wood is Birnam Wood.'

Whomper nodded enthusiastically. 'And?'

'Dunroamin is Dunsinane?'

'Exactly.'

'There is no *exactly*, Whomper. It's just a coincidence.'

'You've said that before but our visions are always correct.'

'But what does it mean?'

'Just like the play, Toby. When Bernard Wood comes to Dunroamin, Macbeth shall no longer be king. When Lawrence finds out, he'll know the game is up.'

Toby wasn't convinced. 'I can't sell this nonsense to Fred and Beeching, they'll have me sectioned!'

'You don't have to. Just get the information out there, it will unsettle him. Maybe cause him to make a mistake.'

'You think so?'

'Of course, actors are superstitious creatures. If he thinks that he is Macbeth this will be a terrible omen for him. Might make him do something foolhardy.'

'Like what?'

'Well, if I was him, I'd kill Bernard.'

'What?'

'It makes sense.' Whomper thought for a moment before qualifying his statement. 'Actually, it makes perfect sense if you're a homicidal maniac who thinks he's Macbeth.'

Toby considered Whomper's advice. Fred had always told him to try and get inside the mind of the killer. If he was Lawrence, killing Bernard would make a kind of sense. It was the logic of madness but when you had already killed seven victims and been responsible for the death of Chief Wilson, maybe the only logic you had was that of a madman. 'You think we should give Bernard police protection?'

'Absolutely. He should be in a safe house right now. Get him in protection and then announce that he is back in town. Make it an innocuous statement in an article in *The Herald*.'

'Like, "well-known agent returns to Stratford and is going to live in his old family home on Sanctus Road?"'

'Exactly. Set the trap, he'll come running. What have you got to lose.'

It made sense; what had they got to lose?

'I can't sell it to the boss with the prophesy though,' said Toby.

'You don't have to. Just tell Fred and Beeching that Bernard Wood was very close to Lawrence and they'd clashed before he disappeared.'

'Did they?'

'I don't know, I just made that bit up. If you do the same, they'll put Bernard in protective custody and the trap will be baited and set.'

Toby didn't have to think about it, it just felt right. Crazy, but right. To catch a madman you had to think like a madman. 'OK, I'll do it.'

Whomper sighed with relief. 'Thank God, I thought for a second you were going to let the rational side of your brain overrule you.'

'I've never been guilty of that,' smiled Toby. 'See you later, Whomper.'

'You will,' he grinned. 'Why don't you meet me in the Garrick for a spot of dinner later.'

'I can't afford it, Whomper,' chuckled Toby.

'No, I'm paying.'

Toby stepped back in mock surprise. 'Is this a late April Fool's joke?'

'No. I've come into a bit of money, happy to share it with a friend.' Whomper shot him his most winning smile which, despite the gold teeth and occasional missing item, was still somewhat charming. Like the graveyard of a once noble estate, elegantly decayed.

'I'm tempted, Whomper. Let's see if we have any murders this afternoon. If the body count's low, I'll consider it.'

Whomper sighed. 'Wow, that went dark.'

'Yeah, well, if it wasn't for my sunny disposition I might be getting a little depressed.'

Toby turned up his collar against the sudden chill he felt and headed back towards Guild Street, knowing he had to get Bernard

Wood into police protection without actually explaining exactly why to his superiors.

Chapter 23
A Performance Of Grief

Beatrice was proud of her performance. She had tried to underplay her role, casting doubt on whether she really believed that Oliver could return to the stage one day. Gently convincing him that the killing was not over. It had been a subtle planting of a poisonous seed and Oliver's crazed mind was the perfect soil in which to grow it.

All she had to do now was stand back and wait to see what happened, only then would she know her path.

For now, she had the business of grieving to perform, the nation expected it. Lady Beatrice Oxford had to face the world's press and pretend that she was lost without her husband. How would she keep the smile from her face?

There was a knock on her door.

'Come.'

The door swung open and in walked Robert Parker, her travelling assistant. He was younger than her, a lot younger, but Morris had allowed her to hire him. He would do anything to please Beatrice, especially if it meant a quiet life.

'The press are in reception, Lady Oxford.'

Beatrice gave him a weak grin. 'That's very formal, *Robert*. Is somebody listening?'

'Can't be too careful, you never know. When I drove into Stratford from Woodstock this morning the traffic was terrible. Police and press everywhere.'

'So what do you think I should do?'

Parker paused for a moment. He ran his fingers through his long, lustrous locks.

Watching him, Beatrice felt a long-forgotten itch that she so wanted to scratch.

'I think we should issue a statement.'

Beatrice nodded. 'That would be the sensible thing to do, but I don't feel very sensible today.'

'Why would you. Your husband has just died a horrible death. You're still in shock.'

'Yes,' she said distractedly. 'I suppose I am.' She looked at Parker as he bent down to pick up his notebook. He had a nice bottom; pert and firm. It hinted at the possibilities her new future could hold. Disappointingly, with the benefit of youth, he straightened up smoothly and that lithe rump, so ripe for slapping, disappeared as he turned back to her.

'Hudge up, Beatie. Let's get this written.'

'Well that formality didn't last long.'

He shrugged. 'Like you said, nobody's going to hear us, so we can just be ourselves.'

Beatrice looked at him as he opened his notebook and wrote something at the top of a blank page. Maybe, when a suitable period of mourning had passed, she could make a move on him. She knew he was from somewhere near Liverpool but that wasn't a deal breaker for her. She had always been open to mixed relationships.

'I think you should open with, "This has been a terrible week. First the stabbing and now, just as Sir Morris seemed to be out of danger, the fire. It's almost too much to bear."'

Beatrice nodded her approval. 'That's not bad, Rob, let me try.' She took the notebook from him and began to read. 'This has been a terrible week,' she paused and bit her lip, seemingly fighting back her tears. 'First the stabbing,' she let out a stifled sob and her hand went to her mouth. She took a convulsive breath and fought to continue.

'Just when Sir Morris was out of danger … the fire.' A tear trickled from the corner of her right eye. 'I'm not sure I will ever be able to come to terms with the events that have occurred.' Her bottom lip trembled and, through tear-stained eyes, she looked straight at Parker. 'Could I ask to be left alone to mourn my dear, sweet husband in private.' She burst into tears and turned away, as if leaving a microphone.

Parker could feel tears welling in his eyes. 'That was so moving, Beatie.'

Beatrice turned to face him, a big smile on her face. 'Yeah. It wasn't bad, was it? I can be quite convincing when I want to be.'

'You were acting?'

'Of course. You knew Sir Morris. He was an old, self-centred git.'

Parker shrugged. 'You have a point, but I think we need to maintain the grieving widow act for the time being. Don't want anyone casting aspersions, now do we.'

Parker picked up a box of handkerchiefs from the table and offered them to Beatrice.

She shook her head. 'No, thanks. I want to look suitably distressed. Tell them I will be down in a moment to give a short statement.'

Parker nodded. 'Keep it short, just like that. Maybe a bit more sobbing?'

Beatrice shook her head. 'No, I'm British. Stiff upper lip, it'll impress the hell out of the Americans. I may even get a film offer off the back of it.'

Robert Parker looked at his boss with renewed admiration. She really was a cold and calculating operator. He admired that, desired it even.

Perhaps now, with Sir Morris gone, he could make the move he had so longed to. Not now though, it was far too soon. There was an age gap of nearly fifteen years, but that wouldn't be a problem. It was the geographical gap that worried him.

He'd never dated a southerner before. The idea of a

relationship below the Watford Gap would have been unthinkable growing up in Warrington, but this was 1972. The world was changing and everything seemed possible. He tore the page out of his notebook and offered it to Beatrice. 'You want to have a read on the way down?'

'No. I think I know my lines.'

When they reached the lounge of the White Swan Hotel, Rob told Beatrice to wait for a moment before entering. 'I just want to set some ground rules first, OK?'

Beatrice nodded and watched Parker do what he was best at: controlling the narrative. As he entered the lounge, journalists with raised voices vied for his attention.

'How is Lady Oxford?'

'When is Sir Morris' funeral?'

'The police think it was her son who set fire to the hospital. What's her reaction?'

They were the usual insensitive and inane questions that he had come to expect from the burgeoning tabloid press.

He smiled and held up a hand to silence them. 'Lady Oxford will be here in a moment. She will be giving a statement and will not be taking questions.'

There was another barrage from the press, all of which Parker ignored as he waited patiently for the noise to die down.

'I will ask Lady Oxford to come in. Please, just listen to the statement and afterwards I,' he put an emphasis on the I, 'will take any questions you have.'

As Parker moved to the door behind him there was a hum of anticipation in the room.

Behind the journalists stood Fred Williams; he wanted to hear this. Like Toby, he thought there was something about Lady Beatrice Oxford that didn't ring true. Maybe witnessing her press conference would give him a clue.

Parker opened the door and Lady Oxford entered the room. Fred had forgotten how attractive she was. An elfin beauty that rendered her ageless, she could have passed for mid-thirties and yet he knew she was nearer sixty.

Parker guided Beatrice to the microphone and stood back to allow her to speak. She stepped forward and took a deep breath to compose herself.

'This has been a terrible week,' she paused. 'My husband was stabbed on-stage and that was awful. We didn't know if he would survive.' She let out a sob which she stifled with a handkerchief.'

Parker stepped up and put a reassuring hand on her shoulder. Fred noticed this. A little over familiar?

'Just when we thought dear Morris was out of the woods … this happens.' The first tear ran down her cheek. 'Burned to death, what kind of monster does that?' Along with the tears there was now shocked disbelief. 'I can't even see him, hold him. There are just his teeth.'

For some reason, Fred found this amusing; the great Sir Morris Oxford reduced to a set of teeth. He remembered how his grandad would leave his false teeth in a glass beside the sink in the kitchen every morning. He looked around at the gathered press; everybody else was hanging on Lady Oxford's every word.

'Whoever did this is a monster. He needs to be caught.' She trembled visibly and tears ran down her cheeks, falling to the floor. She tried to compose herself but all she found was anger. Looking up at the gathered press she narrowed her tearful eyes, her face now a mask of rage.

'He took my husband, my love, my life … I hate him.'

Everyone in the room knew she was talking about her son; it was painful to watch.

Some looked away in discomfort but not Fred. He watched intently as Parker moved closer and put a supportive arm around her. She buried her head in his chest and clung onto him.

'That will be all for now,' he said as he guided her from the room in total silence.

None of the press said a word, silenced by the raw emotion on display. Fred watched them depart, unaffected by the scene he had just witnessed. The one word that popped into his head was *choreographed*. That had been a performance, a brilliant one, but a performance nonetheless. Toby was right, there really was something of the night about Lady Beatrice Oxford.

On the other side of the door, Beatrice's tears had stopped. She wiped her face with the handkerchief and looked up at Parker.

'How was I?'

'Amazing.'

She smiled. 'I was, wasn't I.' She reached up and ran her fingers through his hair. 'I couldn't have done it without you, Rob.'

'My pleasure,' he grinned. Maybe he would be going south of Watford Gap sooner than he thought.

In the foyer of the hotel the amassed ranks of the press drifted away in search of phones to call their story in. Outside two TV journalists were setting up to do a piece to camera.

Fred Williams allowed all this activity to pass him by; he was still processing what he had just witnessed. He had changed his mind about Beatrice Oxford, realising she was a very fine actress indeed. He needed to get back to the station and speak to Toby.

Chapter 24
No Blood On The Parquet

Oliver stood outside the Post Office in Old Town. He wasn't sure why; it was just a feeling. He knew Ting Hu from his early years in Stratford. She had secrets, lots of them, and he had a feeling that one of those secrets included Felix. He had no evidence, only intuition. But, of late, intuition had served him well. He pushed open the door of the shop and entered. Ting Hu stood behind the counter as if she had been expecting him.

'Hello Ting, remember me?'

Ting looked at him without expression. 'Sorry, no. Should I?'

'Suppose not.' Oliver glanced around the small Post Office. He had heard rumours about a huge warehouse full of stolen goods. It was a local legend; never proven, just rumoured.

'Can I help you or are you just here to look?'

Oliver smiled at the sarcasm in her voice. This lady took no nonsense from anyone. 'Well, I guess that depends.'

'On what.'

Oliver stepped back towards the front door and slid the shoot bolt, locking them in. He turned back to Ting. 'Whether you want to answer my questions.'

'Why don't you ask them, then I'll decide if I answer.'

Oliver smiled. This woman had spunk. 'I have a friend.'

'You surprise me.'

He ignored the barb. 'He's called Felix Richards, has he been in?'

'It's a Post Office, not a dating agency. How would I know?'

'Oh, I think you know everything, Mrs Hu.'

'I'm nobody's missus.'

'I believe that but I'm not so sure that I believe you about

Felix.' Oliver edged slowly towards the counter.

Ting held up a hand. 'That's close enough. Tell me what you want and then get out of my shop.'

Oliver could see that she was not intimidated. He pointed to the bolt that he had slid shut. 'I think you're forgetting that you are locked in here with me. I give the orders.'

'No, you're locked in here with me.' Ting slowly raised her right hand from beneath the counter. In it she held a Beretta with a suppressor. She motioned Oliver towards a chair by the door to her warehouse. 'Sit down. I want to ask you some questions.'

'Easy, I was only joking.' Oliver reached for the bolt on the door. 'Maybe I should just go.'

'Sit down!'

He heard the click as Ting cocked the gun. He sat down. 'Listen—'

'No, you listen. I don't know who you are but if you come into my shop and threaten me you're making a big mistake. Why'd you lock the door?'

'I didn't want any interruptions,' said Oliver, telling the truth for the first time since he had arrived.

'Maybe I interrupt your thought process by shooting you in the head?'

Oliver held up his hands, this was not going how he had hoped. 'Listen, Mrs Hu—'

'I'm not anyone's Mrs,' snapped Ting, angrily shaking the gun at him.

'OK, I'm sorry. I think we've got off on the wrong foot.'

'I think I'm going to shoot you in the foot. You start telling me the truth or I will.'

Oliver studied Ting's face. She looked angry and her eyes were stone cold. This woman really would shoot him. This upset him; he had presumed that he was the only killer in Stratford. He hadn't bargained for this gun-toting sub-postmistress. Who would have?

'I came here because my friend, Felix, has taken something that belongs to me. I know you look after stuff for a fee. I also know that you fence stolen goods. It seemed like a logical place to come.'

Ting's gun was trained on him but he could see she was considering his words. 'This is a Post Office. You want stamps or pencils you're in luck. Anything else, try Woolworths.'

'But I have cash.'

Ting heard the word she loved so much but it didn't soften her nature in the usual fashion; today it just made her angry. 'Your cash is no good here, Mister. I've got nothing you want, and if I did it's not for sale.' She waved the barrel of the gun towards the door. 'I suggest you undo that bolt and get out of my shop before I change my mind.'

Oliver nodded calmly and slid off his chair. 'No problem. I can see you're having a bad day so I'll get out of your hair.'

Ting nodded. 'That's a good idea. And don't come back. Ever.'

'But what if I have a telegram.'

'Nobody has telegrams these days, it's 1972.'

Oliver reached up and drew back the bolt before turning to Ting. 'I'll be off then. It's been an absolute pleasure to meet you.'

Ting shrugged. 'Likewise, now piss off before I shoot you.'

Oliver slid through the doorway and, pulling the door closed behind him, made his escape. That had not gone at all as he had hoped. Ting Hu's reaction, however, told him everything he wanted to know. Felix had definitely been there and left something with Ting. He didn't have a clue what yet, but he would soon find out.

Back in the shop, Ting put down her pistol as Claude appeared from behind a bookcase clutching a machete.

She looked at his weapon. 'You weren't thinking of using that on him, were you?'

'But of course,' said Claude.

Ting pointed at the floor. 'That's oak parquet flooring. How would I get the bloodstains out of that?'

Claude shrugged. 'We could paint it Post Office Red.'

Ting shook her head. Claude had been with her a long time. He was very reliable and one hundred per cent loyal. All he lacked was imagination, which normally wasn't a problem but, in this case, some lightness of touch was definitely needed.

She didn't know who the man was but if it was the one that Felix was running from, she realised he was in very real danger. She turned to Claude. 'That man, would you recognise him if he came in here again?'

'Of course I would,' said Claude eagerly.

'Good. Next time he does, kill him!'

'Even if he just wants stamps?'

'Especially if he wants stamps ... just remember one thing.' Ting held up a hand. 'No blood on the parquet.'

Claude nodded. 'No blood on the parquet.'

Chapter 25
A Little Knowledge

Felix had finished loading his fridge and on-board pantry with food. Lots of cans and frozen stuff; he needed to eat on the go. There was no time for long stops, he needed to put miles between them, remove himself from Oliver's orbit.

Felix had planned his route. He would follow the Avon down to Tewkesbury and then turn north on the River Severn. Soon he could lose himself on the rivers and canals heading north, leaving this nightmare as far behind as possible.

His journal was now safe with Ting Hu. He trusted her. More truthfully, he trusted the deal they had done together. He had got the impression that if she took your money, she would uphold her side of the deal.

Felix was correct in that assumption. Ting would do as he had asked her but, with her pragmatic head on, she had to know what she was facing. With that heavy burden, she found herself in her locked warehouse staring at the safe where Felix's journal lay quietly ticking like an unexploded bomb.

'You going to read it, boss?'

Ting looked at Claude. 'You think I should?'

'Doesn't matter what I think, does it.'

'No, I never listen to you and I doubt I ever will, but I'd be interested in your opinion.'

Claude brightened. 'Really?'

Ting scowled. 'No, of course not. But it's good to get a second opinion, just for a bit of perspective.'

Claude rubbed his chin thoughtfully. 'If Mr Felix is being chased by the man who was here this morning, I'd say he's in big trouble.'

Ting looked at Claude impatiently. 'Obviously, but do you think I should look at his journal?'

'Might give you some information on the crazy man.'

'My thoughts exactly.' Ting stared at Claude.

Claude stared back, looking more uncomfortable as the seconds passed. Clearly, Ting wanted him to do something. He shook his head. 'Should I be doing something, boss?'

'Turning around, Claude. You can't be seeing the code to this safe, you know the rules.'

Claude did know the rules but an awkward question sprang into his mind. It was one of those questions he knew he should never ask but, to his horror, he heard the words coming out of his mouth. 'But what if you die, boss? How do I get into the safe then.'

'I'm never dying, I have too much to do. Now bugger off into the shop and let me get on with this.'

Claude could feel another question forming at the back of his throat but managed to choke it back and escape the warehouse without adding to the black marks against his name.

Ting watched him go. Claude was a good man; uncomplicated, loyal and able to commit acts of great violence when requested. With his slim build and Gallic demeanour he was the living definition of the word innocuous. Dig beneath that bland exterior and, if you knew which buttons to press, you would find a web of controlled violence that could be switched on at a moment's notice.

The warehouse door closed behind Claude and Ting triple locked it. Now she could read the confession of Felix Richards, in full and without interruption. She settled down and opened the envelope.

Forty minutes later she knew who the Shakespeare Killer was, how he had murdered them all and who was still on his kill list. She closed the book and stared up at the high ceiling of her warehouse. What should she do with this information? Lives could still be saved.

She knew the answer: nothing. She had entered into a deal with Felix, and Ting, being old school, never went back on a deal. There had to be a way she could use this information to save some lives but, right now, she didn't know how she could do that without breaking her promise. Not to mention the fee they had agreed. No, she would say nothing for now. She would find a way to use the information without compromising her customer. She was treading a tightrope between the right and wrong side of the law; getting it wrong could cost her the money … or her life.'

Chapter 26
A Meeting Of Minds

The death of Sir Morris Oxford in the fire at Stratford Hospital had made the news, not just in England but in America and Australia. Anywhere Shakespeare was performed in English, you would find news about Sir Morris. He had travelled the world for over fifty years, performing to millions of theatregoers who all bought into the carefully crafted legend he had woven about himself.

This world was in shock and the sharks of Fleet Street had come out to feed. The biggest shark – the Great White himself – was now at the reception desk in Guild Street: Patrick Fryer of *The Daily Globe*.

No one had wanted it to come to this. Fryer was a nasty piece of work whose acerbic prose had torn many a sound reputation to shreds.

Safe behind his desk, with his office door firmly closed, Acting Chief Constable Beeching took the news well. 'Who the hell let that man into the station?' he screamed down the phone at poor Frank Whittall.

The sergeant couldn't say much. 'It's a public place, sir. To serve and protect, et cetera.'

'Not his sort, sergeant. The man's a hyena, get rid of him.'

'I can't throw him out, sir, he's done nothing wrong.'

'Don't bother me with technical details, sergeant, just get rid of him.'

Frank replaced the phone gingerly on its cradle and looked up at Fryer with an expression that resembled a calm exterior; it wasn't. The corner of his mouth was twitching, as was his left eye. To the untrained observer he could have appeared to be in the early stages of a stroke. To those who recognised the signs, he was about to tell a lie.

Patrick Fryer recognised the signs and they were all there as clear as day; the desk sergeant was about to feed him an alternative truth.

'I'm afraid that ACC Beeching isn't available at the moment, sir. Can I help?'

'You can tell me the truth and you can ask him to get up off his fat arse, come down here and answer my questions.'

Frank thought for a moment about trying to reason with him but he didn't look the reasoning type. 'Let me see if I can get him out of his meeting, Mr Fryer.'

'You do that, sergeant. I'll wait.'

It sounded more like a threat than a promise and Frank Whittall didn't feel like taking a verbal beating from this Fleet Street hyena. Beeching got the big bucks, let him earn them. Frank backed away from Fryer and disappeared through the door behind the front desk. Once out of sight, he took a moment to gather himself at the bottom of the stairs that led up to CID.

As Frank was mopping his brow, Fred Williams appeared through the back door from the car park.

'All right, Frank? You look like you just saw a ghost.'

'Vampire, more like. He's waiting at reception, leaning on the desk and failing to cast a shadow.'

Fred smiled at Frank's comment. 'You think we have a member of the vampire family out there?'

'Dunno, but I reckon he likes blood.'

'This vampire have a name?'

'Patrick Fryer.'

Fred suddenly felt cold. Here was a name from the past that

came with only bad memories. Patrick Fryer had put Fred on the front page of *The Daily Globe* ten years ago when a suspect he had been questioning accidentally fell down some stairs. Twice. He was accused of police brutality.

Fred had tried to explain, somewhat naively, that it was only police brutality if the accused was innocent. That Tony 'The Hatchet' Gambaccini had never been innocent of anything in his life and they all knew it.

This had made no difference to Fryer, who had smelled blood and made Fred front-page news for two weeks. It had been touch-and-go whether Fred would be disciplined, but his boss back then was made of stern stuff and backed him up. Claiming it as self-defence was maybe pushing it a bit far, but that was in the early sixties and the rule of law was taken more seriously by the police back then.

'Leave him to me, Frank. Don't bother the chief with it.'

Before Frank could stop him, Fred had pushed past him and disappeared through the door that led to the duty sergeant's desk.

Fryer looked up as Fred burst through the door like a wild boar scenting blood. 'Sergeant Williams. What a nice surprise.'

'I'm sure it is. What do you want, Fryer?'

Fryer chuckled. 'I see that media training seems to have passed you by.'

'Go boil your head, Fryer. We've got enough on our plate without you adding to it. In case it's escaped your notice, we have a serial killer on our hands. Now tell me what you want and get lost.'

'I'd like to know what you bunch of country bumpkins are doing to catch our killer?'

It was a fair question but Fred didn't feel like being fair. 'There will be a press conference at four p.m. Why don't you wait until then like everyone else.'

'I don't care about anyone else. *The Daily Globe* does not wait. Surely you understand that, Williams?'

Fred bridled but kept his temper. 'I understand that you're a twat, Fryer. Now bugger off before I come around the desk and give you an assisted passage.'

Fryer wasn't intimidated; he smiled smugly. 'Really, DS Williams. What kind of a welcome is that for a visitor to your beautiful, body-laden town.'

'You're not funny, Fryer.'

'Humour can be subjective, sergeant, dead bodies less so. Why not talk to me? I might be able to help raise public awareness.'

'We've got eight victims and Stratford's Old Town is looking like an abattoir. I think we have all the awareness we'll ever need.'

'Only if you count Chief Constable Wilson ... but he wasn't a victim, was he?'

Fred shook his head sadly. He took a deep breath and let it out. Fryer had got to him last time, he couldn't let it happen again. 'Chief Wilson was a suicide.'

'Hmm. Is that the official line?'

Fred felt his hackles rising. 'What's that supposed to mean?'

Fryer pulled a notebook from his pocket and opened it. He glanced down at his notes. 'I have it on good authority that he fell into the River Avon while trying to, um, apprehend the man he thought killed his wife.'

Fred, for once, had no answer.

Nor did Toby, who had just walked into reception. He looked at Fred questioningly and Fred gave the slightest shake of his head.

Fryer didn't miss it. 'Thanks for confirming my information, gents. Would you like to elaborate?'

Fred turned back to Fryer. 'Chief Wilson committed suicide. We believe his wife was murdered by our killer.'

'I agree his wife was a victim of your killer. A case of mistaken identity … It should have been Clarissa Pidgeon.'

Once again, Fryer had both Fred and Toby on the back foot. Toby glanced at Fred but stayed quiet.

How the hell did Fryer know that it should have been Clarissa? They had tried very hard to keep that out of the press and succeeded.

'I don't know where you're getting your information from, Fryer, but it's wrong.'

'I suppose you're going to tell me that he wasn't trying to kill Phil Townsend at the time.'

Fryer had lit the blue touch paper and now stood back to watch the fall out, but Fred had learned his lesson. The angry denials, the accusation of interference with a police inquiry, the fireworks … they never came. He gestured towards the door that led to Interview Room One. 'Come through, Mr Fryer. I think we need to talk.' Fred nodded to Toby who opened the door that led to the interview room.

'Mr Fryer? You're being polite, sergeant. I'm guessing this is more serious than I thought.'

Two minutes later they were sitting around the desk with mugs of tea and hostile looks.

Fred opened the conversation. 'Would you mind telling me where you got your information, Mr Fryer?'

'I can't disclose my sources, sergeant, you know that.'

'I know you think that, but if you want me to work with you there isn't a choice.'

'You want to work with me? Am I sensing a gesture on your part?'

Fred grinned. 'I suppose I might be offering an olive branch. I don't like you, you know that, but I think there may be something to be gained by working with you.'

This came as a surprise to Toby. 'You think this is a good idea, boss?'

'Not to put too fine a point on it, I'd rather have Mr Fryer on the inside of the tent pissing out as opposed to the alternative.'

'Wise choice. I have been known to create quite a deluge in my time.' Fryer leaned back in his chair; he appeared to be considering something. 'Tell you what, sergeant. In the spirit of our new-found co-operation, I do feel inclined to share my source.'

'Go on then,' said Fred.

'A local gentleman called Whomper Smith. I think you know him.'

The look on Fred and Toby's faces acknowledged the fact.

'I can confirm we know him, but I doubt that he gave you this information.'

'He didn't give it to me, I paid him for it. Quite handsomely, as it happens.'

Toby realised where Whomper's new funds had come from; the meal he had offered to buy him was Judas money. Thirty pieces of silver with which he had betrayed them.

'Whomper Smith is a known fantasist in Stratford, eccentric to say the least. I'd take everything he says with a large pinch of salt,' said Fred.

Fryer nodded. 'I do, DS Williams, but you seem to put some store in his information. The barman at the Green Dragon tells me that you and DC Marlowe are often seen consorting with him.' Fryer raised an eyebrow. 'Care to explain?'

Fred didn't but he knew when the game was up. Denial would waste precious time when they could be catching a killer. He sighed. 'Off the record?'

Fryer nodded.

'Very well. I can't deny that Whomper has been useful in the past and his theory does not appear to be a million miles away from the truth. We do think that the murder of Chief Wilson's wife was a case of mistaken identity. Heather Wilson's figure and hair were very similar to Clarissa Pidgeon's. We believe that Oliver Lawrence has a score to settle with her.'

'But how did he manage to kill the wrong woman? He did it with his bare hands.'

Fred shook his head. 'Nice try, Mr Fryer. I cannot confirm or deny how Mrs Wilson was killed at this time, nor what the circumstances were that may have allowed Lawrence to kill the wrong victim. All I can say, off the record, is that we think Clarissa was the intended victim.'

'Can I assume that you are using Pidgeon as bait to catch him?'

It was a tricky question for Fred to answer. 'Are we still off the record?'

'For now.'

'In that case, yes. We have several sets of eyes on her 24/7, all done through concealed surveillance.'

'Why don't you just chain her to a tree by the river and wait?' Fryer leaned back and smiled. 'You really haven't got a clue, have you.'

'To be fair, no. We are certain it's Lawrence, but if he passed me in the pub I wouldn't know it. We don't have any recent photos of him, no fingerprints. I've asked permission for a house-to-house but it's been denied. We just have to watch our potential victims closely and be ready to pounce.'

Fryer looked at Toby. 'And what about you, DC Marlowe. What do you think?'

'Same as the boss. It's Lawrence, I'm sure of it.'

'So when will all this be over?'

'This is *Macbeth*, it won't be over until either he is dead or everyone on his hit list is.'

'*Macbeth*. What does that mean?'

Toby looked at Fred, who gave him the briefest of nods.

He took it as permission to continue. 'We, I mean I, think

Lawrence is convinced he is Macbeth. He's lost the plot, and the murders up to now seem to have touched on both *Hamlet* and *Othello.*'

Fryer looked genuinely surprised. 'You can't be serious, DC Marlowe. Have you any idea how crazy that sounds?'

'We do,' said Fred. 'I laughed at DC Marlowe when he first suggested it, but since then his theory has matched the pattern of the murders. We have a madman out there, Mr Fryer. A madman who is a great Shakespearian actor. He knows all the characters and all the plays. What he has done, and the way he has killed some of his victims, is very much in line with those plays. If you were a crazy actor with a grudge, it might make sense to do your killing in character. Don't you think?'

Fryer nodded. 'I suppose it would. Can I write this down?'

'No, said Fred. 'But if you help us, I will give you all of this as an exclusive when he's caught.'

It was a good offer and Fryer bit. 'How soon do you think that will be?'

'Very soon,' said Toby. 'If this is *Macbeth,* we're approaching the end. Everyone dies, even Macbeth.'

Fryer considered this. 'I can see why you might think that. How many more murders do you think he has planned?'

It was a good question and Toby wasn't going to sugar-coat his answer. 'Between two and four.'

'Jesus Christ,' exclaimed Fryer. 'You really think that?'

'We're not going to let that happen,' said Fred. 'But it could be what he's planning. All those we believe to be in danger are being watched and protected. If he moves on them, we'll have him.'

'Like you did all the other times?'

Fred didn't react to Fryer's caustic comment. 'The case has been evolving. It's taken time to work out who it could be and what his motivation is. I honestly don't think another nick would have been any closer.'

'Really?'

There was no disguising the doubt in Fryer's voice.

Fred leaned towards him. 'Ninety-five per cent of murders happen in the heat of the moment. Anger, betrayal, drink. When you kill in hot blood you don't make plans. You have no alibi, it's hard to cover your tracks. But this killer—'

'Oliver Lawrence?'

'Yes,' agreed Fred. 'He is acting in stone cold blood. He's killing to a plan, following a script, taking his time. He's like a ghost. We don't know what he looks like and, even if we did, he's an actor. He can change his appearance day-to-day.'

'You're not filling me with confidence here, gents.'

'The net's closing, Mr Fryer. You're going to have to trust us.'

Fryer looked at Toby. 'Believes he's Macbeth, does he?'

'I think so,' agreed Toby.

'So who is Banquo,' asked Fryer.

'I wish I knew.'

Fryer stood up and tucked his notepad into his pocket. 'Very well, gents. I'll give you a week to catch him. If you don't, I'll write what Whomper Smith told me. I won't use your off the record comments, but I will print his story. That sound fair?'

Toby looked over at Fred. He could see the blood vessel pulsing at his temple, the clenched jawline. Fred was indeed angry but he kept his temper in check. 'Very well, Mr Fryer.'

'And I get the exclusive when you catch him?'

Fred nodded. 'Yes.'

Fryer gave them both a big smile, turned on his heel and headed for the door. As he reached for the handle, Fred spoke. 'Just one thing, Mr Fryer.'

Fryer turned back to Fred.

'In exchange for this exclusive, there is something I need you to do.'

'I knew there was going to be a catch.'

'It's not much of a catch, it's sort of an exclusive.'

'Two in one meeting, I'm honoured.' Fryer went back to his chair and sat down. He took out his notebook, pulled the top off his pen and looked at Fred expectantly. 'Go on then, what's the favour?'

'I'm going to rearrest Phil Townsend in about an hour and I want you to write an article about it.'

This was news to Toby. 'Arrest Phil for what?'

'Aiding and abetting our murderer in the commission of his crimes.'

'That's ridiculous! We know Phil isn't guilty.'

Fred nodded. 'We know, but Oliver doesn't know that we know. Mr Fryer, here, is going to make it front-page news that Townsend has been arrested.'

'What's he being charged with?'

'Nothing,' said Fred. 'He's just going to be helping us with our enquiries.'

'And this helps us how?'

Fred looked at Toby with genuine sympathy. 'It's simple, Toby. We pull Phil in, and Oliver thinks he's in the clear.'

'But how does that help us,' demanded Toby.

'He might get careless.'

'That's not right, boss.'

'Phil's ex-Job, he'll understand. It'll give him another yarn to spin from behind the bar at the Windmill.'

Fryer looked up at Fred with a satisfied grin. 'Well, this is one for the books. You're going to arrest a man you know to be innocent … and you want me to report it?'

'Yep, you got a problem with that?'

Fryer grinned. 'No, I've been making stuff up for years. Just remind me what my reward is here.'

'You get the exclusive that Townsend has been rearrested, which I assume will be front-page news?'

'It will be the way I write it.'

Fred winced. 'Nothing too salacious, Fryer. Don't forget he's an innocent man.'

Toby was shaking his head in disbelief. 'This isn't ethical, boss.'

Fred and Fryer looked at each other and burst into laughter.

'Ethics. Not heard that one for a long time,' said Fryer.

'Young Toby has very high standards, hasn't been around long enough to realise just how low you sometimes have to stoop to get a result.'

'But I know, Williams. I've read your career history.'

Fred shrugged. 'It's a tough game. Justice is best served in any way you can. It's not so much how you get there as long as you do.'

'Can I quote you on that, sergeant?'

'Get lost, Fryer. Go and get your article sorted and we'll arrest Townsend.'

'And I get first dibs when you catch Lawrence?'

Fred leaned over to Fryer and shook his hand. 'You do. Now piss off and let me and DC Marlowe get some work done.'

Fryer nodded, gave Toby a big grin and left the office. For a few seconds, Fred and Toby stood looking at each other without saying a word. The silence was broken by Fred. 'Get it off your chest, son.'

'That was totally out of order, boss.'

Fred sat at his desk, put his feet up and placed his hands behind his head. 'Why?'

'You know why, sir.'

'I do, I just want you to tell me why you think it was.' Fred raised a questioning eyebrow.

'Because Phil Townsend is innocent.'

'Of murder, maybe, but have you tried his pies?'

'This is no joking matter, boss. You've just admitted to a

member of the Fleet Street gutter press that you're arresting an innocent man. It's …' Toby struggled to find the correct word to describe his outrage.

Fred waved him quiet with the waft of a hand. 'What you're suffering from, young Toby, is a nasty outbreak of principles. If there is anything this job has taught me it's that sometimes you have to do wrong to do right. Arresting Phil is wrong, but we're not going to charge him.'

'We'll be putting a stain on his character.'

'Phil Townsend's character has more stains than a schoolboy's underpants, this won't harm him. I'll tell him the score, get him a cuppa and a bacon sarnie and all will be right with the world.'

'You think Lawrence will fall for it?'

'I dunno, but it may make him think he has a little breathing space. We need to draw him out, help him make a mistake. We're grabbing at straws here.'

Toby knew that much was true. 'Tell me the plan.'

Fred smiled. 'Plan is going a bit too far. Let's just make a big thing of pulling Phil back in and then we'll take Clarissa shopping.'

'We're not really going to use her as bait? That's risky.'

'Not if we have several plain-clothes officers nearby keeping a close eye on her. If Oliver makes a move, we'll grab him.'

'What if he shoots her with a sniper rifle,' suggested Toby.

Fred's brow furrowed. 'Hmm, I hadn't thought of that one. Let's just hope he's a terrible shot.'

Chapter 27
Loose Ends

Oliver was in the kitchen at Trinity Street. So much had happened in the last few months. He had gone from being a missing person to a serial killer. Could there have been another way? What if he had just returned – declared himself well and tried to return to his career on the stage – would they have let him?

He was sure that Morris would have tried to contain him, keep him in the background. But Morris was old, he couldn't have kept Oliver back for much longer. That would have been a better strategy. Had all this been a terrible mistake?

He took a sip of his tea and considered it for a moment. The warm liquid sliding down his throat seemed to clear his mind, clarify his thoughts. It had been the wrong thing to do, he knew that now. But he had never wanted to do the right thing; this whole adventure had never been about doing the right thing. He wanted revenge and he wanted to kill.

It was quite a realisation and shouldn't have been an easy thing to admit to himself, and yet, here he was. Sitting in Felix's kitchen, planning his next move; the final act was getting near.

There was a knock on his door. He knew who it was; only one person other than Felix knew where he lived. Maybe that had been a mistake. She may be his mother but he didn't trust her. It was a terrible thing to have admit to himself but it was true.

Beatrice had been under the control of Sir Morris for far too long. He may be dead and gone but Oliver sensed she was going to struggle to break free of his influence.

Oliver slipped the catch back and opened the door a crack. Beatrice was wearing a running outfit, with the hood pulled up, and a pair of sunglasses. He glanced behind her. He could see the wall surrounding the graveyard at Holy Trinity and a couple of dog walkers. Apart from that the street was deserted. He opened the door. 'Come in.'

A few minutes later they were seated at the kitchen table. His mother had a large mug of strong coffee. She stared at him through the steam that rose from it. It felt like a scene from *Macbeth*, looking at each other through the mist rising from the drinks.

'Double, double toil and trouble,' said Oliver.

'Cut the crap, this is serious.'

'My, we are touchy today.'

'What did you expect? You've just burned my husband to death.'

'You knew from the moment I came back that he would be toast. Well, now he is!'

'That's disgusting,' snapped Beatrice. 'And quite funny.' She smiled and took a sip of her coffee. 'What now then, Oliver. Is your little trilogy of plays at an end?'

Oliver leaned back in his chair to consider her question. 'No, I don't think it is. I have my Banquo to kill, and his wife. I'd kill his children too, but I don't think he has any.'

'My God,' sighed Beatrice. 'You really are quite mad.'

'Do you think? I prefer thorough. If you're on a revenge mission you might as well be hanged for doing them all rather than just a couple. They can only hang me once.'

'We don't do hanging any more. It was stopped while you were missing.'

'Really? So even if I get caught, I'll only end up in prison with three square meals a day?'

'Yes.'

'Brilliant! I could start a theatre group in Wormwood Scrubs.'

'It'd be Broadmoor for you, my boy. You're barking mad.'

'Even better, we'd do Shakespeare's tragedies. Hamlet was nuts, Othello went off his rocker and the Macbeths were both a sandwich short of a picnic.' Oliver rubbed his hands together with glee. 'Getting caught mightn't be as bad as I feared.' He took a big gulp of tea and grinned. 'Not that I'm planning on getting caught though, obviously. I want to be back up on that stage with you, Mother.'

'And how the hell do you think you'll manage that? You've killed half the actors at the RSC. I can't see Pierre Corridor having you back. He's going to be a bit miffed, to say the least.'

'You know, I bet I could bump into him on the streets of Stratford, have a chat, and he'd never even know who I was.'

'You'd have a job. He handed the day-to-day running of the RSC over to Trevor Convent back in sixty-eight. He's like a puppet master, manipulating everyone from the shadows.'

'Even better, he won't have a clue who I am.'

Beatrice could see that her son really believed he could make a return to the stage when his killing spree ended. She knew she could never allow it; he could ruin everything. At some point soon he would have to go. She could betray him to the police or kill him. There were plenty of options, she just had to choose the right one.

'You never answered my question, Oliver.'

'Which one?'

'Who are Mr and Mrs Banquo?'

Oliver winked. 'All will be revealed in the fullness of time.'

That was no good to Beatrice; she needed to know who and when. Partly to protect herself, but more importantly to give her chance to frame her son. The career she had craved for so long was now within touching distance and she realised that she would do anything, literally anything, to grasp it. She drained her cup and got up. 'Well, this has been lovely, Oliver. We must do it again sometime, preferably before you are in prison.'

'Don't worry, Mother, they'll never catch me. No man that's born of woman can harm old Oliver.'

'You do know you're not Macbeth, don't you?'

'I actually kill people. I'm the realest Macbeth you've ever seen.'

Beatrice grinned weakly. 'Yes, I suppose you are.' She disappeared through the front door and headed towards the theatre; her mind filled with foreboding. After everything she had done, he could still destroy her carefully laid plans. There were a lot of loose ends to be tidied up … and the biggest of those was Oliver.

Chapter 28
Thou Shalt Get Kings

The shadows were enfolding Stratford Old Town, wrapping themselves like a blanket around the inhabitants. Making the night darker and the fear of stepping out alone more intense. Death had stalked these quiet streets and alleys for many weeks and the simple charm of an evening stroll had been lost upon a wave of fear.

This was not the case for Oliver; he *was* the fear. He strolled out, content in the knowledge that he was the only serial killer operating in Stratford. The odds of there being another one were too astronomical to contemplate. He walked with caution. He didn't want to be stopped or questioned. Any exposure to the police would make his life more difficult and increase his risk of being caught.

Oliver slipped past the entrance to Holy Trinity. He made his way down to the riverside, to where *the Styx* was moored on the opposite side. The moon was out so he would be able to see what Felix was up to.

When he reached the bank, he stared across the water to where Felix's boat had been. Now there was a big empty gap. For a moment he felt a sense of rising panic. Felix had gone without saying a word. This could not be a good omen. What was he up to?

He remembered the prophesy from Act I, Scene III of *Hamlet*: *Macbeth shalt be king hereafter.* But how long would that take, and what of Banquo? He was told he would have kings. Felix wasn't married but there had been rumours. Felix was his Banquo, of that he was sure.

And what of Mauldvina, Banquo's wife? Felix and Clarissa had once been close. Was she his Mauldvina? Speculation was pointless. He could leave no stone unturned. He would find Clarissa and kill her … but Felix? He was his best friend, the yin to his yang, the man who had made all of this possible. Did he really believe that Felix would betray him? It was a question he didn't need to ask; he had seen it in Felix's eyes the last time they had met. He was done with wondering. Now was the time to close the wound before he bled to death. Regret had been evident in Felix's words and actions, and that regret would inevitably lead to betrayal. He was looking at the bigger picture and, in that frame, there was no longer a place for Felix.

He knew Felix's boat had been there less than twenty-four hours before. Its maximum speed on the river would be four miles per hour. As chases go, this was going to be fairly pedestrian.

The only real question he had was which way he had gone; he thought he would probably head north. He could have gone down the Avon towards Evesham but that would mean heading south-west. If Felix wanted to get away, what would be the quickest way north? Oliver looked down the river towards the marina. The answer was there. From that point, the Stratford Canal went north and when it reached the Birmingham Canal, some twenty-five miles upstream, Felix would have the whole of the Midland network open to him. If he made it onto that he would become a lot harder to find. There had to be a place where he could catch him.

The Edstone Aqueduct! He hadn't been there in years, but if Felix wanted to find the quickest route north, it was the obvious choice. If Felix had gone that way he would have to go through the Wilmcote Lock system. That would take hours on his own. It was a long shot, but if he raced up to Edstone he could be there in time to greet Felix as he arrived.

Time was against him. He knew that Ting had been lying when he questioned her. Felix had been there; he smelled the betrayal in her words. He turned from the river and ran towards Trinity Street and his Morris Minor van. He could be there in ten minutes. The question was, had Felix already been and gone?

As he sped down Stratford Road towards Henley, he felt the first real pangs of fear since his return. Was he about to fail? After everything he had achieved in these few short weeks, would Felix escape and bring the past crashing down on him? He pressed harder on the accelerator, driven by desperation; he had to get there before Felix. If he did, he would end it right there. Banquo would not be the father of kings; Felix would die.

Chapter 29
The Edstone Aqueduct

Felix looked up into the moonlit sky. The sword belt of Orion stood out clearly, he could see the Plough too. He remembered the last time he had looked at the night sky; it was the night Oliver had strangled Lizzie Birchwood. It had been a terrible thing to witness and yet, to his shame, he had felt a buzz. Oliver's murders were a performance. Lizzie's had been too much though; in the end, she hadn't deserved to die. His own reaction to the moment had sickened him and the realisation that he was actually enjoying the thrill of murder had brought with it the shocking notion that he was becoming infected with Oliver's madness. It had been the beginning of the end for him; Oliver was now on his own.

Once he cleared the flight of locks at Wilmcote he had breathed a sigh of relief. It had taken an age to get through them. At every lock he felt sure that Oliver was hiding somewhere in the shadows, waiting for him.

For a while he regretted his late decision to go north instead of heading for Tewkesbury but now he was cruising steadily northwards, every minute taking him further away from the horror he had helped to create in Stratford. It felt good. Oliver had changed, become darker. The quest for revenge that once seemed so pure, righteous even, now seemed squalid, petty. Oliver had become everything he hated; vindictive and uncaring.

When he got to Scotland he would wait until the news came through that Oliver was either dead or in prison. It was only a matter of time and he didn't want to be around when it happened.

Half a mile upstream, Oliver had reached the small car park at the foot of the Edstone Aqueduct. It looked massive in the moonlight, casting long shadows down the lane and across the hedgerows. Oliver had forgotten just how big it was.

He climbed the steps to the footpath. It ran along the side of the cast-iron trough that formed the aqueduct and looked northwards. The waters of the canal sparkled in the moonlight and seemed to be a ribbon of light reaching out across the fields. There were no boats. He looked southwards and could see nothing. Was he too late?

He sat down and waited. It was a beautiful night, a night worthy of the death of Banquo. He quietly reviewed the events of the last few weeks. Was it only three months ago that he had slid the bayonet into Desmond Tharpe's heart? So much had happened since.

Tabitha Tharpe, Terry Fibbs, Gerard Soames and Lizzie Birchwood … all dead. And Heather Wilson; the wrong Desdemona. That had been unfortunate, especially as her husband was the chief constable of Warwickshire. Luckily, he had accidentally drowned himself while trying to kill the bloke he thought had killed Heather.

Oliver chuckled to himself. Sometimes luck is just on your side. And then there was Sir Morris … That had been almost poetic. He had been annoyed when Morris survived the on-stage stabbing during Julius Caesar; it had been so perfectly staged. The knives with blades that didn't retract; Brutus and his fellow assassins repeatedly burying their blades into Caesar, believing his screams were derived from great acting and not real agony.

Oh, how sweet it would have been if Sir Morris had died on-stage, but things don't always go to plan. Setting fire to the hospital had been a blast. Watching the fire take hold and engulf Sir Morris had, if anything, been a more satisfying conclusion.

Cremating him alive, reducing every bit of him to ashes, he had enjoyed that. Oliver stared up at the night sky once more. He was a changed person. Things he would never have dreamed of doing he now did without remorse. Did that make him a bad person? Of course it did. He was a killer, not delusional.

He looked downstream towards Stratford; there was still nothing coming his way. And then he heard it ... the gentle throbbing of a motor. Could this be Felix? He stepped back from the path and went down two steps so that he couldn't be seen from the canal.

The throbbing of the motor was a little louder now. The sound echoed across the fields and bounced around the steel columns of the aqueduct. It was impossible to be sure from which direction the sound was coming. He waited. Seconds turned to minutes and then he saw it, coming from the direction of Stratford: *the Styx.*

He recognised it straight away. He had been aboard many times, he had even killed Gerard Soames aboard it, drowning him from the aft of the boat. He smiled to himself as he remembered the burbling sound Gerard's drowning lungs made as they filled. Sounded a bit like a motorboat engine. Kind of ironic when he thought about it.

He leaned forward. *The Styx* was only about two hundred yards away now. He looked at the cast-iron trough which formed the aqueduct. It was just over three feet high and the side of the boat was another eighteen inches above that. Getting aboard would not be a simple matter; it would require an element of surprise.

He needed to get ahead of the boat, climb up onto the side of the canal and wait for Felix to arrive. Then he could just step aboard. If he waited until Felix was about ten yards away it would be impossible for him to stop the boat.

Oliver crept out onto the path, ducking to stay hidden from the moonlight. He positioned himself against the side of the aqueduct in a crouched position and waited. For once he did not feel the tingle of anticipation.

Killing Felix would not be a pleasure. He liked Felix. No, it was more than that. He loved him like a brother, but he had betrayed him once and he would do it again. Tonight, beneath the judgement of a full moon, he would cut out the cancer before it could hurt him. Like all surgery, it wouldn't be pleasant but it was required.

Aboard *the Styx*, each passing minute seemed to relax Felix. For a fleeting moment, he actually believed he had made his escape. Just a couple of days earlier he had thought there would never be a way out of Stratford and the nightmare he had embroiled himself in. How wrong he had been. The locks at Wilmcote had been slow and scary but now he was free and motoring north, he began to sing.

> 'When that I was and a little tiny boy,
> With hey, ho, the wind and the rain,
> A foolish thing was but a toy,
> For the rain it raineth every day.
>
> 'But when I came to man's estate,
> With hey, ho, the wind and the rain,
> 'Gainst knaves and thieves men shut their gate,
> For the rain it raineth every day.'

Felix had a fine voice and his song floated out across the moonlit meadows of the Warwickshire night. It echoed gently across the fields and into the woods to weave its enchantment with the creatures of the night.

As Oliver listened, it brought a tear to his eye; he had forgotten how well Felix could sing. It was from *Twelfth Night*; he had heard him perform it when he was a young boy.

The words of the song peeled back the years. He sat on the

steps and marvelled as the voice of a man he had called his friend serenaded the night in all its beauty. So many memories stirred from a well that he thought was dry. It was 1934 and he was just four years old, sitting in the wings at the Royal Shakespeare Theatre listening to Felix singing Feste's song.

'But when I came, alas, to wive,
With hey, ho, the wind and the rain,
By swaggering could I never thrive,
For the rain it raineth every day.'

Felix had lost himself in the memories the song held. He, too, was back in Stratford in 1934, when they were all young and everything seemed possible. The words and memories felt cleansing, scrubbing away the dark horrors he had committed. It felt like a return of innocence, or at the very least a view of it once more. It had been lost beyond the horizon all summer. And then, as he was about to sing the final verse, he heard another voice ringing clear and true across the night air.

'A great while ago the world begun,
With hey, ho, the wind and the rain.'

Felix spun around. The voice seemed to come from behind him but there was no one there.

'But that's all one, our play is done,
And we'll strive to please you every day.'

Felix hurried to the front of the boat. He didn't need to steer now; his boat had entered the narrow, raised channel of the aqueduct. It was just wide enough to allow *the Styx* to pass. There was no way to turn back now. He scanned the expanse of the Edstone

Aqueduct and saw a familiar figure rise from the shadows. It climbed up the side of the channel and stood there motionless. At that moment, Felix knew his attempt at escape had failed. Just a few yards ahead stood his fate; Oliver, the keeper of his secrets.

Oliver held out his arms as if in greeting.

'But that's all one, our play is done,
With hey, ho, the wind and the rain,
And we'll strive to please you every day.'

The Styx glided slowly through the water until the bow drew level with Oliver. Felix watched speechless as death boarded. This would be his last night.

'You're a hard man to find, Felix. Trying to avoid me?'

'I clearly need to try harder,' whispered Felix.

'Clearly,' smiled Oliver. 'If you'd taken your car, you'd have been well away.'

'For now, maybe, but what's the point of driving when you can sail?'

'About forty-six miles an hour. You'd have been north of Birmingham by now, I'd never have caught you.'

'Why are you here? I told you I was finished.'

Oliver smiled but there was no warmth in it. 'Let's not play games, Felix. Leaving is one thing but betrayal, well, that's a different matter altogether.'

'I've not betrayed you. I'm your only true friend. Have you forgotten everything we've done over the last three months?'

'Course I haven't. And I appreciate it, I really do. You helped to make all those murders possible.'

'Exactly.'

'So … What did you leave at the Post Office?' Oliver studied Felix intently. 'In Ting's safe.'

It wasn't a question; it was an accusation. Felix wanted to

answer, Oliver could see it in his face.

Felix had been silenced by the truth; that silence had condemned him and he knew it. 'My journal, that's all. I wanted it somewhere safe.'

'Safe from what,' demanded Oliver. 'From me, or the police?' As he spoke, he was slowly edging down the boat towards Felix.

'It's my insurance policy in case you decide to go after me.'

Oliver laughed. 'And how is that supposed to work then, Felix. Is Ting going to take it out and beat me over the head with it?'

'Ting doesn't know what's in it or what it's about.'

'I'm confused, Felix. How exactly does it protect you, then?'

'If I die or go missing for more than three months, Ting takes it to the police.'

Oliver nodded slowly. 'And there it is. Betrayal. I knew we'd get there in the end.'

'There's no betrayal if you don't kill me. Let me go and you won't ever need to worry.'

Oliver shook his head sadly. 'I wish it was that straight forward but it just isn't. You have put our secrets in the hands of Ting and Claude. They're not stupid. At some point, Ting will open that safe and take a look. Curiosity killed a lot of cats. And now it seems it's going to kill a postmistress.'

'No, you can't do that. She has nothing to do with the theatre, you're forgetting what this was all about. This was revenge for you and Richard. Settling old scores.'

'It was but it's not over, is it. So much more to do, I can't let anyone or anything get in the way. Not even you.'

Before Felix knew what was happening, Oliver threw himself across the gap that divided them. Felix grabbed for a wine bottle that sat on a shelf at the side of the cabin. He was too late. As his fingers tried to grasp the neck of the bottle to swing it, Oliver's full weight slammed into him.

Oliver drove his shoulder into Felix's stomach and smashed

him onto the deck. Air exploded from his lungs and he lay helplessly, gasping for breath.

Oliver pulled himself up and stood over Felix. 'I think we need to have a little chat.'

Felix wasn't going to be able to talk for some time. As he struggled for breath, his thoughts seemed detached from his body. He looked up at Oliver; there was a cold finality in the way he was looking down at him. There was no way he could talk his way out of this situation. Only one of them would see the sunrise.

Chapter 30
Bernard Wood At Dunroamin

'Are you sure about this, Toby? Whomper has been known to wind folks up,' said Fred.

'I don't know, boss. Remember when you told me to trust my instincts? Well, my instincts are telling me that this could be important.'

'Fair enough, but why? Is it because Bernard Wood sounds a bit like Birnam Wood and Dunsinane sounds a bit like Dunroamin?'

'Not really, boss,' sighed Toby.

'Good, because – apart from the Dun – there is sod all that sounds the same. I'll grant you the Bernard Wood bit, though. That is a coincidence.'

'It's more than that. Bernard was closer to Oliver than his mother.'

'Well, that wouldn't be hard, would it. From what we have discovered, our Beatrice had the parenting skills of Medea.'

Toby looked at Fred. 'Who the hell is Medea?'

'Greek mythology, Toby. I thought you of all people would know that.'

'Why, because I took A levels?'

'No, because Medea was a sorceress who killed her children.'

'Beatrice Oxford didn't kill Oliver, did she.'

Fred considered this for a moment. 'No but she gave him some pretty hard stares.'

'You're not taking this seriously, boss.'

Fred shrugged. 'I'm trying to, but you're asking me to come and interview a bloke because his name is Bernard Wood and he has come to Dunroamin. I don't ever want to try and explain this in a court of law.'

'Why don't you go back to the car and I'll speak with him.'

'Fair enough,' said Fred and promptly turned around and walked back down Sanctus Road to the car.

Toby really was on his own with this interview.

He walked up to the front door of Dunroamin, peered through the stained glass, and knocked. A few moments later he saw the outline of a man walking down the hallway. The door swung open and a tall man, who looked far more vigorous than a man in his late sixties had a right to look, smiled warmly at him.

'Mr Wood?'

'That's me.'

Toby took out his warrant card. 'DC Marlowe from Stratford CID. Could I have a few words?'

Wood nodded and ushered him in. 'Of course. Come through to the kitchen, I've just made a pot of tea.'

Toby followed Wood into the kitchen and saw biscuits open beside the teapot. Fred was going to regret not conducting this interview.

A couple of minutes later, Toby was sitting at the kitchen table with a mug of tea and a chocolate digestive.

Bernard had waited until they were both sitting comfortably before asking Toby why he was there. 'Is this to do with the murders, officer?'

'Yes, it is, Mr Wood. You're probably aware that we believe Oliver Lawrence is responsible for these killings.'

Wood nodded gravely. 'Yes, I'm afraid I am. I find it hard to believe that the Oliver I knew could be capable of such terrible acts of depravity.'

'People change, Mr Wood. I've seen a lot of it in this job and he had reason to be bitter, didn't he?'

Wood sighed. 'I'm afraid so. He was treated very badly, just like his father.'

'You knew his father?' There was a note of surprise in Toby's voice.

'That's a requirement of an agent.'

'You were Richard Jenkins' agent. How did we not know about it?'

Wood grinned. 'To be fair, I hardly knew about it. I'd tried to be an actor back in the day but I wasn't really up to it. Trouble was, I loved the theatre and I wanted to work in the industry. Becoming an agent was the next best thing.'

Toby was scribbling notes down, filling in gaps he hadn't known existed.

'Were you there at the very beginning, after the fire?'

'I was there when the fire happened in 1926, playing the gravedigger in *Hamlet*.'

'Wow, how did that go,' asked Toby.

Wood smiled. 'Not as well as I'd hoped. Rumour had it that one of the critics started the fire after seeing my performance.'

They both laughed.

'I'm sure that's not the case, Mr Wood.'

'No. To be fair, I was OK. But when you're acting with the likes of Richard Jenkins, and you see what's possible, it makes you reassess your future.'

'And you chose agenting?'

'Yes. I've always had a talent for doing deals and, having been an actor, other actors trusted me.'

'And you signed Richard?'

'Yes, he was my first client. I didn't even have to ask him. Soon as he heard I was going to do it, he approached me.'

'When was this?'

'1926. The theatre had burned down and all of us were out of work for the rest of the season. I went down to the Old Vic at Bristol and that's where I teamed up with Richard. He was already making waves then.'

'So, what happened? Why did he join Morris Oxford's players?'

Wood shrugged. 'I really don't know. In twenty-six Richard was probably a bigger talent than Morris. Always was really. He should have started his own company or stayed at the Old Vic. Birmingham Rep wanted him to lead their company. When he didn't, Laurence Olivier joined them and his career turned out pretty well.' Wood looked at Toby. 'You're from Birmingham, aren't you.'

'Is it that obvious.'

'Not really, but there are some Brummie vowel sounds still lurking amongst those Stratford tones.'

Toby smiled. 'I can't deny it. Brummie born and bred.'

'You know who Sir Barry Jackson is then?'

'Of course. He started the Birmingham Rep.'

'He did and he wanted Richard. If only he had gone there he would have become a huge star and Sir Morris would have been an also-ran. Funny how things work out.'

All of this was news to Toby. 'I don't understand. Why did Richard go with Sir Morris if he could have led his own company?'

'There's a simple answer to that question, DC Marlowe. Richard was hopelessly in love with Beatrice Smallman. I tried to persuade him but he just wouldn't listen. Lovestruck. Ruined his life and crashed his career.' Wood shook his head and took a sip of his tea. 'That's why you didn't know about me being Richard's agent, it never really got going. Once he signed up with Morris he had a job for life. He just had to toe the line.'

'And that would have been hard when it was obvious that he was better than Sir Morris.'

'Impossible. They resented each other. It took a few years to come to a head, but once it did, it was vicious. Morris hated the fact that Richard could act anyone off the stage, including him.'

'And Richard hated the fact that Morris took all the glory when he was clearly the better actor.'

'Correct. It was always destined to fail.'

Toby scribbled down notes furiously. All of this information was really shedding new light, admittedly on things he already had a suspicion about, but it made his next question a lot easier. 'What was your opinion of Beatrice Smallman?'

Bernard Wood leaned back in his chair and considered Toby's question. 'You want the honest answer or the political one?'

'I'm a policeman, Mr Wood. I want the truth, whatever it is.'

Wood nodded. 'Very well, you can have it. Please bear in mind that this is only my opinion.'

Toby nodded. 'I realise that.'

'I always thought Beatrice was driven by ambition. She wanted to be famous. Back in twenty-six Richard had looked like the best bet but ten years later Morris looked a much better bet.'

'You think she was having an affair with Sir Morris?'

Wood looked uncomfortable. 'This is still only an opinion, you understand?'

Toby nodded.

'I would bet my house on the fact that something went on.'

'That's a big assertion,' said Toby.

'Not if you had been around them at the time. Richard was already starting to have problems in 1932 and Beatrice was getting closer to Morris. It was obvious to me where that little trio was headed.' There was a note of bitterness in Bernard's voice. 'That's part of the reason I signed Oliver all those years later. He had it, just like his father.'

Toby didn't have the heart to tell Wood the truth about that; he didn't need to know. 'The talent was that obvious?'

A broad smile spread across Wood's face. 'Oh, he was magnificent. He had a confidence that his father didn't possess offstage. He could mix socially and he knew how to schmooze the press and the impresarios.'

'And on-stage?'

'Just like his father. When he spoke, it was real. The acting vanished, it couldn't be seen. He morphed into the character he was playing. There was nothing declamatory, he was just in the moment. Lost in the role. You should have seen him, officer, it really was something to behold.'

There was wonder and reverence in his voice. Clearly being Oliver's agent had left its mark on him.

'What went wrong?'

Wood took another sip of his tea and scowled. 'Morris Oxford and his ego. As Oliver got the bigger roles, and frequently shared the stage with Morris, it soon became apparent that Oliver had that something special that Morris would never have. Morris had seen off Richard and now he had to contend with his son, who was equally as gifted.'

'And that's when he tried to crash Oliver's career?'

'I'm afraid so.'

'Was it obvious?'

'If you knew what you were looking for you couldn't miss it. Morris Oxford deliberately sabotaged Oliver's career. And you know what made it worse?' Wood looked angry. 'That ... that bitch of a mother helped him.'

'Beatrice?'

'Yes, she deliberately conspired with Morris to undermine him. I actually heard them feed him an incorrect line. Not just once, several times. It was cruel. How could his own mother do that to him?' There was disbelief in his voice.

Toby knew that Beatrice was a hard, cold, ambitious woman but the more he heard, the more apparent it became that she had been the driving force in the Oxford partnership.

'No doubt you've seen *Macbeth*?'

Toby nodded. 'Of course, many times.'

Bernard put down his cup and leaned towards Toby. 'Lady Beatrice Oxford is the living embodiment of Lady Macbeth. She wants the fame, the power. She wants it all and she doesn't care who she hurts to get it. Mark my words, now that Morris is gone, she'll return to the stage and take the lead with his company. Why do you think he sidelined her all those years ago?'

'Because she couldn't act,' said Toby.

Wood chuckled. 'Oh, she can act, trust me. Her forte is comedy. Sir Morris made her do the tragedies until he broke her confidence, just like he did with Richard and Oliver. The Oxfords are terrible people. Back in the day we christened them Mr and Mrs Macbeth. Seemed funny at the time but, as the years passed, that's what they became. Ruthless, crushing anything that threatened their dominance. Maybe they didn't kill anyone but, that apart, they were the very embodiment of the Macbeths.'

Toby didn't look up from his notes. He suspected that the Oxfords were guilty of at least one death but now wasn't the time to say so. Toby was about to speak but Bernard Wood hadn't finished.

'That's why I went to London. I just couldn't stand being here any more.'

'So what brought you back to Stratford?'

'I've decided to ease up. My schedule has been ridiculous for the last few years. With my mother dying I thought it was time to move back home, take it easy.'

'Sir Morris' death has happened at just the right time for you then.' As he said it, Toby watched Wood carefully to see his reaction: he didn't smile.

'I didn't like Morris but I wouldn't wish him dead, especially like that.'

'And Lady Oxford?'

'Beatrice? She won't be dying any time soon, the Devil looks after its own.'

'You really don't like her, do you.'

'There is absolutely nothing to like. She's poison.' Wood looked Toby in the eyes. 'You must have interviewed her, officer.'

'I have.'

'And what did you think?'

Toby didn't have to think, the answer was on his lips. 'She has something of the night about her.'

Wood smiled. 'Couldn't have put it better myself. Whatever it is that Oliver has become, she's the main reason for it.'

'I'm starting to form the same opinion,' agreed Toby.

'I'd watch her very carefully if I was you. If she finds Oliver before you she could make him worse.'

'He's responsible for the deaths of eight people, it couldn't be much worse.'

'Never underestimate Beatrice Oxford. She gets inside people's heads.'

Toby closed his notepad and looked at Bernard. 'Do you think you would recognise Oliver if you saw him again?'

'Fifteen years is a long time, officer, but I think I would.'

'People can change a lot in fifteen years.'

'Of course they can but Oliver had a little tell. If I saw it, I would recognise it.'

Toby's ears pricked up. 'What kind of tell?'

'When you spoke to him, he would always look away to your left. He just couldn't make initial eye contact. It never affected him on-stage though. He tried to break himself of it but there was still a momentary glance before he spoke.'

Toby had pulled his notepad back out and scribbled down this new information.

Wood watched him. 'Do you think it's relevant?'

Toby nodded. 'Could be. Right now we don't really know what he looks like. The most recent photo we have of him is nearly sixteen years old. Like we said, people can change a lot in that time.'

'Especially someone like Oliver, he knows how to use make-up. A dark line here, a touch of rouge there, and he can age himself years or make himself look younger. As an actor he could change his whole persona on-stage just by getting into character. It was like watching a different person.'

'That "look away" could be useful. If we ever get a suspect into the interview room, I'll watch out for that.'

'I'd be happy to try and identify him for you if you ever do get him in to custody,' said Wood.

'You sound doubtful.'

Wood chuckled. 'Oliver won't settle for being in jail, officer. He'll either get away or die during the attempt. I can't see a scenario where you take him alive.'

'I'm beginning to realise that.'

Wood held up the teapot. 'Another cuppa?'

For a moment Toby was going to refuse it, and then he thought about Fred sitting out in the car and decided to accept. He helped himself to another chocolate digestive. 'Do you think Oliver would hurt you, Mr Wood?'

Wood looked genuinely surprised by the question. 'Why on earth would he? I only ever had his best interests at heart. If he'd have gone to London like I told him, everything would have been fine.'

'When was this?'

Wood considered for a moment. 'Late fifty-six, early fifty-seven, just when everything was going wrong for him in Stratford.'

'How did you know it was going wrong?'

'Haven't you read the reviews?'

'Yes, I went back and read them all. They were bad.'

'They were,' agreed Wood. 'I didn't know what was going on at first. My agency was taking off and I was in London more than I was in Stratford. Without the heads up from Felix, I would never have known what was really happening.'

'Felix?'

'Felix Richards. You must have interviewed him, surely.' Wood seemed surprised that Toby didn't appear to know who he was.

Toby flipped over the pages of his notebook looking for Felix's name. He couldn't find it. 'One of the other officers may have interviewed him. Do you think he's important?'

'Very. He was the one true friend that Oliver had.'

Toby leafed through his notes but could find no record of Felix Richards. 'I don't understand this. We've interviewed everyone that was part of the company when Oliver was there, from 1970 through to 1972 when he disappeared.'

Wood bit his lip. 'There's your problem. Felix wasn't part of the company then, he had moved on to television.'

A cold, hollow feeling lodged itself in the pit of Toby's stomach. Could Felix be the missing link that pieced this whole puzzle together? He hurriedly closed his notebook and stood up. 'Thanks very much for your help, Mr Wood. It's been very useful.'

'You're welcome, officer.'

Toby turned to go but then paused. 'Don't go out at night, Mr Wood. Not until this is all over.'

'You think I'm in danger?' Wood looked amused.

'To be honest, we don't really know who is in danger right now. My advice is to be careful. Oliver is out there and clearly not the person he once was.'

Chapter 31
The Missing Link

As Toby approached Fred's car, he could hear a low rumbling. At first, he thought it was the motor. As he reached the car he looked inside and there was Fred. The passenger seat was fully reclined and Fred was lost in sleep, his snoring, deep and sonorous, sounding not unlike a V6 motor at tick over.

Toby slapped his hand down hard on the roof of the Granada and Fred shot up like he had been hit by a wet kipper.

'What the …' He saw Toby looking through the windscreen at him. 'Very funny. You trying to kill me?'

Toby climbed into the driver's seat and fired up the engine. 'We've been missing a vital piece of the puzzle, boss.'

Fred pulled the back of his seat up and tried to compose himself. 'And I was dreaming of Mel Townsend.'

'Jesus, boss. Didn't you hear what I said? I've just discovered something we've been missing.'

The urgency in Toby's voice got Fred's attention. 'Go on, I'm listening.'

'Felix Richards.'

Fred looked confused. 'Who's he?'

'Exactly. We didn't even know he existed.'

'Should we?'

'According to Bernard Wood, he was Lawrence's closest friend.'

'There was nobody called Richards listed as part of the company when Lawrence was there.'

'No, he was there before Oliver arrived. He'd gone off to do TV by then, after that he became a critic. Apparently, Richards told Lawrence to listen to what Bernard was telling him about getting away from Stratford.'

'You think it's important?'

Toby shrugged. 'I think it's strange that we haven't heard of this guy. We've said from the very beginning that Lawrence must have had help. Maybe Felix Richards is the one who's been helping him.'

Toby could see that Fred agreed with him. 'We need to find him, boss.'

Fred nodded. 'We do. Let's get back to Guild Street and take it from there.'

It didn't take them long to get to the station. Fred and Toby made their way to CID. Toby grabbed a red pen and wrote "Felix Richards" on the whiteboard. It was only then that they noticed the desk lamp was on in Beeching's office. Beeching had stationed himself over at HQ in Coventry for the last couple of weeks, preparing to replace Wilson as chief constable of Warwickshire.

Before Fred could warn Toby, Beeching opened the door to his office.

'Evening, gents.'

Toby spun around. 'Um, evening, sir.'

Beeching glanced at the board. 'Who the hell is Felix Richards?'

Toby was about to explain but Beeching held up a hand to silence him. 'Don't answer that, Marlowe. If I know about it, I'm culpable. Sometimes ignorance is bliss.'

'You should know, sir.'

'I heard that, Fred.'

'You were meant to, sir.'

Beeching gave them both a withering look. 'You two, in my office, now.'

'Didn't expect to see you here, sir.'

'I'm sure you didn't, Fred. Close the door after you.'

Beeching sat down behind his old desk and pointed to the two chairs opposite. 'Sit down. I've a little announcement to make.'

They sat and waited.

Beeching looked from one to the other and shook his head sadly. 'It's not going well, is it?'

'What's not going well, sir?'

'The bloody case, Fred,' snapped Beeching. 'Every time I'm here there's another murder in Stratford.'

'Maybe we'd all be safer if you just stayed in Coventry, sir.'

Beeching didn't rise to Fred's baiting. 'See this desk, Fred? It could be yours. Don't you want it?'

'I don't think I do, sir.'

'And why would that be?'

'It's a poisoned chalice. Whoever sits in that chair is technically in charge of the hunt for the Shakespeare Killer.'

Beeching let out an exasperated sigh. 'Fred, we've been doing this job a long while. If this case was a game of football, it'd only be half-time.'

'Yeah, and we're eight-nil down!'

Beeching winced. 'That was a poor analogy but I'm sticking with it. You're right in what you say, this chair is the hot seat. The press and the public are starting to get restless. Instead of blaming Lawrence for the murders they are starting to blame us for not catching him.'

'So, sticking with your analogy, sir, you are the manager of the team?'

'That's right, Fred.'

'Why don't you resign before they sack you?'

Toby tried to keep the smile off his face but failed.

'That's very funny, Fred, but you're forgetting I'm not in this chair any more.'

'But you want me to be?'

'No, not at all. I want you in this chair when the case is solved and Oliver Lawrence is either dead or under lock and key.'

'So what are you suggesting?'

'More a question of who, not what.' Beeching winked conspiratorially.

Fred knew exactly what Beeching was suggesting. 'You want to put in a fall guy to take the heat.'

'More a fall girl, actually.'

Toby realised who Beeching was proposing. 'You bastard!' The words were out of his mouth before he could stop himself.

Beeching raised an eyebrow. 'I'd choose your words very carefully, DC Marlowe.'

'Sorry, sir.'

Fred looked slightly shocked; he didn't think he had ever heard Toby swear before.

Toby looked at him. 'Don't you see what he's going to do, boss?'

Fred shook his head.

'He's going to put Mel Townsend in charge.'

'You bastard, Beeching.' The words shot out of Fred's mouth – a clear accusation – but Beeching didn't appear to take offence. Instead, he smiled.

'I can see why you might think that, Fred, but consider this.'

Fred looked like he was considering punching Beeching, who continued unruffled by the air of impending violence that was emanating from Fred.

'I know you boys think this is a stitch up but let me explain.' Beeching waited for a moment.

Both Toby and Fred looked angry but at least Fred had unballed his fists. He took this as a good sign.

'There is a vacancy for a detective chief inspector here in Stratford, as a long-serving DS you should have a chance at it.'

'I don't want it,' snapped Fred.

Beeching held up a hand. 'Hear me out.'

Fred bit his lip and sat back on his chair.

Beeching continued. 'I am taking over Chief Constable Wilson's role at HQ in Coventry. DI Townsend would probably have been in with the chance of an interview under normal circumstances, but these aren't normal circumstances. Wilson tried to murder DI Townsend's brother. Can you imagine the repercussions if that ever came out?'

Fred and Toby glanced at each other; Beeching did have a point.

'If that happened, her position as chief would be untenable. The top brass were not prepared to take the risk, and besides …' Beeching held up his hands. 'We all know she'd never get the job.'

'Because she's a woman,' said Toby.

'Exactly,' agreed Beeching, totally failing to pick up the sarcasm in Toby's words. 'This is 1972 and women have come a long way but we can't have them ordering men around, can we.'

'She does a pretty good job of it every day in her role as a DI, sir.'

Beeching nodded at Fred. 'She does but she's hit the old glass ceiling.'

'And now you want to smash her head into it.'

'No, Fred. I want to give her the chance to break through. Admittedly, it will probably be a case of breaking it as she falls through it on the way down. This chair is, as you quite rightly put it, a poisoned chalice at this precise moment in time.'

Beeching opened his arms. 'So, what do you think?'

'I think you're a cunning bastard, sir.'

Beeching smiled. 'I think we've established that, Fred. When you get to my position it's less about policing and more about politics.'

'That much is obvious.'

'Look, I know you don't like this but DI Townsend would be the first female chief inspector in this force. I'm guessing that she would jump at the chance. What say we give her the opportunity?'

Toby and Fred said nothing; they both knew that if Mel was offered the role she would take it. Beeching was going to drop her in the hot seat and step away.

'You both seem to be forgetting something.'

'What's that, sir,' asked Fred.

'You have it in your power to make her a hero.'

'Heroine,' corrected Toby.

Beeching nodded distastefully. 'Yes, that's why we have a glass ceiling, DC Marlowe, words like that. Be that as it may, if you fine detectives catch the killer after she is appointed, you're going to make her look a hero.'

Toby went to correct Beeching again but he held up a hand. 'I know, Marlowe, but I'm not a member of women's lib, so I'll confine my politically correct comments to public events where lip service is required.' Beeching turned back to Fred. 'Well, do you and your team think you can catch Lawrence?'

'I do, sir.'

'Fast enough to save DI Townsend?'

Fred and Toby nodded.

'We have a new lead, sir,' said Toby.

'Felix Richards?'

'Yes, sir. I think we interviewed him early in the case but we never realised there was a close link between him and Lawrence. It could be important.'

Beeching stood up. 'You better hope it is, boys, for DI Townsend's sake. I'm interviewing her tomorrow with some of the top brass and the general feeling is that we are going to give her the job. Clock's ticking.'

Beeching grabbed his briefcase, put on his cap and headed for the door without looking back.

Fred stood up and watched him go. 'How far do you reckon I

could throw him through that window, Toby?'

'Right now, boss, he'd probably reach the car park.'

They watched Beeching walk out to his car. The driver was waiting and got out to open the back door for him.

'Look at him,' scowled Fred. 'Lord ruddy Muck. He's going to be even more of a nightmare now he's in charge.'

'Never mind about him, we need to warn Mel.'

'Do you think we should? Mel's not going to like us warning her off a big promotion. She's a clever woman, she knows what's at stake. I reckon we say nothing unless asked.'

Fred's words made sense but Toby had a horrible feeling Beeching was setting her up to take the fall. 'OK, boss, it's your call. Better make sure we solve the case.'

Fred nodded thoughtfully. 'Oh, with all this excitement there was something I forgot to tell you.'

'What's that?'

'Our grieving widow.'

'Which one?'

'Lady Beatrice Oxford.'

'What about her?'

Beeching's car pulled away and headed off down Guild Street. Fred turned to face Toby. 'I don't think she's grieving any more.'

'Well, it's been a couple of days. She had to move on sooner or later.'

Fred chuckled. 'You don't like her much, do you.'

'She's evil, boss. There's something wrong with her.'

'I'm starting to think you might be right, Toby. I watched her press conference at the Swan, and unless I'm very much mistaken, she was acting. After she left the room, I saw her getting very flirty with her personal assistant. One second, she was all tears, the next all smiles. She probably thought nobody was watching her in the corridor, but I was and I saw the change. She's glad to see the back of Sir Morris.'

'We making her a suspect then?'

'No, but she's certainly a person of interest and we are not going to believe a single word she says from now on. Agreed?'

Toby nodded. 'Agreed.'

Fred was finally seeing what he saw: Lady Beatrice Oxford was a creature of the night with secrets to hide.

Chapter 32
The Ghost Boat

Oliver watched *the Styx* float off down the canal, headed northwards with no crew on-board. It was a shame. Felix had made a wonderful job of the renovation and he felt bad letting it float away unattended. He just didn't have time to moor it at a marina.

He hurried down the steps that led from the Edstone Aqueduct. As he approached his Morris Minor van he could hear the muffled cries of Felix. He opened the back door and hit him hard in the stomach, driving the wind from his body and silencing him. As Felix lay there, desperately trying to suck air through his gagged mouth, Oliver leaned in close.

'One more sound and I will really have to hurt you. Do you understand?'

Felix continued to writhe on the floor of the van.

Oliver slapped his face. 'Do you understand?'

He shouted it this time and Felix stopped; there was a slight nod of his head.

'Good.' Oliver took a deep, calming breath. 'We're going for a little drive now, Felix. And, just so we understand each other, if you make one sound or struggle in any way, I will kill you.' Felix's eyes widened. 'Do you understand? I will kill you, friend or no friend.'

Felix nodded.

Oliver smiled at him and then slammed the back doors of the van shut. He took out his keys and locked them; it was too late in the proceedings to leave anything to chance.

He leaned against the van and looked up at the night sky. All the enchantment seemed to have gone. The belt of Orion looked down on him coldly and the moon seemed to sit in judgement. Everything that was beautiful about this night had been tainted by his actions. He had become the darkness, the evil that walks in the shadows.

His friend lay tied up and terrified in the back of his van. It would have been better to kill him quickly and set fire to *the Styx* – let it burn like a warning to everyone that might oppose him – but he couldn't do that. If Felix died, the journal he had left with Ting Hu would be opened and his revenge would be ended. No, Felix had to live for now and he knew just the place: the Witter Lock below Holy Trinity.

There was a small island beside it, that lay between it and the weir at Lucy's Lock. Many years before, as a teenager, he had discovered its secret and tonight he would use it to his advantage.

As he headed down Stratford Road, he couldn't quite believe that he was taking Felix back into town. It was a huge risk but what choice did he have? He needed a place to hide Felix until ... until when? He really wasn't sure. At this moment there were so many loose ends and the walls were closing in. Could he pull them all together in time? He glanced at his reflection in his rear view mirror; the smile he saw reflected told him he could.

When he reached the centre of Stratford the streets were deserted. It was 3.30 a.m. He would stand out like a sore thumb if any police spotted him. It could all end right here. He drove slowly across the river and turned right onto the drive that ran behind the boathouse.

He turned off the lights as he approached the cricket and hockey club. It would make him harder to spot but it would also look very suspicious if anyone saw him. As he reached the end of the car park he bumped gently up the kerb and drove slowly across the grass towards the Witter Lock. He had to get close, he couldn't carry Felix that far.

After what seemed like an eternity he reached the gateway to the lock. He slipped out of the driver's seat and went round to the back of the van, fumbling the keys as he hurried to get the back doors unlocked. He forced himself to take a deep breath. 'Calm, Oliver. Calm,' he whispered. He opened the doors, pulled Felix roughly from the van and slung him over his shoulder. 'Come on, Felix, old son. I'm taking you to my secret place.'

Felix bounced along on Oliver's shoulder. Despite the darkness, and being upside down, he recognised where he was. He was on the playing fields opposite Holy Trinity. He heard the water and fear took hold of him. Was Oliver going to throw him in? He was bound hand and foot with gaffer tape. He began to struggle.

Oliver stopped. 'Remember what I told you, Felix. If you cause me any trouble, I'll kill you. Choice is yours.'

Felix stopped struggling. There was a coldness in Oliver's voice. He'd heard it before, though never directed at him. At this moment there was nothing he could do to save himself. All he could pray for was time; time to plan, time to be saved. His life was at the mercy of his friend and he wasn't looking very merciful.

He heard the metal gate swing open and realised they were on the little bridge behind the Witter Lock. Oliver passed over it and then they were moving up the path onto the small island between the lock and the weir. He'd seen it many times but never been on it. The signs said "No Access" and he had always followed the rules … until he had teamed up with Oliver. He felt the leaves and branches scraping at his back and head as Oliver pushed off the path into the undergrowth.

Oliver stopped and dropped him to the ground without warning. He couldn't even put out an arm to try and break his fall and he hit hard, knocking the wind out of him for the second time that night.

'Sorry about that, old chap, but I'm in a bit of a hurry. Can't make an omelette without breaking a few eggs.'

Felix was now on the other side of events. In recent weeks he had stood alongside Oliver, watching his victims. Now that he was the victim, he didn't like it. Not one bit.

Beside him Oliver was scrabbling away at the undergrowth. 'I know it's here somewhere. It has to be.'

He turned his head to see what Oliver was doing. The undergrowth was deep and Oliver had torn away big chunks of grass, wild flowers and weeds. He worked with the desperation of a man who knew that time was running out.

As he watched, fear began to overwhelm him. What was he looking for? He didn't have to wait long for an answer.

'Found it!' Oliver turned to him, a triumphant smile on his face. 'I'm just going to park you here for a bit, Felix. I've got a bit of business to take care of.'

He turned back and Felix watched in horror as he dragged a round metal cover off what appeared to be a hole in the ground. He tried to scream but the gag muffled his cries.

Oliver turned to him; an index finger raised to his lips. 'Quiet. I'm not burying you, just storing you for a while.'

He leaned over and began to drag Felix towards the black hole. Felix struggled but Oliver was too strong.

Oliver pinned him down and leaned close to his face. 'You need to listen to me very carefully, Felix. I'm going to lower you into this culvert.'

Felix shook his head frantically and Oliver slapped him hard across the face. He stopped struggling; despite the surrounding darkness he could see the manic determination on his friend's face. Resistance would be futile and probably fatal. He stopped struggling and Oliver continued.

'There's a ledge about eight feet down. Make sure you land on it or you'll be straight into the river below the lock.' Oliver looked him up and down. 'Tied up like that, I'm guessing you'd sink like a brick.'

Felix tried to plead with Oliver but all that came out were muffled, terrified grunts.

Oliver held an index finger to his lips once again. 'Remember what I said, Felix. Silence really is golden. If I'm still alive at the end of it, I'll come and get you. If I'm not, you'll just have to hope that someone hears you. Afraid that's going to be unlikely with the roar of the water over the weir.'

He hooked his arms under Felix's and dragged him past the dark void of the culvert, then took his feet and fed them down until he had Felix perched on the edge. 'Remember to feel for that ledge as you go down. Miss it and you're fish food. I'm going to untie your legs, give you a better chance of landing on it.'

Oliver began to lower him into the darkness. As his head was just above ground, Oliver whispered in his ear. 'Good luck, old friend. I hope we'll meet again, but if not ...' He looked off into the distance, his eyes glistening. 'It's been a lot of fun.'

With that, he let go and Felix dropped into the void. For a split-second he thought he was going to fall into the bubbling waters of the Avon but his feet found the ledge. He nearly toppled off it but managed to push his weight back against the wall. It took a second for him to realise that, for the moment, he had made it. He breathed a sigh of relief too soon. There was a scraping sound from above as Oliver clunked the culvert cover back into its frame. Felix shuddered as he found himself in a place of perpetual night.

Above him, Oliver considered re-covering the culvert with undergrowth but decided against it. He would leave it clear, give his friend a sporting chance of being discovered. It was more than he deserved. He shook his head and hurried away. He sun would soon be coming up and he needed to be safely within the walls of Trinity Street, free from the prying eyes of the police and locals.

Events were gathering pace and there were many loose ends to be drawn together as his revenge headed for the final curtain.

Chapter 33
Star-Crossed Lovers

Dame Suzy Tench could not sleep. The events of recent weeks had destroyed the normality of her life in Stratford. She reached for her alarm clock: four a.m. There was no way she could go back to sleep now. She climbed out of bed and peeked through her curtains.

From her window she could see the chain ferry. The River Avon slid by; a silver ribbon shimmering in the moonlight. Despite the recent murders, she thought a walk in what remained of the night would be a good idea. Suzy had no fear, or, apparently, common sense. She pulled on her jeans and a jumper, slipped on her pumps and headed downstairs.

Two streets away, Oliver was parking his van in the little garage off Ryland Street. He breathed a sigh of relief as he snapped the padlock closed. He had been out far too late. Driving across the recreation ground to secure Felix in the Witter Lock culvert had been fraught with risk. Now it was done, and he had made it home unscathed, the pent-up tension began to leave him. But there was still too much adrenalin coursing through his veins to sleep.

He looked up at the spire of Holy Trinity which was now beginning to glint as the sun's rays played fleetingly upon it. The morning sun was creeping around the planet from the east, casting the shadows that signalled morning was breaking.

He needed to burn off some energy and settle his racing thoughts. He headed towards the church and made his way around the path to the right of it. He would head through the graveyard and follow the riverbank, then watch the sun come up from the bench where he had stabbed Desmond Tharpe all those weeks ago. So much had happened as spring had turned to summer. His life would never be the same again.

Suzy had made her way down Church Street. She would turn right down Chapel Street and then cross Southern Lane into the trees at Avon Dell. She, too, wanted to watch as the sun rose over the river.

Further along, Oliver walked slowly through the graveyard. He smiled. He feared no evil because he was the evil; it was a comforting thought. He reached 'Desmond's bench' and plonked down. From here he could see the spot where he had persuaded Tabitha Tharpe into the river. Happy memories. At a moment like this he wished he smoked. Instead, he contented himself with remembering all those he had killed in Stratford during the course of late spring and summer. It gave him a warm glow of satisfaction.

As Suzy entered The Dell it felt like a scene from *A Midsummer Night's Dream*. The first shards of light were beginning to filter gently through the trees, casting everything with a silvery phosphorescence. It should have been magical but, as she walked past the entrance to the tunnel that ran under Southern Lane, she thought of her friend, Lizzie Birchwood, who had been strangled there.

She shivered and silently chided herself for being silly. The dead are dead; they are never coming back. That was not the case for whomever had made them dead. They could still walk the shady passages of the night.

Suzy headed down the slope towards the perimeter of the graveyard. There was a doorway in the wall near the top of the riverbank. Should she go through it? She hesitated for the first time. Desmond and Tabitha had died there. Maybe this walk wasn't such a good idea.

She stood at the bottom of the slope and looked up at the darkened doorway into the graveyard. This was irrational. There would be no ghosts there, they only existed in the corners of your imagination.

'Come on, Suzy, it's only a graveyard. Everyone's dead and the dead can't hurt you.' She balled her fists and headed up the slope, still unsure if she was being brave or foolhardy. She knew if she turned back, she would think herself weak, and she didn't do weak.

She stepped through the doorway. As she turned left onto the riverside path, she saw someone sitting on the bench where Desmond had been killed.

Oliver could hear footsteps approaching. For a moment he thought about hiding. What if it was a policeman, how would he explain himself? But as whoever it was walked briskly up the steps on the other side of the wall, he realised the footsteps sounded too light for a man. The chance to hide had come and gone, it would look suspicious if he was caught. On the upside he knew it wasn't the Shakespeare Killer. The thought made him smile.

Figuring it was now or never, he slowly turned his head. Relief flooded through him, followed by something else. 'Ill met by moonlight, proud Titania.'

Suzy stopped dead and looked from left to right. He thought she was going to run but, instead, she called out, 'Is that you, Francis?'

Oliver cringed; why had he used Francis Bacon as a false name? 'It is, Suzy. What on earth brings you here at this ungodly hour?'

'I'm not afraid of the dark.'

Oliver smiled. 'Though she be but little, she is fierce.'

She recognised the quote from *The Dream* and smiled. 'I am

not Hermia, though I am like her.' She walked towards the bench. 'Mind if I join you?'

Oliver gestured to the space beside him. 'Of course not but … you know which bench this is?'

She nodded. 'It's where Desmond died.'

'And yet we choose to sit here in the dark. Lord, what fools these mortals be!'

'Puck?'

Oliver nodded.

'You are definitely an actor, Francis.'

Oliver laughed. 'Not any more.'

'I think you could be, there's something about you.'

'Is there, Suzy? You think I should give it a try?'

'I do. I would love to share a stage with you one day.'

'Yes,' Oliver grinned. 'I think I'd like that too.'

As they enjoyed a comfortable silence, a shaft of sunlight burst through the overhead branches and the silvery light was slowly warmed as the daylight spread.

'Soon the cock will crow and the sleeping world awake. Time for me to be away to my bed.'

Suzy looked questioningly at Oliver. 'Who said that? I don't recognise it.'

'I just made it up, although I can't claim it as original. There are so many words and phrases in my head that I can never be sure what is coming out and in what order.'

'We actors have heads full of lines we have learned but can never forget.'

'We actors?'

Suzy looked at Oliver with affection. 'You're an actor, Francis. I just know it.'

He looked into her eyes. Here was a woman he admired – could even love – but now wasn't the time. His chance of being with Suzy lay in the future; a promised land that existed on the other side of murder.

He stood up. 'Would you like me to walk you back to Sheep Street?'

'I don't live on Sheep Street.'

'Maybe not but I won't leave you alone here before the night has truly ended.'

'You frightened the Shakespeare Killer will get me?' Suzy grinned as she said it.

'No, I'm not frightened of that. I'm quite sure you'll be safe from him.'

They walked together through the doorway in the graveyard wall and down the slope into the hollow. The sun's rays illuminated the clearing and Oliver's heart swelled with joy. The words he had used to lure Lizzie Birchwood to her death came flowing from his lips, but this time they were recited with love.

'I know a bank where the wild thyme blows. Where oxlips and the nodding violet grows. Quite over-canopied with luscious woodbine. With sweet musk-roses and with eglantine: There sleeps Titania sometime of the night. Lulled in these flowers with dances and delight.'

Suzy turned towards him and her face reminded him of Titania in the golden rays of the early morning sun. 'I knew you were an actor, I just knew it.'

Oliver shook his head. 'In another life, maybe. Not in this one.'

Suzy took his hands in hers and looked so deeply into his eyes that he felt she saw his very soul.

'Let's act together in this life, Francis. Now I've found you, I can't lose you.'

As he stood, gazing into the eyes of Suzy, he knew that here was a woman he could love, and it seemed she could love him too. It was so cruel, fate had dealt him a winning hand in a game he could not play. There was too much blood, too many dead, and more to come.

He shook his head. 'I'm sorry, Suzy. I don't think that will ever happen.'

She squeezed his hands tightly. 'You don't know that, none of us know for sure what our future holds.'

Oliver did. He smiled sadly. 'We are such stuff as dreams are made on, and our little life is rounded with a sleep.'

Oliver took Suzy's hand. He led her through the hollow and towards the exit to Southern Lane. He pointed down towards Waterside where the first signs of morning life were stirring. A milk float from Loxley Dairies was delivering to the houses and hotels.

He gave Suzy a gentle nudge. 'Go into town and walk home from there. You'll be safe.'

Suzy checked left and right before crossing. When she reached the pavement on the other side, she turned to speak to Francis just as he slipped into the trees at Avon Dell, disappearing like a dream she would never catch.

A moment when everything had seemed possible was lost forever; only Suzy didn't know that yet.

Chapter 34
Too Good To Be True

Mel Townsend could not remember the drive from HQ in Coventry to Stratford. The whole morning had been surreal and she needed to talk to Fred. She pulled up on Guild Street Station's car park and made her way to CID.

Fred was waiting for her at the top of the stairs. 'Detective Chief Inspector Townsend, is it?'

Mel was surprised. 'How did you know? I've only just been offered the job.'

Fred nodded his head towards Beeching's old office. 'Come with me. We need to talk.'

Mel followed, her head full of questions, Such as how did Fred know and why did he look so bloody miserable? As she entered she saw that Toby was already there and three mugs of tea were steaming on the desk.

'How did you know I'd be coming?'

'I'm a bloody detective, Mel.'

'That's Detective Chief Inspector Mel to you,' she smiled.

'It's a trap, don't take it,' blurted Fred.

The smile left her face. What was Fred talking about? She turned to Toby. 'What's he on about?'

'Beeching and the top brass. They're setting you up.'

'Setting me up. What do you mean?'

Toby pressed on. 'Beeching has taken himself away from heading up the case. If we don't catch the killer soon, who do you think is going to carry the can?'

Mel was about to make light of it but registered the looks on her friend's faces; they weren't smiling.

'But I've only just arrived. Nobody can blame me for an

inquiry that wasn't mine, can they?' She bridled as she realised they could.

'Beeching offered me the job but I didn't accept. It's a poisoned chalice. He's trying to distance himself from failure,' said Fred.

As Mel listened it all started to make sense; she hadn't even applied for the role. After Wilson's death, Beeching had taken over his role, seemingly on a temporary basis but it had soon become apparent that the top brass wanted him there. He was a useful buffer between the press and a case her colleagues in Stratford were struggling to solve.

'Did you know I didn't even apply? They just wheeled me in and offered it to me after a very cursory interview.'

Fred nodded. 'Same as me, Mel. They just want a fall guy in place.'

'Fall person,' corrected Toby.

Fred looked distastefully at Toby. 'Don't bring your socialist, liberal opinions to work.'

'I'm just trying to be balanced and fair.'

'We're the police, we don't do balanced and fair.'

Mel shook her head but there was a smile playing on her lips. 'And that, boys, is why I have to take the job. It may be a poisoned chalice but I'll be the first woman detective chief inspector ever on this force.'

'For about five minutes.'

'Doesn't matter, Fred. One of us has to break that glass ceiling.'

'You ever seen a glass ceiling, Mel? When it breaks it sends shards of glass everywhere, you're going to get cut to pieces!'

Fred was very clear that he didn't want Mel to take it; Toby had said nothing.

'What do you think, Toby?'

'Unfortunately, you're both wrong. The first female detective chief inspector was in 1935.'

'Really?' Fred sounded like he didn't believe Toby.

'Lilian Wyles, 1935. She was in the Met.'

'How do you know all this stuff?'

'Always wanted to be a copper, boss. I did a lot of research.'

'But what about me, Toby? It would still be something to be the first female DCI in Warwickshire.'

Toby didn't answer. He looked at Fred and then back to Mel.

'Don't bother about what Fred thinks, Toby. I stopped listening to him years ago.'

'Charming.' Fred looked like he was caught somewhere between hurt and a man suffering from terminal wind.

'Well?'

'I think you should take it, Mel.'

'Give me one good reason, Toby,' snapped Fred. 'You know Beeching is slipperier than a greased second-hand car salesman.'

'Because I think we are on the verge of cracking this case and when we do it's going to make Mel look good. If we do that, she's going to be our boss.'

Fred visibly winced but said nothing.

'And with Mel as our boss, I reckon you'd finally want the promotion to DI you've been avoiding.'

Fred considered it for a moment. 'You really think we're close?'

'Yes, I do.'

'Based on what, exactly?'

'Don't be so negative, Fred. You and Toby are getting close and I'm betting my career on you doing it.'

'No pressure then,' said Fred.

Chapter 35
Unsex Me Here

When Beatrice arrived at the house on Trinity Street, morning had well and truly broken; the sun filtered through the trees and the morning chorus was coming to an end. She watched as Oliver appeared, tired and dishevelled.

'Where have you been?'

Oliver jumped at the sound of her voice. She smiled; he hadn't been expecting her.

'What are you doing here?'

'Waiting to see you. Is it done?'

'Is what done?'

'Felix. Is he dead?'

'He's sorted.'

'And what does that mean?'

'I've buried him. That clear enough for you?'

It was. Beatrice smiled. One more piece of the jigsaw had fallen into place. Now she just had to get her son to finish the project and she would be free. Truly free for the first time in her life.

'So what's next, Oliver? Have you finished your revenge?'

'Well, my Banquo is gone … and now for his wife.'

'And who is your Mauldvina?'

'You know, Mother. Clarissa.'

'Ah, the lovely Clarissa. Good choice, she does need killing.'

'I thought you two were friends.'

'We were never friends.' Beatrice could not disguise the contempt in her voice. 'That little trollop would have loved to get Morris into the sack. Who knows, maybe she did.'

'And that bothers you?'

Beatrice looked hurt. 'Why would you even ask that?'

'Because you never really cared about him, did you. He was a stepping stone after my father.'

'What kind of a woman do you think I am, Oliver?'

'A bad one, Mother. That's why you're still alive.'

Beatrice watched as Oliver washed his hands and then poured himself a cup of tea. He had become a very strong man; he would be hard to kill if it came down to it. She had to find a way for the police to either arrest him or kill him without implicating herself. If Clarissa was the last piece of the jigsaw, she didn't have much time. 'Do you think we should kill Suzy Tench?'

Oliver was visibly shocked. 'Kill Suzy. Why?'

Beatrice shrugged. 'Well, she's very good, isn't she.'

Oliver's face hardened. 'Isn't that a good thing? We want a great company.'

'Not if I'm there, too much competition. I want the spotlight, Oliver. I've been out of it long enough.'

'Absolutely not. Suzy has done nothing wrong and we need her.'

'Do we though? She's too famous now. She won't want to toe the line for long.'

Oliver's face soured; he looked at her with disgust. 'You have no scruples at all, do you?'

'I'm ambitious, Oliver. Is that so awful when I've missed out on so much.' Beatrice struggled to keep her face neutral, to hide the emotions within. Where did he think his dreadful desire for revenge had come from! Hers was an ambition so raw and ruthless that there were no limits to what she would do to satisfy it.

'Did you betray my father?'

The question caught her off guard. 'No, of course not. I loved your father.'

Oliver knew that was a lie; Beatrice could see it in his eyes.

In that moment they both realised there was a very good chance that, before this was all over, one of them would have to kill the other. Beatrice knew Oliver had considered it and now she decided upon it. She would unsex herself; forget she was a mother and kill what she had created. She needed to guarantee her future. But motherhood is more complicated than that and the blood ties that bind us run deep. There was also another piece of the jigsaw that Beatrice didn't realise was missing.

Big Al was still smarting over the stabbing of Sir Morris. Someone had got into the theatre and tampered with his knives. He wasn't having that. He had thought about little else since it had happened. Who had access to them and a motive?

Obviously, the killer must have a motive. The police thought it was Oliver Lawrence but no one had seen him. Then there was Beatrice; she wanted to return to the stage and Sir Morris had stood in her way. Would she kill for that? Big Al wasn't so sure. There was one nagging doubt in the back of his mind. The man he had seen in the Memorial Gardens a few days before Sir Morris was stabbed seemed very familiar. He had a feeling that man was something to do with it. No one messes with his theatre without repercussions. Lady Beatrice was going to get a visit.

Chapter 36
The Coming Storm

The day soon became hot and sticky, but the long hot spell of weather was about to break.

'You seen the forecast for tomorrow,' asked Fred.

Toby nodded. 'Yeah, looks like the end of the world.'

'That'll be a relief.'

They stood in front of the whiteboard in CID. Felix Richards' name stood out like an unanswered question.

'We need to find him.'

'Already on it, boss. Apparently, he has a boat on the Avon.'

'Good work, Toby. Where's it moored?'

'According to my information he's on the river, opposite the theatre.'

'What are you waiting for? Get down there and find him. If he's there, bring him in.'

'OK, boss. You coming?'

Fred shook his head. 'No. Mel will be here in a while.'

'Romantic lunch?'

'Sod off, Toby. She's coming to take over from Beeching. It's on a temporary basis for now and that's how it will stay unless we catch Lawrence.'

'I'd better go and find Felix Richards then.' Toby grabbed his notes and headed for the river.

'Let me know what you find.'

'What if I don't find anything, boss?'

'If he's not there find out when he left, where he was headed and what the name of his boat is.'

Toby held up his notebook. 'I've got that already. It's called *the Styx*.'

Fred's brow furrowed. '*The Styx*? That's the river of death from Greek mythology.'

'Well, considering the number of bodies we've had in and around the Avon recently, I reckon that's quite appropriate.'

As Toby walked over the footbridge towards the boathouse, he looked down the river towards Holy Trinity. There were several boats tied up along the embankment that ran alongside the recreation ground. Excitement welled in the pit of his stomach; this was the first time he had felt optimistic for a while. He felt sure that Felix Richards really could be the key that unlocked the whole case.

The first boat was called *The Tempest*. You found a lot of that kind of thing in Stratford. It was locked up. Clearly the owner wasn't in so he made his way down the embankment. On the next boat an old boy sat on the back smoking a pipe. His white beard had been stained yellow by the frequent exposure to the smoke. If he was a fish, he would have been a kipper.

'Good morning,' said Toby.

The old boy considered it for a moment before deciding that he agreed. 'For now, but I don't think you'll be saying that tomorrow.'

'Oh, the storm?'

'Bit more than a storm, I reckon. Looks like the end of days.'

Toby frowned. 'You think it's going to be that bad?'

The old boy took a long pull on his pipe, giving the air of an old man of the sea. This was somewhat undermined by the fact he was seated on a canal barge called *Trevor's Folly*. 'When the river rises there will be no stopping it. I'm moving *Trevor* up the Wilmcote Locks to get above the flood.'

Toby pointed to the empty berth downstream of his boat. 'Do you think that's what the owner of the boat that was moored there has done?'

The bowl of his pipe glowed like a furnace as he inhaled, and Toby wondered if sucking something that hot into your lungs could be good for you.

'Left in the middle of the night, was spooked by the weather forecast when I warned him. He was going to take the Avon down to Tewkesbury but I told him to go up the flight of locks at Wilmcote to get above the storm. Besides, it's a quicker way to get north. Why do you want to know?'

Toby pulled out his warrant card. 'DC Marlowe, Stratford CID.'

The old boy took another deep draught of his pipe.

This could be a long conversation, thought Toby.

'Like I said, he left in the middle of the night.'

'Can you remember the name of his boat?'

'Yes.'

'Feel like sharing?'

'Something about twigs.'

Toby's heart gave a lurch. 'How about *Styx*?'

'That's what I said.'

Toby wrote it down on his notepad and held it up to him.

'That's it. I told him that's not how you spell sticks.'

'It's from … Never mind.'

He looked again and nodded.

'That's the boat we're looking for.'

'Why, are you the spelling police?'

Toby smiled. 'No, sir. This is part of a murder inquiry and he is a person of interest.'

He drew deeply on his pipe once more. 'I reckon he left at about two this morning.'

'Are you sure?'

'Nope. I was asleep. I went to bed at half one and woke up at about five. He was there when I went to sleep and he was gone when I got up.'

'Can you describe his boat?'

He thought for a moment but this time without taking a draw on his pipe. 'Biggish.'

'Could you be more specific,' asked Toby.

'Yes, I could.'

Toby was beginning to feel like a dentist; this interview was like pulling teeth. He tried to hide the irritation in his voice. 'Would you mind describing the boat, please.'

'A riverboat, not a canal boat. Been recently refurbished, looks nice.'

'Anything else?'

'Yeah, fancy calling it *the Styx*. Bloke can't spell!'

'Styx is Greek.'

'He didn't look Greek.'

'He isn't.' Toby looked downriver. 'Are you sure he went north?'

He pointed to the lock at the corner of Waterside. 'I reckon he took my advice and went north towards Wilmcote Locks, more options to join the national network up there.'

'Thanks,' said Toby, that's very helpful. Did you speak to him apart from the weather warning?'

'No, not really. We nodded a couple of times but he was hardly ever up on deck. Came and went a lot.'

Well, thought Toby. *You would if you were involved in a lot of murders, wouldn't you.*

He had found Oliver Lawrence's accomplice, of that he was certain. As he went to make his way back to Guild Street a great rumble of thunder crackled across the sky.

The old boy smiled wryly and knocked his pipe out on the side of his boat. The hot ashes hissed as they hit the water. He gestured up to where the rumble was coming from with his pipe. 'That's not rain coming, that's a deluge. I'd cancel any plans you had for tomorrow.'

Four hundred yards downstream Felix struggled with his bonds but Oliver had taped his hands securely behind his back. He had been down in the dark culvert for several hours and still hadn't managed to work the gag from his mouth. Even if he did, with the roar of the weir on one side and the lock on the other it was unlikely anyone would hear him.

He looked down through the metal grille he stood on. The waters of the Avon flowed just a few feet below him and he thanked his lucky stars that it wasn't winter. When the floods came, this island was often underwater. The culvert in which he was imprisoned could soon become a watery tomb.

Felix never heard the rumble of thunder which foretold the coming storm.

Chapter 37
The Mary Celeste

Toby hurried back to Guild Street to give Fred the news. When he arrived, his new boss was behind her desk.

She looked up. 'Morning, Toby.'

'Morning, ma'am.'

Mel shot him a quick smile showing she appreciated the formal greeting while other officers were around.

Fred walked in behind him. 'Creep.' He went over to his desk and slumped down in his chair. 'Well? What did you find?'

'Nothing, sir. He took off in the middle of last night.'

'Bugger.'

Mel wandered into the CID office. 'That Felix Richards' boat you're on about?'

Fred looked surprised. 'Yes, how did you know?'

Mel pointed at the whiteboard. 'I figured if I'm in charge here I'd better bring myself up to speed. Felix is on the board with a big red question mark next to him.'

'He's the missing link, ma'am.'

'I thought that was Fred.'

Fred gave Mel a sickly grin which Toby ignored.

'He's really missing now. Leaving in the middle of the night looks suspicious.'

'North?'

'That's what the old boy on the boat next door reckoned,' said Toby.

'He could be up in Birmingham by now.'

Mel shook her head. 'Doubt it, he'll have to go through Wilmcote Locks first, that'll take him an hour or two on his own. To get to Birmingham there's over fifty locks to negotiate.'

'How do you know this stuff, Mel?'

'Ma'am,' Mel said.

Fred stiffened momentarily. 'Ma'am'

'My ex used to have a narrow boat.'

'No wonder he's an ex then.'

'Just like you, Fred.' Mel gave Fred a smile that wasn't.

'So where do you think he'd be, ma'am,' asked Toby, keen to move the conversation on.

'Probably between Henley and Knowle. Let's get some uniforms from Solihull going down the towpath from there, see if they can spot the boat or its owner.'

'What if he's made it past there?'

Mel looked at the map on the wall. 'He could carry on north but it's more likely he'd head for Gas Street Basin.'

'Sounds lovely,' said Fred.

'Lovely or not, if he gets there he has options. The Grand Union, The Worcester, Birmingham or Stourbridge canals. He could go anywhere. The canal system in Birmingham is like Venice.'

Fred nodded. 'Yeah, whenever I'm in Birmingham I listen out for the singing of the gondoliers.'

Toby smiled. 'On the upside, ma'am, it's not going to be a high-speed chase.'

Mel pointed at the map. 'I'm going to ring Birmingham, I've got a mate at Digbeth. I'll see if I can get some uniforms at the basin and then wait. It's about all we can do for now.'

Dave Lewis was paddling his coracle towards the Edstone Aqueduct, though to say towards was probably overstating it. It was going round more than forward but at least it floated. He had made it in his garage after a visit to Wales had reignited the latent Welshness that lurked somewhere in his consciousness. He had been conceived in a caravan near Bangor, according to his brother, and that had been enough for him to declare his heritage to anyone who would listen.

As he rotated slowly towards the aqueduct, his way was obstructed by a large boat that had drifted diagonally across the canal blocking his passage. It was about fifty yards away and, using his advanced nautical powers of deduction, he reckoned he could be there within twenty rotations.

As he pulled alongside he grabbed the rail; he was feeling dizzy. He waited for a few seconds until it passed before calling out. 'Hello … is anyone there?'

There was no answer. He called again; still no reply. When not in his homemade coracle, he was an experienced sailor. He deftly tied off and, with a litheness that defied his years, pulled himself up and over the rail.

'Hello, can anyone hear me?' He opened the door to the cabin and looked inside. There was no sign of life. Here was an empty boat floating freely down the canal. Like the *Mary Celeste*, it was a ghost boat. He went back on deck and grabbed hold of the bow rope. The bank was only a couple of feet away and on this part of the canal there were some mooring posts.

Dave jumped ashore and quickly tied the boat up, he then went aft and did the same. Once the boat was secured he took a closer look: *the Styx*. Dave was an educated man; he knew *the Styx* was the river of death. It seemed weirdly appropriate for this ghost boat. He needed to raise the alarm. He climbed back aboard and untied his coracle. He would row back down the canal to his house and call the police.

As he leaned down towards it he remembered the number of revolutions it had taken him to get here. He pulled the coracle up and out of the water; it was light, designed to be carried to the river. He pulled out the strap and draped it over his shoulder, climbed off the boat and carried it home to raise the alarm. That would be so much quicker and less disorientating.

Chapter 38
Opportunity Knocks

Beatrice walked down Southern Lane towards the theatre. She had a meeting with Pierre Corridor at 11 a.m. He'd asked her to pop in and though she wasn't sure why, she hoped it was to discuss a juicy part for the coming season. She'd been promised Puck but who knew what else might be on offer.

When she reached the stage door she swept in, barely acknowledging the staff. It had been her way for over fifteen years. She had never been able to fake humility, and after marrying Sir Morris she didn't have to. The hard stares that she got in return showed the feeling was mutual. She proceeded in silence until she entered the hallway that led to Pierre's office. Walking towards her was a familiar figure: Big Al Morris.

'Morning Alan, how are you?'

'Maybe I should be asking you that question.'

Beatrice smiled weakly. 'Oh, life must go on. It's what Morris would have wanted.'

'I think Sir Morris would have liked his life to go on.'

It was a blunt statement and Beatrice was taken aback. She wasn't sure how to respond; that's the trouble with lying. 'Don't blame yourself for the knife, Alan.'

'I don't. Your son did that.'

Again, the bluntness of his reply was disarming and Beatrice took a beat before responding. 'I'm not sure what to say to that. Why do you think it was Oliver?'

'Because I think I met him last week by the Remembrance Garden. There was something really familiar about a man I passed at the gate. I didn't recognise him but there was something about him. Since Sir Morris was stabbed I've thought of little else.'

'You believe the press then?'

Big Al looked at Beatrice with concern. 'Not just the press, Beatrice, the police think so too. I'm beginning to think they're right.'

Beatrice nodded. 'I can see why you would think that but I'm just hoping it's not true. I can't lose my husband and my son.'

Big Al nodded.

Beatrice mused that there wasn't much he could say to a woman who had just lost her husband in terrible circumstances and now had a missing son who appeared to have returned to Stratford as a full-blown serial killer.

'What are you going to do now?'

Beatrice forced a smile. 'I'm going to take your advice, Alan, and throw myself back into the work. I'm going to see Pierre about playing Puck.'

He nodded. 'Great, I think you should.' He smiled and started to walk away but then paused and turned back to her. 'Just so you know, Hugh Pitt is in there.'

Beatrice tried to hide her surprise but her face must have shown it for a split-second because Big Al smiled. 'I know, I was wondering why he was there too.' He turned and walked away. He had seen that momentary look of shock on Beatrice's face. She was upset and for the first time, he began to wonder if she could be trusted.

Beatrice watched him go and then turned towards Pierre Corridor's door. As she walked the few steps towards it she breathed deeply. Whatever was about to happen behind that door she had to show the right face; grieving widow trying to carry on. It was a hard role to pitch correctly, especially in front of one of Europe's greatest theatre directors. She knocked.

'Enter!'

Beatrice swung open the door.

Pierre stood up from his chair and walked around his desk to greet her with a hug. 'Thank you so much for coming, Beatrice. I know it's a difficult time.'

Beatrice smiled bravely and, as she did so, saw Hugh Pitt smiling at her over Pierre's shoulder. 'Oh, hello Hugh.' She wanted to add *what the hell are you doing here?* but left those words unspoken.

'Hello, Lady Oxford. Can I just say how terribly sorry I am about Sir Morris.'

Beatrice nodded weakly and allowed her eyes to moisten. 'Thank you, Hugh.' *You're not sorry,* she thought. *You hated him and now you're here to try and take his place.*

Beatrice stepped back from Pierre's embrace and waited to see what was about to unfold. She had to hold her cards close and not betray herself. Play the role that was expected of her. Lies and secrets corrupt and corrode but they can also make you a better actor.

'Please, take a seat, Beatrice.'

Pierre ushered her towards the chair next to Hugh. He remained standing, waiting for her to sit first. The perfect gentleman. *You're playing a role too,* she thought as she sat down and waited.

Pierre walked around the desk and sat down. 'Can I get you a tea or coffee?'

Beatrice shook her head. 'No, thanks.' She didn't want to play games, delay things. She needed to know what was going on. Her mind was spinning out all the scenarios that could possibly happen but she tried to block them, concentrating on repeating the same mantra inside her head: *stay in character, stay in character.*

Pierre sat back in his chair and steepled the fingers of both hands together, then leaned his head forward until his lips were touching the tips of his fingers. This was his thinking pose, *gravitas* on steroids.

The silence lasted for nearly fifteen seconds, which isn't really long but when your whole future may depend on what he was about to say, it felt like a lifetime.

Finally, he looked up. 'You may be wondering why I've asked you here today.'

Too bloody right, she thought but again remained silent, letting Pierre set the agenda.

'The loss of Morris is terrible, horrendous. I can't imagine how you are feeling but I knew Morris for nearly twenty years and if I know only one thing, it's that he would want the show to go on. He was the greatest actor of his generation.'

That was a lie. It was Richard, always had been. Again, Beatrice kept her thoughts to herself and listened carefully to Pierre; her future could depend on it.

'You may be wondering why Hugh is here.'

Beatrice turned her head and smiled at him. 'I was a little.' She heard herself say it. Calm, gentle, enquiring. It was perfect.

'We can never replace Morris.'

And now she knew; here it was, the big speech. The torch was about to be passed on and, somehow, she had to become a part of the torch bearer's company. Her thoughts raced and she calmed them with the mantra. *Stay in character. Stay in character.*

Pierre had paused, looking at Beatrice for a negative reaction, but her face remained calm. She was listening and seemingly open to his proposal.

'We don't need to talk about this now, Beatrice.'

She shook her head. 'No. You're right, Pierre. The show must go on. It is what Morris would have wanted.' Beatrice smiled at the perfect pitch of her response. It had been flawless; her acting was getting better by the moment.

Pierre reached across, laid a hand on hers and squeezed gently. It was a patronising squeeze; she knew she was being played but maybe not in a bad way.

'I'm fine, Pierre. Let's just say what needs to be said. Life is for the living, looking back is pointless.'

Hugh nodded his agreement. He had never liked Lady Beatrice Oxford. When he had been a young actor coming through the ranks she had been cold, even dismissive of him. And then he had become a star in Hollywood and she had suddenly seemed to soften towards him. He really didn't like her but he had to admit, given the situation, the way she was handling herself was remarkable.

He also noticed that despite being in her late fifties she looked twenty years younger. Other thoughts then began to occupy his mind. What a lovely way to get back at Sir Morris. He allowed those thoughts to drift away, they could be revisited at a later date. For now he needed to concentrate on what Lady Beatrice had to say; his future at Stratford depended upon it.

Pierre sat back in his chair and looked from Beatrice to Hugh and back.

Here it comes, thought Beatrice.

'There are seminal moments in theatre where a new direction is taken,' he paused. 'This is one of those moments.'

His words were full of *gravitas*. Beatrice and Hugh listened intently, both fervently wishing Pierre would just get on with it. That wasn't his way, he also loved the sound of his own voice. This, too, was a performance, planned and performed just for them.

'I want to build a new company around the two of you. Trevor Convent and I have discussed it at great length and we feel this is the way to go!'

And there it was, out there. This was music to Beatrice's ears. She wasn't so keen on the Hugh Pitt bit, but at least she would be part of the new company. She waited for Pierre to continue.

'You have been wickedly under-used. I know you stepped back to support Morris but you are a great comic actress.'

I'm an even better serious actor now, thought Beatrice. *You don't even know I'm acting.*

'I want to make you Puck in *The Dream* and I also want you to play Rosalind.'

Beatrice was taken aback. 'I'm too old to play Rosalind.'

Pierre shook his head. 'I don't think so. Your beauty is timeless, Beatrice. What do you think, Hugh?'

'Er, yes. Timeless. And of course the audience is mostly quite far away.'

Beatrice laughed. 'Well, that's me damned with faint praise.'

Hugh looked horrified. 'No, no. I didn't mean that. You're beautiful, Lady Oxford and … and I'm sure you could pull it off.'

Beatrice fixed him with a long smile, looking deeply into his eyes and she could see it; hidden behind the embarrassment was desire. Maybe everything was possible in this strange new world that her son was creating.

'What do you say?'

'I'm astounded.' She was.

'And?'

'Yes. Whatever you want, Pierre. I want to throw myself into the work, lose myself in it and try and make something good out of this terrible situation.'

Pierre clapped his hands together. 'That's wonderful. Isn't it, Hugh?'

Hugh nodded. 'Yes, marvellous,' he said distractedly. He was imagining playing Orlando opposite her. The hugs and kisses, the …

'Hugh, Hugh!'

He snapped out of his daydream and focused on Pierre. 'Sorry, I was just imagining us playing Orlando and Rosalind.'

I bet you were, thought Beatrice. She had Hugh in her orbit and he was hers to control. For now.

Pierre was very happy. He hadn't expected Beatrice to be so

positive; given recent events, he hadn't even expected her to show up. She was remarkable. He was desperate to get the show back on the road. This was a business and they needed to put on plays to pay the staff and keep the whole thing going. He turned to Hugh. Here, he needed to be delicate.

'Hugh has kindly offered to stay for a couple of seasons to help us rebuild.'

That was true but it was mainly because the decent offers in Hollywood had dried up. *Four Dates and a Christening* had made Hugh a huge star but the subsequent films he had been shoehorned in to had filled his bank balances but tainted his box office appeal.

Returning to Stratford had been a great way to rebuild his reputation. His agent had sold it as, "Returning to his first love." It was true that he had been outstanding in *Much Ado*, not an easy play to be outstanding in. This had got the offers to start trickling in again. Two seasons at Stratford could rebuild him. As they say, absence makes the heart grow fonder.

Beatrice was well aware of the reasons for Hugh's return but never showed it.

'I can't wait to share the stage with you, Hugh. I've long been an admirer of your work.' That was a lie but she sold it so well she could see that Hugh, despite evidence to the contrary, believed it.

'And me of yours, Lady Beatrice.'

She laughed. 'I doubt that, Hugh. I was retired before you left drama school.'

'I meant by reputation.'

That too was a lie but Beatrice ignored it. She turned to Pierre. 'So, this is the new beginning.'

'It is.'

Beatrice leaned over the desk and offered her hand. 'Honoured to be a part of it.'

Pierre took her hand and placed his other hand over it. 'We are lucky to have you, Beatrice. I think this could be wonderful. I will introduce you to Trevor when he gets back from his holidays. He will be your director.'

Beatrice looked from Pierre to Hugh. Hugh was smiling warmly too and, in his eyes, Beatrice could see unspoken possibilities. She smiled back and, as she did so, she realised that they would never share the stage. She had an idea that would solve all of her problems. It was dark and unthinkable, but she had thought it and now, like a terrible road accident that happens in front of you, she couldn't unsee it. She didn't want to.

Chapter 39
Bad Feeling

The call from Dave Lewis had galvanised Fred. He looked at the whiteboard. *The Styx*/Felix was marked out in red. He turned to Toby and Mel. 'Lawrence has taken Felix Richards and we have to find him. He's the key.'

'Do you think he's still alive?'

Fred looked at Mel; it was a fair question. 'According to SOCO there was no blood on the boat and no sign of a struggle.'

'He's been kidnapped then,' said Toby.

Fred nodded. 'It looks that way, but why would he kidnap him? Surely killing him would make more sense. Tie up the loose ends, once and for all.'

'Maybe they're friends. Hard to kill a friend, even when you're mad.'

Mel glanced at Toby. 'I think he's right, Fred. It looks like they were close, maybe he's been helping Lawrence all along.'

'I think he's got him locked up somewhere until this is all over,' said Toby.

'If that is the case, he must have more murders planned. Sir Morris is dead so, apart from Clarissa, I can't think who.'

'I can. He could kill his mother.'

Fred looked at Mel. 'Boys don't kill their mums.'

'Read the papers, Fred, it happens more than you'd think. That's why I never became a mum.'

Fred knew that wasn't the only reason. He and Mel had been an item for quite a while but Mel had decided that Fred wasn't parent material. She had been wrong in that; Fred would have made a great father but now wasn't the moment to debate it. 'So, we think that Lawrence has stashed Felix somewhere.'

Toby nodded. 'Yeah, I think he must be near here. Lawrence is going to wait and see how this plays out before he decides whether to kill him or not. The only question is where?'

Toby went over to the map on the wall. 'He's close, I can feel it. Felix is our Banquo but Lawrence couldn't bring himself to kill him yet.'

'He's not had much trouble with anyone else,' observed Fred.

'Let's keep close to Beatrice and Clarissa, and I want every lock-up, garage shed and empty building in Stratford searched. If Felix is here we have to find him.' Mel turned to Toby. 'Get uniforms out there and do a street by street. Check anywhere someone could be concealed. Start by the American Fountain and work your way out.'

'That's going to take a lot of men, ma'am.'

Mel looked at Toby. 'You can have forty. Get moving.'

Toby nodded and headed out to gather the officers he needed, a lot of whom would have to come from Coventry. As he made his way down the stairs he glanced out of the window. The sky to the east had gone dark. He could feel the pressure dropping. There was a storm coming and it was going to be big.

Back up in CID, Mel and Fred stood side by side looking at the board.

'You think Felix is dead,' she stated.

'I would have killed him. Why take the risk of him being found alive? I think we're looking for a body.'

'Not another one, my career prospects won't survive it.' Mel walked back into her office and sat down behind her desk. 'Come in here, Fred.'

Fred followed and sat down opposite her.

'Do you think I've made a mistake?'

'Taking the promotion?'

'Yes. Have I bitten off more than I can chew?'

Fred thought for a moment. 'Maybe, but it's not really about ability, is it. All you need is a bit of luck.'

Mel smiled weakly; she didn't feel lucky right now.

Within an hour, Toby had gathered together sixteen uniformed officers and given them their instructions. The search for Felix Richards had begun.

Just half a mile away, Felix had given up on trying to escape his bonds. Oliver had bound him well, there was blood seeping from the skin on his wrists where he had struggled against his restraints. His mouth was sore and his tongue swollen from trying to work the gag out of his mouth. It had been hours and he had lost track of the time. His mouth was so dry that every time he coughed he retched.

He looked around what could soon become his tomb, unless he could get free. It was dark but his eyes had become accustomed to it, and a sliver of light reflected from the Avon. From where he stood, precariously balanced, he could see the waters charging beneath him. There was daylight reflected in them; he must have been here all night.

The metal mesh platform on which he perched was reached by four rudimentary metal hoops that were fixed into the wall of the culvert. Clearly, they were designed for inspection access. On their top surface the steel hoops had been filed flat to allow the engineer's feet to sit safely without slipping. He edged over to the step that was just above his face. If he stood on his tiptoes he could try and hook the edge of his gag on the top of the step and use it to pull it out of his mouth.

The edge of the step looked rough and corroded. There was a real risk of cutting himself but what choice did he have? As he stretched up towards the step he realised that he would have to try and remove it by pushing up. He had to force it out of his mouth and back down and over his chin. He angled his mouth up until he could feel the step snagging the gag at the side of his mouth. He felt a downward tug, it was working. He poked at the gag with his tongue and pressed his cheek harder into the step. It was moving. His calf muscles were starting to scream but he had to keep going, it was his only chance. He struggled on for another thirty seconds, feeling the gag move slowly, fraction by fraction, from his mouth. Just as he felt certain he was going to make it, agonising cramp hit his left calf like a blow.

He dropped down in pain and his cheek scraped hard against the step. His skin tore on the rough metal and the pain was instant. Staggering backwards, he felt his left foot slip on the edge of the platform and fell backwards. The culvert was only three feet wide but it felt like he was falling into a deep black well from which there was no hope of return.

He braced for the impact, knowing in an instant that if he fell he would tumble into the dark waters and drown; with his hands tied behind his back and his mouth gagged there would be no hope.

This all occurred in a split-second but everything felt like it was happening in slow motion. His back hit the wall of the culvert and he felt his body begin to fold into a sitting position. He held his core with every bit of his strength; he mustn't fold or he would drop down into the river. His feet were still on the platform and his shoulders were backed against the wall. For a few seconds he fought to straighten his back and slowly push himself up. It took a supreme effort but he managed to get his back and legs straight.

He had managed to stabilise himself but he was now leaning backwards at about a ten-degree angle, his feet on the platform. He couldn't move but he knew he couldn't hold this position for long. He tried to push his weight forward but only managed to get his back a couple of inches from the wall. As he fell back the impact forced him down. Gravity was sucking him towards the dark waters, folding him back into a sitting position and, once he had gone too far, his feet would slide across the platform and he would fall into the darkness.

He cried out, more in frustration than fear; he couldn't die like this, alone in the dark. Fear and anger gave him a strength he didn't realise he had and, inch by inch, he began to straighten his legs again. His quads burned with the strain, his stomach muscles forced his torso straight, and little by little he edged his shoulders back up the wall until his body was braced, stiff as a board. Like a plank leaned against a wall he realised the angle of lean – without his hands to assist – was too much. The realisation hit: when his muscles could no longer stand the strain he was putting them under, he would fall.

He felt hot tears of despair in his eyes; he was going to die. The voice of defeat whispered in his ears. *Give up, Felix, you can't escape.* He shook his head, knowing he wasn't ready to accept that as his fate. Another voice broke through, and this one he listened to. *Think. Breathe and think.*

He drew several deep, slow breaths and the terror that had clogged his mind began to clear. There had to be a way. He tried to assess his situation. How could he get vertical enough to get back on the platform? He looked at it and then felt the circular wall of the tunnel against his back. Suddenly, it was obvious. All he had to do was inch his way around the culvert, bracing his feet against the edge of the platform for grip. His hands were tied behind him but his palms were faced against the wall.

He pushed carefully backwards, just enough to allow his shoulders to shuffle a bit, then a bit more. As the angle changed he felt his right foot begin to slip but adjusted it and repeated the process. His left calf was screaming and he could feel it threatening to cramp again; if it did, it would be game over.

He paused, took several deep breaths and began the exhausting process again. For the next ten minutes he edged around little by little, feeling that at any moment his muscles would cramp and he would fall. He was so immersed in the effort, the pain and the sheer will to survive that he hadn't noticed he was no longer leaning backwards but was standing vertically on the platform. He had done it, he was safe!

For a moment he was filled with joy but that soon passed as he was overcome with the sickening realisation that he had only got back to where he started twenty minutes ago. His hope died as he too in the scene before him; he wasn't quite back to where he had been, he was worse off.

His face was cut open and bleeding, his energy had been massively depleted and his calf was cramping so badly that it felt like he had torn a muscle. There was no way he could get up on his toes again. He slumped back against the wall. He wanted to give up but somewhere in his head that little voice was talking. *Chew. Chew the gag. Bite through it.*

He began to grind his upper teeth against his lower jaw. His throat was dry, moistened only by the metallic taste of blood that was seeping into his mouth from the wound on his cheek. It wasn't much but it was all he had. He worked his teeth back and forward across the material of the gag. This was the only way he had left to fight for his life and he prayed that he would gnaw through the gag before exhaustion took him.

Chapter 40
A Mother's Love

As Beatrice walked back down Southern Lane towards Trinity Street a plan began to hatch in her mind. Hugh Pitt had been a nasty surprise; she hadn't seen that coming. Pierre was seizing the opportunity. Hugh's career in Hollywood had hit a temporary low. He would bounce back, he just needed the right script. His reviews for *Much Ado* had been excellent and he was still a star. Having him at Stratford for a couple of seasons would put bums on seats.

It wouldn't be all bad for her, there would be full houses for every show and the audience would get to see her Puck ... but they wouldn't be watching her. All eyes would be on Hugh.

She tried to weigh up the pros and cons. Hugh fancied her, she had seen it in his eyes. It was more than that though, he wanted to take Sir Morris Oxford's wife as a trophy. She didn't object to it in principle but it would mean conceding her power.

No, the opportunity lay in how Oliver would react to the news; he loathed Hugh, was probably jealous of his film success. With Hugh heading the company, he could never return. As she walked past the Dirty Duck it all became very clear. Oliver had to murder Hugh. It was perfect. And to get rid of Oliver she had to make sure he was caught in the act. She could arrange that. Get rid of both of them in one *foul* swoop. She started to smile when a voice from the patio above her called out to her.

'Beatrice.'

She looked up and there was Alan Morris seated at one of the outside tables, raising a glass of beer towards her.

'Hello Alan, I didn't expect to see you here.'

He winked. 'Always expect the unexpected. Care to join me?'

She nodded and skipped up the steps to the pub patio. 'Don't mind if I do.'

She sat down opposite him and he shook his glass. 'What's your poison?'

'Glass of dry white, please.'

Big Al went to get up but Dick Mayrick was already approaching the table. He had seen Lady Oxford arrive and he always liked to look after the big names himself.

'What can I get you, Lady Oxford?'

Beatrice looked up at Dick and smiled. 'Hello Dick, how are you?'

'I'm good, thanks.'

'And Julia?'

A huge smile spread across his face. 'She's back. We're together again.'

Beatrice feigned delight. 'That's wonderful news, Dick.'

'It is,' he agreed. Not enough time had yet lapsed to remind him of why they had separated.

'Glass of dry white to celebrate then, please.'

'Coming right up.' Dick spun on his heel and headed back into the bar. Big Al and Beatrice watched him go.

'It won't last,' said Al.

'No, it won't,' agreed Beatrice. 'Still, while he's in the optimistic phase, best keep him happy.'

Big Al smiled. 'I'd forgotten what a hard git you are.'

There weren't many people that Beatrice would allow to talk to her like that but Big Al Morris was loyal. She had known him for a long time. They had grown up together in the theatre from her late teens and his early twenties.

She grinned. 'You know it's true. Those two love each other but it's like a night out with the Kray Twins whenever they spend time together.'

Big Al smiled. 'You're right, of course,' he paused and looked over his glass at her. 'That's not why I invited you up here for a drink though.'

Beatrice raised an eyebrow. 'And why would that be?'

'Because I think your son is our murderer.'

Beatrice laughed. 'Everyone thinks that, Alan.'

'I know, but I've met him.' He let that sink in for a moment as the smile faded from Beatrice's face.

'You said you thought you had met him, but that doesn't mean anything, does it?'

'It does if I'm sure. I know what he looks like and I compared him to the artist's impression they did of Oliver based on his old PR photo.'

'The one where they aged him fifteen years?'

'Yes,' he paused and then looked straight into her eyes. 'It was him, Beatrice. I'm certain of it.'

Beatrice desperately tried to process Alan's information. Was this a good thing or not? She hadn't killed anybody. She tried to look surprised, which wasn't hard, and waited.

Big Al looked around before continuing. No one was close enough to overhear what he had to say. 'It was him in the Memorial Gardens a couple of weeks back.'

'How can you be so sure?'

'I wasn't at the time but now I've had time to consider it …'

'You think it was Oliver?'

He nodded. 'I do.'

'Has he changed?'

'Oh yes.'

He said it in a whisper and Beatrice leaned towards him, her face now framed with what she hoped was a look of motherly concern. 'What does he look like?'

'He's big.'

'What, fat?'

He shook his head. 'No, not fat. Powerful. He's built like a rugby forward that's given up beer and hit the gym. He must have two or three stones of muscle he didn't have when he left. It's made his jaw squarer and his shoulders much broader. His hair is longer too.'

Beatrice nodded. Alan had indeed seen him and knew exactly what he now looked like. Again, she asked herself if this was a good thing.

'I wanted to tell you before I go to the police. That artist's impression is still a bit off. They need my help.' He leaned forward and put his hand on Beatrice's arm. 'I'm sorry, Beatrice, but we need him caught,'

Beatrice smiled weakly. 'It's all right, Alan. If it is Oliver, he must be stopped.'

She could see the relief on Big Al's face. Clearly, he had not wanted to break this news to her; he was her friend.

'Are you sure?'

She nodded. 'Positive,' she paused for a second.

Alan picked up on it. 'What is it?'

'Would you leave it until tomorrow? I just need to get my head around it.'

He hesitated; he wasn't sure.

Beatrice beat him to the next sentence. 'The press will be all over me when this comes out, Alan. Just give me a chance to take a breath.'

He didn't like the idea of delay but what difference would one day make? He nodded. 'Very well. Tomorrow morning.'

'Thanks, Alan, I really appreciate it. My son being a killer is a lot to process.' She looked wistfully towards the river. 'He was such a happy child but the loss of his father must have hit him harder than I thought, and I don't think he ever accepted my closeness with Morris.'

Big Al. Everyone knew they were a lot more than close, but he realised that this must be so tough for her. 'Maybe go back to

Woodstock, stay out of the way.'

Beatrice shook her head. 'I can't. Pierre Corridor has just asked me to head up the next season with Hugh Pitt. I need to be here.'

'That's brilliant news.'

Beatrice smiled at Big Al. 'It is and it's all thanks to you, Alan. Without your advice I don't think I would ever have put myself forward.' It was the first true thing she had said since she sat down.

Big Al nodded. 'Glad to be of help.'

As he finished his sentence there was a prolonged rumble of thunder that travelled above them like the roar of an angry monster. Big Al looked up.

'I don't like the look of those clouds, maybe best you don't travel.'

Beatrice followed his gaze. The sky had taken on a blackness which she had never seen before. 'The sky does look angry.' She watched the dark wall of cloud that was approaching from the east. There was an occasional flash of lightning. With the red glow at its edges, the coming storm held menace. It felt like a judgement. She wondered how bad it would be, if there could be enough water to wash away her sins. Or, better still, drown them.

Big Al drained his glass. 'I think we'll be OK for a few hours, it doesn't seem to be moving. It might hold off until nightfall.'

Beatrice nodded. 'You could be right, Alan, but I'm not going to be out on the streets tonight to find out.'

'Me neither. Besides, I have an early appointment in the morning.'

Beatrice was about to ask with who and then realised: the police. He was going to tell the police exactly what Oliver now looked like. If she was going to act, she needed to do it tonight.

Dick Mayrick reappeared with Beatrice's drink. 'Glass of beer for the gentleman and a white wine for the lady.'

'That'll be a catchphrase one day, Dick,' said Beatrice.

'Many things I say will become catchphrases,' said Dick modestly.

'You and Shakespeare,' smiled Big Al.

'Both local boys,' said Dick as he disappeared back into the Dirty Duck.

Beatrice watched him go. 'That's what I missed when I stopped acting.'

'You missed Dick Mayrick?'

'No, Alan. I missed Stratford, being a part of the place. There's something magical here.' Beatrice gazed at the parkland opposite. The trees, now in full leaf, created a filter for the rays of the sun and illuminated The Dell with a light that seemed almost magical. The slow-moving waters of the Avon reflected the dappled sunlight at the edge of the trees. Down to her left she could see the back of the theatre. A deep feeling of contentment descended on her and for a moment all her problems were forgotten.

'Can you see it, Alan, it's …' she paused, trying to find the right words. 'Magical. I used to walk in The Dell at night when I was younger.'

'Weren't you afraid?'

'Of what, the dead in Holy Trinity?'

'I wouldn't walk through that graveyard at night.'

'Oh, Alan, don't be so silly. The dead can't hurt you.'

Big Al shrugged. 'Rather you than me, Beatrice. Wandering around in the moonlight is not my thing. I'll leave that to you and Puck.'

Beatrice leaned forward and touched his hand. 'By the way, Pierre is going to announce me as his Puck tomorrow. It's official!'

Big Al's face lit up. 'That's fantastic news.' He gave her hand a squeeze. 'What did I tell you.'

Beatrice grinned.

'If we shadows have offended,
Think but this and all is mended:
That you have but slumbered here
While these visions did appear.
And this weak and idle theme,
No more yielding but a dream,
Gentles do not reprehend.'

'Been learning your lines already?'

Beatrice shook her head. 'I've known them for years. I've waited to say them on that very stage all my life. I thought my chance had gone … but here we are.'

For one brief moment Beatrice saw the possibilities stretch out before her, a glimpse of a future she had all but given up on.

Little did she know that this was as close as she would get. The coming storm would wash away everything she was trying to build.

Chapter 41
Meet Me At Nine

Toby had managed to gather thirty-six uniforms together and the search of Stratford had begun. Every shed, every garage in which a hostage could be hidden, was being opened and checked. It was a huge task but Toby knew if Felix Richards was still alive, he had to find him; he was the key that could unlock this whole case.

He wanted to go into every house but there was no way the magistrates of Stratford would allow multiple search warrants to be issued on an off-chance. Martial law would need to be in place and, despite the number of dead bodies that Lawrence had littered the quiet streets and riverbanks of Stratford with, it was not a war zone.

Oliver had put on a baseball cap bearing the legend "*2B or not 2B*". He pulled down the peak and slipped on his sunglasses. There seemed to be a lot of police around Old Town and, despite the risk, he wanted to see what was going on. The net was closing and his options were reducing with every moment that passed.

As he walked past the Memorial Gardens, he was shocked to see three uniforms poking around the back of the shelter and over the wall on the far side. He realised they were looking for Felix and felt a momentary pang of guilt.

Poor Felix would be suffering in that culvert. Cramped, cold, gagged and bound. He consoled himself with the knowledge that Felix had brought it upon himself. Hopefully he would get chance to get back to Felix before he died in there but that would be in the lap of the gods. He had too much going on to worry about his friend.

If Oliver had walked down Southern Street he would have seen Beatrice sitting outside the Dirty Duck with Big Al Morris.

They had finished their drinks and Beatrice was about to head for her hotel. 'Thanks, Alan, been good to see you.'

'You too, Beatrice. Keep your head down tomorrow.'

She sighed. 'I will.' Beatrice grabbed her bag, pecked Big Al on the cheek, skipped down the steps and headed towards town.

Big Al watched her go. He liked Beatrice but there was something wrong, he just couldn't put his finger on it. For a woman who had just lost her husband, and had a son who was probably responsible for the Shakespeare Murders, she seemed to be far too happy. Resilience is one thing but Beatrice's clear optimism for her future bore no relation to her circumstances. Here was an ambitious woman who would let nothing distract her from her goal.

As Beatrice turned up Sheep Street she saw a familiar figure seated at a table outside the Vintner.

'Hello again.'

She smiled at Hugh Pitt, he really was a handsome man. 'Hello Hugh. I'm looking forward to working with you.'

He grinned. 'Yes, that was quite the surprise this morning, wasn't it. Who'd have thought that I would take on the mantle from Sir Morris?' He paused, realising how indelicate his words had been. 'I'm so sorry, Lady Oxford, I didn't mean it to sound like that.'

Beatrice gave him what she thought was a brave, philosophical smile. She was getting good at it. 'It's all right, Hugh. I know there was no offence intended. It's a strange time for all of us.'

'Would you like to join me?'

'I'm sorry, I can't. I've just been having a drink with Alan Morris.'

'Big Al, the set director?'

'The very same.'

'He's a bit of a legend, isn't he.'

'He is but he's lovely, just don't muck around with his sets.'

They both laughed and Hugh stood up. 'Are you doing anything tonight?'

She was. Although she didn't know exactly what she was planning, she knew it was going to involve Hugh. Now was the moment to look like the innocent flower but be the serpent underneath. 'I'm going to be at Trinity Street tonight. Why don't you come and meet me there.'

'I'd love to, what number?'

She leaned forward and whispered it in his ear.

Hugh looked up at her with a knowing smile. 'Just the two of us?'

'Of course, we have a lot to talk about. See you at nine.'

Beatrice turned and headed up Sheep Street, leaving Hugh to watch her walk away. She was a good-looking woman and she'd enjoyed letting him think he had a chance with her. He wanted to bed the wife of the late Sir Morris Oxford ... but she wouldn't be a notch on Hugh's bedpost.

As she walked away, Beatrice could feel his eyes watching her. She had him hooked and a plan was forming in her mind. Oliver must be caught and she needed to make that happen. He would hate the idea that Hugh was going to become the leading actor in the company. It would thwart any hope of his crazy plan to return to the Stratford stage. Oliver, being Oliver, would feel the need to kill him.

And she didn't really want to be in Hugh Pitt's shadow, far better to lure him to Trinity Street to die at the hands of her son. It was tough on Hugh but when an opportunity like this presented itself it would be foolish not to grasp it. She smiled and realised that she really wasn't a very nice person. She could live with that, as opposed to Hugh, who wouldn't live to see tomorrow's dawn. Well, not if she had her way.

Chapter 42
The Victim List

Fred was busy going through a checklist he had drawn up. He was trying to work out who could still be at risk from Lawrence. There were four names on the list:

Clarissa Pidgeon
Felix Richards
Beatrice Oxford
Hugh Pitt

There was only one new name and he wasn't sure why he had added it. Having seen *Four Dates and a Christening*, Fred would have dearly loved to strangle Hugh Pitt. To be fair, though his last two films were not commercially successful, Pitt's performance had been critically acclaimed. Fred thought Pitt had talent, so why had he added him to the list?

There was no way that he and Lawrence had ever met at Stratford, so there was no revenge motivation. There was no logic for putting him there but he was getting one of his feelings. He glanced across at Mel; should he tell her? It made no sense but hadn't he told his detectives to trust their instincts?

He grabbed the sheet of paper from his typewriter and wandered over to Mel's office. Unlike Beeching, Mel was operating an open-door policy.

She looked up. 'Hello Fred. Everything OK?'

'Yeah,' he placed the paper on her desk.

She picked it up. 'What's this?'

'A list of anyone I think is still at risk from Oliver Lawrence.'

Mel scanned the list. 'Clarissa makes sense, he's already killed the wrong woman in her place. As for Felix, don't you think he's dead already?'

Fred nodded. 'I do. He's buried somewhere, or under the Stratford Canal.'

Mel frowned. 'Should we be sending divers into the water near the Edstone Aqueduct?'

'Nah, too early yet. I don't think he would dump him there. If he hasn't turned up by this time next week we can take a look then.'

Mel looked back down at the list. 'You really think he'd murder his own mother?'

'I would in his shoes.'

'I'm hoping you're talking about Beatrice.'

Fred grinned. 'Yeah. Not ruling anything out though.'

'Hmm. Beatrice. You really think he could?'

'She's a terrible person, Mel. Dark, calculating. Anything you see isn't real. I think she's been lying to us every time we've talked to her.'

Mel nodded. 'OK, I can see where you're coming from with Beatrice but what on earth have you put Hugh Pitt on here for? Why would Oliver kill him?'

Fred laughed humourlessly. 'Apart from being a serial killer, you mean.'

'Fair point. What do you propose?'

'Maybe put a tail on all of them. We're watching Clarissa already, and Lady Oxford.'

'OK. Who are you going to put on it?'

'Good question. Ginger is still out of action and Kinky has gone into therapy for his sex addiction.'

'Do you think he wants to be cured?'

'No, so I think we're going to need two of your lads from HQ while we get him back on the straight and narrow. All my best lads are already committed.'

Mel nodded. 'OK, I'll get them over first thing.'

The morning would be too late. The coming night would be a long one … and one that the people of Stratford would never forget.

Chapter 43
No Man That's Born Of Woman

'Toby. Toby!'

He turned to see who was calling him, the voice sounded familiar.

'I've been looking for you everywhere.' Whomper slid off his Raleigh Chopper.

'What the hell are you doing riding that?'

'I'm on a health kick.' Whomper said this without irony despite the Woodbine hanging from the corner of his mouth.

'What is it, Whomper? I'm a bit busy.'

'I can see that but I've had another vision.'

'What you, or you and your sisters?'

'Just me, I was in bed at the time.'

'Probably for the best then.'

Whomper looked irritated. 'You have to take this seriously! When have I ever steered you wrong?'

Toby was about to make a smart answer but realised that Whomper had never steered him wrong, no matter how outlandish his visions had been. He sighed. 'Fair enough. You want to grab a cuppa in the White Swan or go to the station?'

'Station,' said Whomper, which took Toby by surprise; he'd never known Whomper turn down an opportunity to go to the pub.

Whomper climbed back onto his Chopper and peddled furiously down Meer Street towards the station. With his long hair and leather waistcoat he looked like a Hells Angel. On a Raleigh

Chopper it was an incongruous look.

Toby jogged along behind but Whomper soon disappeared round the bend towards Henley Street. Toby slowed his pace; Whomper could wait. When he reached Guild Street, Whomper had parked the Chopper on its side stand and was waiting by the door for him. 'Took your time.'

Toby shrugged. 'I didn't have the benefit of a child's bike.'

'It's not a child's bike, it's a design statement.'

'Like Easy Rider?'

'Yeah, but peddling.'

Toby went into the station. 'Come on then, Whomper. Let's get a cuppa and you can tell me what this is all about.'

Five minutes later they were sitting in CID with mugs of tea and some Custard Creams. Fred and Mel had also joined them.

Whomper looked up at Mel with undisguised desire. 'Congratulations.'

'On what?'

'On the promotion. Not many female chief inspectors.'

'Thank you, Whomper. Toby tells me you have some information.'

'One of my visions.'

Mel tried to disguise her disappointment but failed. 'Not anything tangible then?'

'Depends on your viewpoint.'

'Just tell us what you've got, Whomper. There are people dying out there, in case you hadn't noticed.'

'Last night, I thought I was awake. In the corner of my room I heard these voices.'

'Was it your sisters?'

'No, it was just like the witches from *Macbeth*.'

Mel glanced at Fred; her look implied that this was going to be a waste of time.

Whomper continued. 'They kept repeating, "No man that's

born of woman can kill Macbeth. No man that's born of woman can kill Macbeth"... you see?'

The three blank faces opposite him told Whomper they didn't.

'Then they said, "Sorrento. The man from Sorrento will take Macduff's place."'

Fred looked at Toby. 'Didn't Macduff kill Macbeth?'

'He did, but who's Sorrento?'

'Buggered if I know,' said Fred.

'You sure you don't know, Toby? Most of Whomper's visions and prophesies seem to be aimed at you.'

Toby thought there was something familiar about the name.

Whomper saw the recognition on his face. 'Go on, Toby. You know, don't you.'

'There is a hospital in Moseley Village called the Sorrento but that can't be it.'

'What kind of hospital is it?' Whomper seemed intent, as if Toby's answer contained something vital.

'Maternity,' said Toby.

'I think we've heard enough, Whomper,' said Fred.

Mel overruled him, her face looking curious, almost as if she too suddenly thought there could be something serious here. 'Go on, Whomper.'

Whomper turned back to Toby. 'What else do you know about the Sorrento?'

Toby stared blankly at Whomper. 'Nothing.'

'Think, there is something you're forgetting.'

Toby still looked blank. 'I just know that it's the Maternity Hospital in Moseley.'

'Where you were born!' Whomper looked at the three detectives triumphantly. 'Where you were born, Toby!'

Toby laughed. 'Yeah, you're right. I was born there, I'd forgotten.'

'What's the significance, Whomper,' asked Mel.

'That depends on what Toby has to say.'

'What's it got to do with me?'

'The dream! You're the only one with a link to Sorrento. How were you born?'

Toby shrugged. 'The usual way, I guess.'

'Are you sure,' demanded Whomper.

'My mum had me ...' Toby trailed off as a conversation he had been party to many years ago came trickling back in to his consciousness.

'By Caesarean section.'

They all looked at each other; this meant something.

Whomper was ahead of them all. 'No man that's born of woman can kill Macbeth.'

'And a C-section isn't technically born,' added Mel.

'Macduff. From his mother's womb. Untimely ripped. It's you, Toby. You will kill Oliver Lawrence.'

'No, I won't.'

'You might,' said Fred. 'All this other Shakespeare nonsense seems to be actually happening, why shouldn't this?'

'Because it's ... not logical,' said Toby.

Mel stood up and went to the whiteboard. 'I can't believe I'm saying this but everything about your belief that Lawrence is following Shakespeare's plays has been correct, even some of Whomper's prophesies have come true. I believe it.'

'Why would I kill Oliver?'

'Nobody says you will but if Oliver thinks he's Macbeth, he will believe you can.'

Fred sat in his chair shaking his head. 'In all my years, this is the craziest thing I've ever heard. Murder investigation by dreams and the plots of Shakespearian tragedies. Never speak of it outside this room.'

'It is crazy,' agreed Mel. 'But so far Toby has been right and now, mad as it may seem, Bernard Wood has returned to

Dunroamin and Toby is not born of woman. There's an insane logic to it.'

'What's your gut saying,' asked Fred.

'Trust my instinct,' said Mel.

She looked at Toby. 'What about you?'

He shrugged uncertainly. 'Can't believe I'm saying this but … trust my instinct.'

And there it was. The most experienced and high-ranking female detective in Warwickshire and one of the most experienced detective sergeants in the country had now bought into Toby's theory and Whomper's dream. The world had gone mad.

Chapter 44
Waiting For Death

Time had lost all meaning for Felix. He would die here and the culvert would be his final resting place. Everything he was and everything he had ever been would end here in this cold, dark, watery grave. There was acceptance, but still he chewed at his gag; the only defiance left to him in the face of his death.

The blood that had moistened his tongue had long since dried, leaving a harsh rawness to the inside of his mouth and a throat that felt like it was closing. He would probably choke to death. He began to cry; tears of frustration and tears for the fact that it was over. And then, without any warning, the gag dislodged and fell from his mouth. He had done it, chewed his way through that godforsaken gag.

A surge of hope filled him now he could shout for attention. But the fates were not on his side. He tried to shout, but no sound came out; his throat was raw and bone-dry. His call for help was reduced to a hoarse whisper, even somebody standing directly above him wouldn't hear it. His body shook with a soundless laugh. All this water and not a drop to drink. If his hands weren't tied he could climb down and scoop some river water up. He doubted that it would taste very pleasant, given what the Stratford swans do in it.

His eyes had become accustomed to the darkness now and he could pick out things that had been invisible to him before. On the other side of the culvert the bricks stood out more clearly but, to the left of him, there was something glinting in the light refracted from the waters below.

There was a thin strip that ran from the edge of the water and right up the side. It was a flat metal plate that supported the platform he was standing on, and there was another one on the opposite side. He looked closer and suddenly realised why the dark metal was glinting; it was covered in condensation.

He moved to the one on his left. It was rusty and coated in accumulated muck but it was also covered in condensation; he knew he had to lick it. He edged forward until his nose was touching it and tried to ignore the cobwebs. This was his only chance.

He ran his tongue up the cold metal. His revulsion was only momentary. As he felt the cool condensation all other thoughts were washed from his mind. This was what he had to do. He ran his tongue up another part of the metal and was again rewarded with a mouthful of moisture. The third time he did it he was able to swallow. It was working.

He licked every part of the metal plate he could from his seated position and then shifted onto his knees so he could reach more. Suddenly he had purpose, and with that purpose came hope; it galvanised him.

He took several good long licks, one of which tasted suspiciously of spider but he didn't have the luxury of being choosy. This was the only water available and he needed it.

Before he knew it, he was standing up and running his tongue further up the plate, absorbing much needed moisture into his dehydrated body. He felt the energy trickling slowly back into him. There was some hope. He still had the other plate for more moisture and he knew that if they had been covered in it once it would happen again. The whole area was damp and the metal made a great surface for condensation to form.

He took one more long lick, swallowed and then leaned back against the wall to reassess his position. It didn't take him long to realise it was dreadful. His wrists were bound tightly behind his back and the exit would be impossible to reach if he couldn't use his hands. He needed to be able to pull himself up the metal steps to reach the cover. How could he do this? There had to be a way, but at this moment he just couldn't see it.

Time was not Felix's friend. He hadn't noticed it yet but the water below had started to rise. Although it had not yet reached Stratford, forty miles upriver a storm was raging at the point the River Avon rises. Near the ancient battlefield of Naseby, where in 1645 Cromwell's army defeated Charles I's Royalists, the flood was about to begin its descent.

There had been sixty days rain in just eight hours as the clouds had come to a halt and spun above the village of Naseby. All that water needed somewhere to go. It had begun to surge towards Stratford, sweeping everything before it; flooding the plains, closing roads and bursting the banks. Downriver in Stratford it was still dry but the atmosphere had become very close and uncomfortable. The storm may not have arrived yet but Stratford would soon be engulfed by its swell, which would take everyone by surprise.

Felix didn't know it but he only had a matter of hours to escape or he too would be swept away on the storm surge, the likes of which the Avon had never seen before.

Chapter 45
A Moment Of Calm

Oliver leaned back on the settee but couldn't relax. The atmosphere had become very sticky; his clothes clung uncomfortably to him and he felt irritated. Morocco had been hotter than this but it was a dry heat, this sticky heat was more like the tropics. It made him want to kill, which was lucky because that was exactly what he intended to do.

Clarissa Pidgeon needed to die. She had got away with it once before when he had killed Heather Wilson in an unfortunate case of mistaken identity. Time was running out. With every murder his odds for being caught had grown; he needed to finish and move on to the next part of his plan.

He had one big problem. Clarissa was being watched by the police. She was their lure to draw him out. Somehow, he needed to take her from under their noses without being spotted. After the murder of Heather, they had moved Clarissa to a room at the Falcon. There was a policeman in plain clothes outside, watching from the doorway of the Guild Chapel opposite. There was also a uniformed officer inside the hotel. He had seen them going in; the police weren't the only ones that could conduct surveillance.

The uniform would probably be sitting in the corridor outside Clarissa's room. A thought occurred to him: *maybe he could burn down the Falcon too.* Plenty of old timbers to feed the fire once it got going. He didn't really care about collateral damage, there were no longer any innocents in this battle. If you were between him and his victim that was just unfortunate. Revenge has a habit of getting out of control; when hatred fans the flames, logic is left behind.

There was only one thing holding him back from setting fire to the Falcon. He knew that Suzy Tench loved the place, was a regular there. She was one of the few he would never harm. Just the thought of her made him burn with desire. He wanted her and not just in a sexual way. There was something about her; a sparkle, a sense of fun and happiness. He needed to tap into that, to lift himself above the darkness he had created. She could be his salvation. All he needed to do was finish his revenge, move away and then, through other theatres, work his way back under another name. He would probably have to get used to being called Francis Bacon now. That's the name he had given to Suzy and he was stuck with it.

It never occurred to him that he couldn't make this happen. He had the certainty of a great talent and the belief that the police would never catch him. It made him bold, but not stupid. He would kill Clarissa. There had to be a way and he would find it.

He slipped back into the doorway of King Edward VI's School. Shakespeare had once been a pupil there. As Oliver watched and waited; he liked to think that William was standing behind him, looking over his shoulder approvingly. This would be the final act of his revenge.

Oliver noticed a familiar figure walking down Scholars Lane towards him. DS Fred Williams was a big man. Not fat, stocky. He looked like he could handle himself in a fight. If they ever had to match up it could go either way. He hoped it would never come to that; at another time, he and Fred Williams would probably be friends.

Oliver stepped back into the shadows as Fred approached the corner of Chapel Street. He was clearly checking on Clarissa. He crossed over and confirmed Oliver's suspicions by talking to the man at the entrance to the Guild Chapel. That was the plain-clothes detective accounted for, now he would go in and check on the uniform. Fred had a brief conversation with the plain-clothes officer and then headed into the Falcon.

Oliver was about to step out of the doorway to follow him

when he noticed DC Toby Marlowe walking down Chapel Street from Old Town. The clever sods! They had assumed that he would be watching and Toby was hanging back to see if Oliver, or anyone, would follow Fred into the Falcon. He really shouldn't underestimate these two. They had kept Clarissa out as bait and expected him to bite.

He watched as Toby strolled towards the officer stationed in the chapel's entrance. They exchanged a few words and then Toby crossed the road and stood by the entrance of New Place, Shakespeare's old home. He'd died there in 1616 and the house was demolished by the Reverend Gastrell after a planning dispute in 1759. This had made him very unpopular but probably not as unpopular as Oliver would be should he ever get caught.

He watched as Toby scanned the street, waiting for him to show himself. He wasn't going to do that. He edged further back into the entrance of the school. He knew the old building well. He slipped across the courtyard and through a corridor that led to the gardens at the rear, and then to a doorway onto Chapel Lane.

He emerged onto the street and didn't glance back to where Toby was standing. As he walked down the lane towards the theatre he smiled to himself. This was his town, he knew every street and alleyway. He was a ghost who could slip unseen wherever he chose. The knowledge filled him with confidence.

He walked unhurriedly down to Southern Lane and turned towards the Dirty Duck. He crossed over and went into The Dell by the chain ferry. He didn't have time to be spotted by Dick or Suzy; he had much to do that night and the storm was coming. There had been reports of massive rainfall just forty miles away but the storm had stalled and was rotating over Northamptonshire, causing major flooding.

That flooding was flowing into the tributaries of the Avon, and the river was noticeably higher than when he had imprisoned

Felix in the early hours of the morning. He glanced at the island at the back of the Witter Lock. Felix would be aware that the river was rising beneath his feet by now. Oliver sighed. He hoped Felix wouldn't suffer too much; he had been a good friend, he just didn't think he could trust him any more. There was too much to play for. Besides, he couldn't risk going back to the culvert to finish Felix off. Someone had once told him that drowning probably wasn't too bad once you gave up the struggle.

Oliver made his way across The Dell and up through the doorway in the graveyard wall. As he walked past the bench where he had killed Desmond Tharpe, he looked back towards the island where his old friend lay trapped.

'Goodbye, Felix. Thanks for everything,' he whispered under his breath. He turned and headed through the graveyard towards Trinity Street without looking back.

Chapter 46
Time's Winged Chariot

As the shadows of evening began to spread their long fingers across the rooftops of Stratford, Toby and Fred returned to Guild Street and sat in CID looking up at the whiteboard with Mel.

'So what now?'

'We watch and wait,' said Fred. 'Clarissa is protected and Beatrice is safe in her room at the White Swan. If Lawrence makes a move, we'll have him.'

'It's a big if, Fred.'

'I don't think so. He's definitely going to try to bump Clarissa off, she's unfinished business.'

'What about Beatrice, you really think he'll try to kill his mother?'

Fred shrugged. 'I would.'

Mel smiled but Toby pointed to where Felix Richards' name was written on the board. 'But where's Felix?'

'Dead, I reckon,' said Fred.

'So where's his body? Lawrence's never tried to hide any bodies before. Why do it now?'

'He doesn't know that we know about him. Perhaps he's worried that we would make the link between them.'

Mel nodded. 'I think you're right, Fred, he wants him disappeared.'

Toby shook his head. 'I don't think so. I just don't think he's killed him.'

'You got one of your feelings, young Toby?'

Toby looked at Fred; he wasn't sure if he was taking the piss. 'Yeah, I have. I don't think he wants to kill Felix but he knows he's going to have to.'

Mel looked confused. 'Well, that doesn't get us anywhere, does it. All we can do is wait.'

'"But at my back I always hear, time's winged chariot hurrying near."'

Mel looked at Fred. 'What was that?'

'Andrew Marvell. He's one of my favourite poets.'

Mel glanced at Toby and they both smiled. Fred Williams was full of surprises.

The three of them fell into silence. They were all out of ideas, all they could do was wait for a sighting of Lawrence near the White Swan or the Falcon. That wouldn't be easy, it would soon be dark and they still didn't really know what he looked like.

If only Big Al Morris had come in a day earlier instead of tomorrow they would have known exactly what Oliver Lawrence looked like. But he had promised Beatrice that he would leave it until the morning and she was going to take advantage of the time that Big Al's delay would give her.

There was a fire escape at the back of her room in the White Swan. She could climb onto it and slip away without the policeman in the corridor outside her door being any the wiser. The night, she knew, had promises to keep. As she crept down the metal fire escape she calmed herself by whispering her favourite poem beneath her breath.

'The woods are lovely, dark and deep,
But I have promises to keep,
And miles to go before I sleep,
And miles to go before I sleep.'

Beatrice reached the bottom of the steps and made her way through the alley at the rear, onto the square opposite the Shakespeare Memorial Fountain. She paused and looked at it, wondering; if tonight went as she had planned would there one day be a memorial to her in this wonderful old town? She crossed and made her way down Rother Street, scurrying in the shadows like a thief in the night.

In a quiet room behind the Garrick, Hugh Pitt was admiring himself in his bathroom mirror. It was a sight that pleased him and would, he felt sure, impress the dear Lady Oxford.

What a blessed relief for her to see a man whose height exceeded his girth. Making love to Sir Morris must have been like having a wardrobe fall on you. The dear lady was in for a treat tonight. He pulled on his shirt and debated whether he should wear a tie. Too formal? Then he smiled to himself, he could use it to tie her up. The thought made him chuckle. How the tables had turned.

Just ten years earlier he had arrived at Stratford and been cast in to the supporting actors' pit, carrying scenery and holding spears. It was a given that you had to pay your dues but working in Sir Morris' company was akin to being an indentured servant. Unless he took a liking to you there was little chance of progression.

Sir Morris had not liked Hugh. Too good looking, too talented and too keen. He was careful to supress any potential threat to his crown. Hugh knew that his career progression had really enraged Sir Morris. He had once been quoted as saying, when questioned, that Hugh Pitt's success in Hollywood showed how low the bar had become outside of the theatre. It was a mean statement and reflected badly on Sir Morris.

Hugh had a lot of fans and they didn't take kindly to the older actor's comments but Morris ignored the protests, safe in the bubble of a theatre in which he was the undisputed star. Hugh's return had been, against all odds, triumphant. Sir Morris had hated that.

Tonight though, he was going to make love to the old boy's stuck-up wife. What a shame he wasn't around to see it. Still, revenge is best served cold and Hugh was looking forward to it. Technically Beatrice was old enough to be his mother, but she still looked good and tonight wasn't about building a lasting relationship. Hugh winked at himself in the mirror then flicked off the light and went out into the night. Who knew what promises the evening had in store?

Chapter 47
A Sea Of Troubles

Mel had returned to her office and was busy going over her reports. Fred and Toby sat opposite each other, desperate for a call to say there had been a sighting, an attack or even just a rumour of Lawrence. It was nerve-shredding waiting for the hammer to fall, and fall it would.

All this against the backdrop of the huge storm that was circulating above the old battlefield at Naseby, some forty miles away. The mighty River Avon rose near there from a tiny spring but the weather was turning the spring into a mighty torrent. The Avon was surging through Northamptonshire and onward into Warwickshire. The first swell was about to burst across the Alveston Weir. Soon the huge volume of water cascading over and around the weir would swell the Avon and burst its banks as it barrelled towards Stratford. Without a drop of rain falling the town was about to drown, and with it Felix Richards, imprisoned in the culvert at the Witter Lock.

The moisture he had licked from the metal plates had eased his dry throat and rehydrated him; not enough to get back his full strength but enough to enable him to fight. He was barely clinging on and if he gave up now he would die.

He began to call for help but it seemed that the roar of the Avon below had increased. He looked down and realised, to his horror, that in the time it had taken him to chew through his gag, the water level had risen.

He peered at the dark water flowing beneath him. It seemed to be a lot closer. An hour ago he could see the reflection of the sunlight glinting on the surface some two feet below the bottom of the culvert in which he stood. Was it raining? He listened hard but could hear nothing above the roar of the water below.

He looked down and tried to gauge the depth. The river was a foot or so below the base and the mesh platform on which he stood was some two feet above that. He breathed a sigh of relief; the river couldn't rise three feet. Could it?

Less than two hundred yards away, Oliver stood at his bedroom window looking out across the graveyard of Holy Trinity. He wondered if Felix had managed to stay on the mesh platform or, in his struggle to get free, fallen into the unforgiving waters of the Avon. *Radio Four* had warned of possible flooding in the area because storm-waters were feeding the Avon and that surge was heading right towards them.

Outside his window it was a warm, sticky summer's evening. It was uncomfortably close and his clothes stuck to him like the guilt of an unfaithful husband. He wondered; if all went well tonight, would he rescue Felix?

He liked to think he would but that depended on how the events of the night played out. His mother was coming for a visit and she had a surprise for him, he could tell. She was so full of secrets and somehow – he didn't yet know how – he would get her to reveal them. It made him happy. No, that was the wrong word. It excited him. There were answers to be had, solutions to be found. Those answers would show him his course.

He didn't believe he wanted to kill her but he knew that if he had to, well, then he would. It was as simple as that. Betrayal was not an option and explaining to his mother why he had killed her husband was going to be ... tricky. That said, he was sure that she was glad to be rid of Morris. He had seen her press conference after his murder and, to be fair, he had been impressed by her show of emotion. It had been very, very good.

But with a well-trained eye, such as his, you could see the join.

It had been a performance, a fine one. The press had lapped it up and spread sympathy for Sir Morris' brave widow across the pages of the broadsheets and tabloids alike. His mother was lying, the grief on display no more than a performance. Who knew what motives lay beneath that river of deceit. He had come from her, a child filled with her genes and attributes. He recognised the kinship and knew that they both had a burning ambition which had been suppressed for too long. How would it express itself and, when it did, would it permit them both to live?

Thunder rumbled throughout the distant sky. The huge storm moved slowly across the county border and the rains it generated filled the springs and tributaries that ran into the river.

The Avon was swelling, gathering itself to sweep down towards Stratford and onward to Evesham and then Tewkesbury, leaving death and mayhem in its wake. It would eventually run down the Severn and into the sea where the vast waters of the estuary would absorb its bubbling mass unimpressed.

Oliver realised that this would be his opportunity. The radio had warned of the danger of flooding so, in the chaos that it would bring, he could finish his final act. Close the play before moving on to a new life full of promise. Tonight would decide who would still be alive in the morning to share that rich promise with him.

He felt the tingle of anticipation and wondered if he should sharpen a knife. He decided against it; there was no script, tonight would be about improvisation. He would play the cards as they fell.

Chapter 48
A Source Of Optimism

Toby and Fred still sat restlessly at their desks. The call, when it came, was not the one they had been expecting. Fred's phone rang and he snatched it up like a gunslinger in a shoot-out. 'Williams.'

'Whomper Smith wants to see you and DC Marlowe, sir.'

Fred put his hand over the receiver and turned to Toby. 'Whomper's downstairs, he wants to see us.'

Toby nodded.

'OK, send him up,' said Fred. He placed the receiver firmly back on the cradle. 'What do you think he wants?'

Toby chuckled. 'Who knows, maybe he has some info that will crack the case.'

They both shrugged; with Whomper, you never knew.

They heard footsteps coming up the stairs and then Whomper appeared at the door like a Hells Angel who had studied English Lit and Philosophy.

'Greetings, gents.'

'Evening, Whomper. You come to confess,' asked Fred.

'Nah, but I'm going to patrol Old Town tonight.'

Fred looked at Toby and sighed. 'We can't have vigilantes on the streets.'

'I think you're going to need anyone you can get before this night is through.'

'What is it, Whomper,' asked Toby.

Whomper pointed to an empty chair. 'Mind if I sit down?'

'Help yourself,' said Toby.

Whomper sat opposite Toby and looked earnestly at him. 'I really am going to patrol Old Town tonight.'

'Thanks,' said Fred. 'That's very helpful.'

The lack of sincerity in Fred's voice was clear to hear but Whomper ignored it. 'Before tonight is over, everything will be revealed.'

'You think it's that close to being over?'

'Yes. The floods are coming and the killer needs to complete his mission before the rising waters stop him. It's all coming to a head, lads. We need to be alert.'

'We? There is no *we*, Whomper. This is a dangerous situation. Only the police should be out there trying to handle it.'

Whomper smiled at Fred. 'You think you could stop me from being out on the streets tonight?'

Fred looked at Whomper's powerful, though somewhat abused, body. 'No, I don't think so but I'd advise against it. Lawrence is crazy, if you get in his way he'll kill you.'

Whomper smiled and pulled a chrome motorbike chain from his pocket. It was only about fourteen inches long but it was welded to a metal handle covered in a rubber grip. It made a fearsome weapon.

'You're not thinking of using that if you find him, are you,' asked Fred.

'Depends if he provokes me,' said Whomper.

'What if he's got a gun?'

It was a fair question and, for a moment, Whomper seemed stumped but then he shook his head. 'Oliver hasn't shot anyone, why would he start now. Besides, in a small town like this he'd draw too much attention. Last time someone raised their voice in the library it made the front page of *The Herald*.'

Fred and Toby smiled; there was truth in Whomper's words.

'Don't do anything foolish, Whomper.'

Whomper stared at Toby for several seconds before replying. 'You sure you were born at the Sorrento in Moseley?'

'Positive.'

'By C-section?'

'I think so.'

Whomper frowned. 'You think so or you're sure? It's important.'

Toby scratched behind his ear as he thought about Whomper's question. He was almost certain his mother had once told him he had been born by C-section. Or maybe it was his uncle who had told him, he couldn't remember.

'Well?'

'Yeah, I'm pretty sure.'

Whomper nodded. 'I hope you're right, it could make all the difference.' He turned and headed for the door.

As the sound of his footsteps faded, Mel emerged from her office. 'Was that Whomper?'

Fred nodded.

'What did he want?'

'He wanted to confirm where Toby was born.'

Mel looked confused. 'Is that relevant?'

'Apparently,' sighed Fred.

Mel looked to Toby for explanation but only received a blank stare for her trouble. She was holding her notepad.

'What's the message, ma'am,' asked Toby.

Mel looked at her scribbled notes. 'Bad news. They reckon the Avon will burst its banks in the next hour here in Stratford. We're going to have to scramble all officers to help civilians get to safety or sandbag their homes. Waterside could be going under within the hour!'

That was all that Fred and Toby needed. The flood could provide a diversion for Oliver and it would pull officers from their allotted tasks. Soon Stratford would be laid bare, helpless to defend itself against a madman as the flood waters approached.

Chapter 49
A Moment Of Reflection

Beatrice walked slowly through the graveyard at Holy Trinity and made her way over to the plot that had been reserved for her husband. Morris would be so happy to be buried there; near to his beloved Shakespeare and close to his adoring fans. She glanced at the pile of flowers that continued to grow at the gates in the hours since his murder.

If Sir Morris was watching over her, what would he think? She had no guilt about his death, despite the fact that it had been something of a relief. It was only now he was gone that she truly realised what she had been missing. Life had been passing her by, just a bird in a gilded cage.

She looked down and felt momentarily sentimental; it hadn't all been bad. They had lived a fine life together; the travel, the hotels, the acclaim. Everything was first class but now she realised that none of it meant anything, it was just window dressing to hide the cracks in a life unfulfilled. She had been comfortable with Morris, but it was a way to mark time until life – real life – could begin again.

It had only been recently that she realised how much she still wanted to do with her life; she had wasted so much time. Now she needed to grab the future by the throat and achieve everything she had placed on the backburner for too long. Only now had it become clear just what she was prepared to do. A fire burned within her. Ambition possessed her, woke her from her sleep and commanded her to do whatever was necessary to attain her goal. Did that include killing Hugh Pitt and her son?

'He'll be happy there.'

Beatrice jumped. 'Oh, you scared the hell out of me.'

Standing beside her was Theo Cumberbatch, a long-standing member of Morris' company and probably the most talented actor in it, including Morris.

'Theo! I wasn't expecting to see you here.'

He smiled gently. 'I came back for the funeral but I've decided to stay for a while afterwards. I've got a couple of weeks off before we start filming.'

'Oh, of course. You're about to be a big TV star, aren't you.'

He waved her compliment away. 'I think that could be a bit premature but I've been given the chance to have some input on the scripts.'

'What's it called?'

Theo looked a little embarrassed. '*Othello Jones.*'

Beatrice nodded slowly. 'Well, you are mixed-race, Theo, so ...' she trailed off, unable to find anything positive to say about the title.

Theo wasn't offended. 'It's a crap title but they're going after the *Shaft* market. Two-year contract and enough money to buy two houses. Plus the shooting schedule between the first and second season will allow me to come back here and do *Othello.*'

'Well, you'd be a fool to pass that up. Morris would never have given you Othello. He'd have shovelled on the black paint and done it himself.' Beatrice looked down at her husband's future resting place and sighed. 'Sad to say, Theo, but your career prospects are a lot better without Morris. You were always the best of the company, now's your chance to fly.'

'Morris was always good to me. Despite his faults, he always looked after me.'

They stood in silence, staring at the plot reserved for Sir Morris, both having new opportunities opening up to them because of his death.

'What are you going to do, Beatrice? I've heard talk about *A Midsummer Night's Dream.*'

'My, the rumour mill has been busy. Who told you?'

'Everybody.'

They both laughed. It was common knowledge at the theatre that Beatrice would play Puck. It was a brave piece of casting, groundbreaking even.

'You sure about this?' There was concern in Theo's voice.

'Absolutely, I've wanted to get back on-stage for years but Morris wouldn't let me.'

Theo didn't look sure. 'It's a lot to take on and with Morris and—'

'Oliver!' She finished the sentence for him and, once again, they fell silent. It wasn't an angry silence, it was just two people who liked each other but were unsure of what to say next. The awkward silence of the well-meaning.

'Can't be easy.'

'It's not. Everyone tells me that my child has killed all these people. Friends and fellow actors, my husband. Do you think it's him?'

There was desperation in her voice and Theo answered honestly. 'Yes. It's the only explanation that makes sense. I was new to the company then but Oliver was forced out. It was ugly. I'm not surprised he came back.'

'All this, though. It's a bit over the top, don't you think.'

It was a massive understatement and Theo couldn't help but smile. 'He always loved the dramatic.'

Beatrice wanted to spend more time with Theo. She had always liked him, but now wasn't the time. She had promises to keep. She turned towards him and forced a tear from the corner of her eye.

'Do you mind giving me a moment, Theo. I want to remember Morris as he was. There were so many things left unsaid.'

Theo looked embarrassed. 'Oh, I'm so sorry, Beatrice. I didn't think.'

She reached out and laid her hand on his chest. 'It's OK, Theo. I'm just a silly old woman who needs to talk to a dead man who isn't even buried yet. Crazy as it sounds, it makes sense to me.'

Theo took her hand in his and gently squeezed it. 'Of course, Beatrice. I still talk to my mother and she died in sixty-eight. Sometimes the dead make the best listeners.'

'Only because they can't answer back,' said Beatrice.

Theo leaned forward and kissed her gently on the cheek. 'Goodnight, Beatrice, I'll see you soon.' He stepped back, turned and walked away through the graveyard, disappearing through a gateway in the wall by the river.

Beatrice watched him go, admiring his athletic gait and wondering what it would be like to be held in those arms. They were the thoughts of someone who had missed her chance. Theo came from a different age, an age from which she was barred by time. She had made her choices and now was no time for regret. She turned back to Morris' future resting place.

'What do I do, Morris? Do I kill Hugh Pitt?'

She pictured Morris nodding enthusiastically; he had never liked Hugh. That was the easy question. 'What about our son? What should I do about him?' Beatrice paused and listened hard, half expecting to hear the sound of Morris rotating in the ground.

If there was a great beyond, the fact he was Oliver's father would come as a huge shock and give the afterlife a new dimension. It would cast his ruination of Oliver's career into a whole new light. He had destroyed his own son and created a monster that now roamed the streets of Stratford. He was lucky to be dead. For any father to realise he had destroyed his own child would be too much to bear.

Beatrice knew this because she too had been culpable. So many secrets, a sea of them deep enough to drown her. What difference would one more make? Her life, if it was to mean anything, had to become something more. Her foot was on the first stepping stone. There were other people on those steps and she would have to sweep them away before this night ended. Whether Oliver lived through it was up to him, he had a choice. As for Hugh, there was no option; he had to die.

Beatrice sighed. 'I'm sorry, my love. This night may be long and I may have to kill our son. I comfort myself with the knowledge that if the tables were turned, you would do the same. Good night, sweet prince, and flights of angels sing thee to thy rest.'

Beatrice paused for a few moments and then turned and slowly walked away through the graveyard towards Trinity Street.

From the bedroom window in Trinity Street, Oliver had watched Beatrice as she stood in the graveyard speaking to the spirit of her dead husband. She looked so sad, so vulnerable. He felt sorry for her; so much tragedy to deal with, how could one woman cope? If only he had known the secrets that drove her – shaped her actions and formed her lies – maybe his sympathies would have been spared.

He watched her walk towards his house. For a moment he considered calling out to her but she would be knocking on his door soon enough. There would be time for the words they had left unspoken, then it would be a strange evening. They needed to talk and what was said would decide her fate. He had killed her husband, and he may have to kill her too.

Chapter 50
A Clash Of Egos

As Beatrice walked across Trinity Street towards Oliver's house, she saw Hugh Pitt walking down from College Road. All the pawns were being positioned on the board and worlds would soon collide. She pretended not to see him and made her way to the front door.

She paused for a moment outside and then looked up as Hugh arrived. 'You found it all right then.'

He nodded. 'Yeah, just a four-minute walk from the Garrick.' He looked the house up and down. 'Is this yours?'

'No, it belongs to a friend.'

'Oh, is she away?' asked Hugh hopefully.

'No, he should be in.'

Hugh couldn't disguise his disappointment. 'I thought it was just you and I tonight.'

Beatrice gave Hugh her best coy smile. 'My, Hugh, what were you proposing?'

He raised his left eyebrow suggestively. It may have worked in the films but Beatrice saw right through him. Like her, he was playing a part and she would just be another trophy for his cabinet.

She touched his arm gently. 'Let's see how the evening goes … I do have my suite at the White Swan.'

Hugh visibly brightened, this was more like it. He just needed to play nicely with her friend and then he could get her out of there and back to her suite where he would … well, there would be plenty of time to decide that later.

Beatrice knocked and waited, curious to know how Oliver would react when he opened the door to see Hugh Pitt with his mother. It was exciting. Anything could happen and Beatrice was ready for any outcome. Tonight had to clear the path for her future and all options were on the table. She was shocked by how comfortable she seemed to be with the possibility of an impending death, especially that of her son. Ambition really was a tough task master.

The door swung open and Oliver was about to speak when he noticed Hugh Pitt. For once in his life he was rendered speechless.

Hugh wasn't surprised. Since he had become famous he had seen the same reaction a hundred times when people recognised him in public. Fame really did have a strange effect on people. He stepped forward with his hand outstretched. 'Hi, my name's Hugh.'

Oliver shook it without saying anything.

'Are you going to invite us in, Oliver, or do we have to stand out here all night?'

Beatrice didn't want anyone to see them on the doorstep. If events turned fatal she couldn't afford to be placed at the scene by a passing witness.

Oliver nodded and stood aside as Beatrice took Hugh's hand and dragged him into the hallway.

As Hugh squeezed past Oliver he noticed the look in his eyes had changed from surprise to hostility. Was he imagining it? He walked down the corridor towards the kitchen and a thought occurred to him. Oliver; why did that name sound so familiar?'

Beatrice saw the open bottle of Fleurie. 'Can we help ourselves?'

Oliver nodded.

Beatrice poured a glass and offered it to Hugh. He took it and inspected the bottle. 'You didn't buy this from Tesco.'

'No. I bought it in a lovely little shop in Antibes when I was on my way up from Morocco in March. Sixty-six was a really good year for wine in France.'

Hugh took a sip and nodded approvingly. 'That's lovely.'

Beatrice tried it. 'Oh it is wonderful, not saving it for a special occasion, Oliver?'

He looked from his mother to Hugh and back again. 'I think this is a special enough occasion, don't you?'

Beatrice smiled. 'Well, it's not every day you get to meet a real Hollywood star, is it.'

Hugh smiled what he hoped was a modest grin but his acting wasn't good enough to hide his conceit. It made Oliver visibly bristle even more. Beatrice saw it and approved. Tonight was moving in exactly the direction she had been hoping.

'Hugh has just made a triumphant return to the stage in *Much Ado*.'

'Yeah, I'd heard,' said Oliver with as much disinterest as he could muster.

'Not a fan of the Bard?'

'Not a fan of that play.'

Hugh tried to not look bothered but, again, his acting wasn't up to the task.

'Pierre Corridor has asked Hugh and I to front up the new season, what do you think of that?'

Oliver shrugged. 'Underwhelming.'

It was brutally rude; Beatrice approved. She looked at Hugh apologetically.

'I'm sorry about Oliver. He's a man of strong opinions.'

'And no bloody manners,' muttered Hugh.

Oliver leaned back against the kitchen door and looked at Hugh. 'It's only an opinion, don't be offended. It's not like you're Gielgud or Olivier, is it?'

Hugh put down his wine firmly and looked Oliver in the eye. 'Are you an actor?'

Oliver nodded. 'Yes.'

'Well, if you're any good, why haven't I heard of you.'

Oliver laughed. 'Oh, you've heard of me, you just don't realise it.'

Beatrice picked up Hugh's wine and held it out to him. 'Don't take offence, Hugh. Oliver is just jealous. He'd like to be heading-up the new season but you have definitely stolen his thunder.'

Hugh looked confused. 'I don't mean to be rude but who the hell are you? They don't give lead roles to anyone at the RSC, you have to earn it.'

'Earn it, what would you know about that? You swanned off to Hollywood and made *Four Dates and a Christening*! That only qualifies you to do panto at best.'

Beatrice watched the two actors becoming more aggrieved. The atmosphere between Oliver and Hugh was heating up nicely. All she had to do was poke the fire and watch it burn.

'Oliver is a very fine actor, Hugh. He's starred in several plays at the RSC.'

The penny still wasn't dropping with Hugh, who was full of indignation at the dismissal of his most successful film. 'When? I've never seen you.'

'The seventy and seventy-one season, mainly.'

Hugh wasn't a student of the RSC but even he knew that was when Sir Morris and Richard Jenkins had been the big stars.

Beatrice looked at Oliver. 'Shall I tell him?'

It was a tough question: if she did, he would have to kill Hugh. He would leave that decision to his mother; she was playing a dangerous game that could threaten everything. Clearly, she wanted Hugh gone as badly as he did but now wasn't the time.

'Before you answer that, Beatrice, you need to understand that there are implications.'

Beatrice looked at Oliver guilelessly. *Boy, she's good*, he thought.

'It really doesn't matter. Hugh and I are the future and you're … not.'

It was harsh, but fair. There was no way that Oliver could get back to the RSC any time soon. If he went away and did Rep with great success, it would still take three seasons minimum to work his way back into the company.

Hugh had enjoyed Oliver's clear discomfort as Beatrice put him right in his place. He drained his glass and put it down on the kitchen work surface.

'Thanks for the wine, Oliver. It was delicious.'

'I know,' agreed Oliver.

'You coming, Beatrice?'

'Not yet, Hugh. Oliver and I have a lot to discuss.'

'What, more than we already have?'

'Yes, I would say so.'

'You thinking of doing panto too?'

Hugh's question was a clear put-down and Oliver rose to it. 'I could outact you in the back-half of a pantomime horse, Pitt.'

Hugh hadn't been expecting such open hostility. 'What is your problem? There can only be one king and Sir Morris is dead and gone. I'm next in line and Beatrice is going to be my leading lady. You should be happy for her.'

This was good news for his mother but, despite being one step ahead of him, Oliver realised that Hugh was correct. There could only be one king and it was clear Hugh felt he was it.

Hugh, on the other hand, was astounded by Oliver's high opinion of himself. It was borderline delusional and, if truth be told, a little intimidating. 'I think we should go, Beatrice. Your friend clearly doesn't like me and, I have to say, the feeling's mutual.'

'He's not really my friend, Hugh, we've just known each other for a long time. Haven't we, Oliver.'

'All my life.'

There was something in the way he said it that sent a shiver down Hugh's spine. Something here was very wrong.

Beatrice looked questioningly at Oliver. 'Do you want to tell him or shall I?'

'Tell me what?' asked Hugh, unable to hide the rising anxiety in his voice.

'Now's not the time. Think about it.'

'I have, I thought you wanted to clear the decks.'

'Not now, think it through.' There was a tenseness in Oliver's tone that seemed to chill the atmosphere of the room by several degrees.

Hugh had a horrible feeling that this conversation, between Beatrice and Oliver, was about him, but how could it be? He and Beatrice had only got to know each other in the last couple of days and he had never met Oliver before.

Beatrice walked over to Oliver and pushed the door shut behind him, blocking the only exit from the kitchen. She turned to him and cupped his face in her hands. 'There can only be one king, Oliver.' She pointed and looked scornfully at Hugh. 'And he is not it.' She fixed her gaze on Oliver. 'Screw your courage to the sticking place, and we'll not fail.'

Hugh recognised the quote. 'What the hell are you talking about, Beatrice? I'm leaving. This is all getting too weird for me.'

Oliver opened the kitchen door, pushing Beatrice out of the way as he did so. 'Go on then, don't let me detain you.'

She stepped forward and kicked the door closed. 'Nobody is leaving.'

A stunned silence descended. Hugh was now scared, and Oliver had begun to realise that his mother had her own agenda for how the events of this evening would unfold.

She could see in her son's eyes that he did not want to kill Hugh Pitt, but she needed him to. It had all become clear to her, watching Oliver and Hugh face each other and seeing the intense dislike. The old prince about to face the new king. If Oliver killed Hugh, it would place her as the leading actor in the company, and Oliver would be in prison for the rest of his life. Hugh had to die and Oliver had to kill him. It was so obvious and yet when she considered the thought it sounded crazy. There was only one way to bring this stand-off to a conclusion. She stepped towards Hugh. 'I don't think you two have been properly introduced.'

Oliver shot her a frightened look. 'Don't.'

'But it would be rude not to.'

'Don't, now is not the time.'

'On the contrary, now is exactly the time.' Beatrice smiled at Hugh. 'This is Oliver and he is—'

'Mother, no!' The words left Oliver's mouth before he could stop them.

Beatrice looked at Hugh and raised an eyebrow. 'Whoops! I think Oliver has gone and said it for me.'

Both she and Oliver stood and watched Hugh as the reality of Oliver's words began to register.

'You're his mother?'

Beatrice nodded slowly and smiled. 'Hard to believe, isn't it?'

'Then he is ...' Hugh looked from one to the other, unwilling to acknowledge the terrible position that revelation had put him in.

'He's the Shakespeare Killer. I'm afraid he's been a very bad boy.'

Oliver was shaking his head sadly. 'What have you done, Mother? What have you done?'

'Nothing. You said it, not me. The question is, Oliver, what will you do?' She looked again at Hugh and gave him a weak grin. 'This isn't personal, it's just a question of mathematics.'

'Mathematics?'

'Yes. Two into one doesn't go and I'm afraid that means you're expendable. This theatre has belonged to my family for forty years and, with Morris and Richard gone, it's up to me and Oliver to take the reins.'

Oliver looked at his mother, appalled. 'What's happened to

you? You're as mad as me.'

'It must be in the genes.' Beatrice nodded her head towards Hugh. 'He needs to be gone.'

'You stupid woman,' he snapped. 'I told you now wasn't the time. The river is bursting its banks, there will be rescue and flood workers everywhere. I can't get the body away from the house tonight.'

'What body,' asked Hugh, now looking truly terrified. 'You can't be talking about me.'

They both glanced at him with a look of pity. 'Who else?' demanded Beatrice.

Hugh turned and looked out on to the courtyard garden at the back of the house, desperately seeking the door.

Oliver smiled. 'Afraid there's no door, Hugh. Felix has been changing the layout somewhat and the door into the garden is at the side of the house.' He watched as Hugh's eyes tried to find it. 'It's behind me, old chap, you have to go through the front door. Bit inconvenient but apparently when the extension's done there will be French windows from the kitchen. That doesn't really help you now though.'

For a moment Hugh considered trying to smash a window and break out but they were leaded and the panels of glass were tiny. He turned back to face Beatrice and Oliver. 'You need to think about this. Harming me would ruin your life, Beatrice.'

'Not really,' there was a nasty smirk at the corners of her mouth. 'If you were to disappear, who would ever know?'

Oliver was desperately trying to think of a way to avoid killing Hugh. Now wasn't the time or the place; his mother really had gone quite mad … and then it came to him and he began to laugh out loud. He raised his hand at Hugh and pointed. 'Look at your face, you believed every word.' Oliver laughed even harder. 'If only you could see yourself. Bloody hilarious.'

Beatrice did not join in and stared at Oliver as if he had gone mad.

Hugh looked numb. 'This was a joke?'

'Of course,' laughed Oliver. 'And a bloody good one.'

Still Beatrice wasn't laughing. Hugh wasn't sure what to think. Oliver could see his doubt. 'She's bloody good, isn't she. Once she's in character you can't get her out.'

Again Hugh looked desperately at the two of them. 'Beatrice isn't your mother?'

'God, no,' said Oliver disdainfully. 'She once played my mother and I don't think she's moved on. Hasn't lost her sense of humour though.' Oliver looked at Beatrice. 'Have you, darling?'

She looked into his eyes. She could see what he was doing, using everything he knew to stop her killing Hugh. She didn't know why but, for now, she would opt to say nothing. She would let the scene play out and then choose her part.

Slowly the tension drained from the room. After another minute Hugh let out a long breath and looked at them both reproachfully. 'That wasn't very funny.'

'Oh, I think it was,' smiled Beatrice.

'No, it was sick. Especially given what's been going on in Stratford of late.'

'Oliver, here, wanted to see if you could play shock. I have to say you've passed with flying colours.'

Hugh shook his head. 'You pair of absolute bastards, you could have given me a heart attack.'

'We're not that lucky,' sighed Beatrice.

'Another glass of red,' asked Oliver.

'Please, I think I need it after that.' Hugh held up his glass. 'So, if you're not Oliver Lawrence, who are you?'

Chapter 51
Great Neptune's Ocean

Just two hundred yards away from where Hugh Pitt was breathing a deep sigh of relief, Felix Richards was starting to panic. The water that had been three feet below the platform on which he stood was now beginning to lap around his feet. It was rising at an incredible rate. He knew that the island was now barely a foot above the level of the upper river; surely it could not rise any further.

If he had been able to climb up the ladder rings and push off the culvert cover he would have seen an inland sea that had spread across the recreation ground. The bandstand was now an island and the shops and cafes of Waterside were no longer at the side of the water, they were in it.

Fred Williams had never seen anything like it in all his years in and around Stratford. He'd seen flooding before but that was usually after a lot of rain. Not a drop had fallen here, it was surreal. The storm circulating forty odd miles away had turned the Avon into a raging torrent. He turned to Toby. 'This could be an opportunity.'

'How? It's chaos.'

'We can knock on every door, tell people to leave, and enter without a search warrant.'

Toby looked at Fred and smiled. 'Why didn't I think of that?'

'Because you haven't been bending rules as long as I have. It's an art.

There's only one rule you need to remember.'

'What's that?'

Fred winked at Toby. 'Don't get caught.'

'Shall I get uniform to start down Waterside and then up Southern Lane?'

'Yeah, but get them to go all the way to the end of Southern Lane.'

Toby paused. 'But the ground rises after the chain ferry, that part of Old Town never floods.'

'You know that and I know that, but with the water rising so fast folks aren't going to question us. If you get any challenges, remind them that the tin shed rehearsal room was once flooded back in the sixties.'

'Really?'

Fred nodded. 'Yeah, the water tank split.'

Toby couldn't help laughing. 'You're some role model, boss.'

'I know. Now get those uniforms moving. I want them to go into every property and check every room upstairs and down. It's our duty to make sure there is nobody trapped inside.'

Toby turned and strode down Waterside. He was wearing waders and the water was already over a foot deep. If they found Oliver hiding in one of the houses, the pursuit would be a slow one.

Fred turned and headed for the high ground. He was going to check out the area that was free of water. Age and rank had its benefits. As he waded towards the chain ferry he saw a familiar figure standing on the slope opposite the tin shed.

'What you doing here, Whomper?'

'Something's going to happen, I can feel it.'

Fred wanted to dismiss Whomper's fears but he couldn't; he felt the same. 'What's your intuition saying?'

'Oliver's a local, he's going to be on the high ground. Wherever he's stopping it's going to be in a house of someone who knows Stratford. No local would buy a house on the low ground.'

Fred shrugged. 'Estate agents can be pretty persuasive.'

'No, Old Town feels right. Look where all the murders have occurred. It's someone staying close, just slipping in and out. He's been walking amongst us, hiding in plain sight.'

They both stood and looked out across the Avon; it had begun to look like an inland sea.

'Will all great Neptune's ocean wash this blood clean from my hand?'

Whomper nodded. 'It feels like the end, doesn't it.' He shuddered. 'The final scenes of *Macbeth*. Bernard Wood has come to Dunroamin. The king is dead and the reckoning is at hand.'

Fred wanted to say something silly but he couldn't; he felt it too. This night felt like an ending. Everything that had happened over the last few weeks was now concluding. The warm, humid air was full of menace.

Whomper turned to Fred and grabbed his arm. 'Remember Sorrento.'

'But what does it mean, Whomper? All we know is there's a maternity hospital in Moseley Village called Sorrento and Toby was born there. I can't believe that's relevant.'

Whomper shook his head. 'I don't know, I just know it is,' he paused and bit his tongue.

Fred could see he wanted to say more but was holding back. 'Go on, Whomper, say what you're thinking.'

He hesitated for a moment. 'It's Toby, he's the key. No man that's born of woman can kill Macbeth. Whatever you do, stay close to him tonight. I think he's in danger.'

Fred would have liked to laugh off Whomper's warning but he felt it too. He nodded slowly. 'OK, Whomper, I hear you. What are you going to do?'

'Stay around Old Town. I'm going to walk the streets till morning, see what the storm washes out. If I see him again, I'll know him.'

Fred knew that Whomper thought he had met Lawrence on top of Meon Hill. He trusted his instincts; he had been right so many times before. 'OK, Whomper, you do that. Try and get back to me and Toby every hour or so.'

Whomper nodded and turned to go but Fred grabbed his shoulder. 'Be careful out there tonight. I have a bad feeling.'

Whomper winked at Fred. 'I'm the king of careful.' He turned and jogged off up Southern Lane towards Holy Trinity.

Fred watched him go until the shadows of the night swallowed him.

On the island by the Witter lock, Felix looked down. The water in the culvert was up to his knees. How could it be rising so quickly? Panic had set in. Only a couple of hours before he had been desperate for water and now he was about to drown in it. He tried to calm the fear, it was stopping him thinking. What could he do?

His hands were still behind his back. He'd tried to get out but the tape was bound too well. Think, there must be a way out. It was hard to be rational when you were trapped inside a culvert in rising water with no way to escape.

He needed to climb up the hoop ladder but he couldn't do that, he couldn't escape his bonds. It seemed hopeless.

If only his hands were in front of him he could at least hold the rings and try to pull himself up. That was it! He needed to try and lower his hands and step through his bonds, but to do that he would need to lower himself into the cold black water and sit down on the platform. The idea filled him with horror, but if he didn't get out he would die of hypothermia.

The water was now over his knees, if he didn't try something soon it would be too late. He took a deep breath and lowered himself onto the platform. The water was cold but not unbearably so. It came up to his nipples, if he didn't manage to step through soon it would be too late. He leaned back and started to work his bound hands under his bottom and down the back of his thighs. As he leaned back the water lapped up around his neck. This was it, the moment that would decide if he lived or died. It was all up to him.

He pulled his right foot back and felt his heel catch on the tape around his wrists. He was close, very close, but to get his foot through he needed to roll onto his back. Everything in his mind screamed against it; he couldn't put his head under that cold, frigid water. Its inky blackness looked like death and its cold embrace felt like death. And yet, in a tiny corner of his rational mind, he knew this was his only chance. Felix took a deep breath and rolled backwards into the darkness of the Avon and beneath its rising waters.

Chapter 52
Out, Damned Spot

At Trinity Street the tense atmosphere had eased. Hugh now believed that he had been the victim of a very dark practical joke. The second glass of Fleurie had also helped.

'So who are you then? There is something familiar about you.'

Beatrice looked at Oliver. 'You going to tell him?'

It was a challenge, she wanted the truth to come out. Oliver did not.

'Felix Richards.'

Beatrice looked surprised, she hadn't seen that one coming.

'Oh, I think I've heard of you. Weren't you part of Morris' original company?'

'Not until the fifties.'

Hugh nodded. 'Well, you're looking good for your age.'

'Moisturising, it's the key.'

Beatrice couldn't help but laugh. Oliver's lie wouldn't bear any scrutiny. The moment Hugh asked about Felix, he would realise Oliver had lied. Felix was sixty-three, there was no way Oliver could be sixty-three, even if he slept in a vat of moisturiser.

'So, why haven't you been acting?'

Oliver shrugged. 'Been doing voice-overs, far more money in it. Made an absolute fortune and now I want to come back to the theatre.'

Hugh nodded. 'Bit like me. I went to Hollywood and made enough money to retire. It's the reason I can afford to come back to Stratford.'

'That and to rebuild your career,' said Beatrice.

'That's harsh, especially coming from an actor who's been riding on the coat-tails of her husband for thirty odd years.'

Oliver could see Beatrice's hackles beginning to rise; he needed to calm the mood. 'Wow, you two are so competitive. Let's forget the theatre for a while and relax.'

They both nodded and Hugh put down his glass. The evening wasn't going the way he had hoped but he wasn't about to give in; the thought of Beatrice in his bed was too much to let go without a fight.

'Could I use your toilet?'

Beatrice was about to say no – she didn't want Hugh escaping – but Oliver pointed towards a door in the corner of the kitchen. 'There's a downstairs one in there.'

'Great, thanks.' Hugh headed over and closed the door.

Beatrice turned angrily to Oliver. 'What the hell are you doing? We need to kill him.'

Oliver held a finger up to his mouth. 'Quiet, he'll hear you.'

'I don't care,' snapped Beatrice. 'He needs to die.'

'That may be true but now isn't the time.'

'Why so picky? You've killed plenty of others.'

Oliver gripped his mother firmly by the shoulders. 'Listen to me, this can't happen tonight. I have a plan and killing Hugh Pitt isn't part of it.'

'Well it's part of my plan.' She didn't reveal that blaming Oliver for it was the other part.

Oliver pushed her back against the wall and pinned her there, his face just inches from hers. 'Listen, you stupid woman. If we kill him now there is no way we can get rid of his body. The water is rising. I had a police officer knock on my door earlier this evening warning me of flooding. We could be evacuated or even flooded and then what would we do?'

'This part of Old Town never floods,' said Beatrice.

'Maybe but it won't stop us being evacuated. Can't you see? The police will use this as an excuse to enter every house in town. A body in here will ruin everything I've been working towards. I can't let you do that.'

'Are you threatening me?'

Oliver grabbed his mother by the throat. 'Does this answer your question?'

She would have answered if she could. 'Now, shut up and do as you're told or you will be on my list. Do you understand?'

Beatrice did understand and pretended to agree. She nodded and then gasped as Oliver released her throat. Her agreement was all part of an act. She was now more convinced than ever that everything would have to come to a bloody conclusion tonight.

The lock shot back on the toilet door and Oliver moved quickly. He held up the bottle. 'Another glass of wine, Hugh?'

Hugh nodded. 'Why not, I've made some room.'

He chuckled and Oliver joined in. Beatrice leaned back against the kitchen counter glaring at both of them. Oliver had lost his courage and she would have to take matters into her own hands.

She watched Hugh take a large glug of Fleurie, its dark redness reminding her of blood. She felt her own blood run hot. Now was the moment to screw her courage to the sticking place. If Oliver would not do it, she had to.

There was a carving knife lying on the sink drainer. She moved without hesitation, grabbed the knife and plunged it into Hugh's chest as he was taking another sip of his wine. She noticed a momentary look of surprise, but he had no further time to react as the knife slid into his chest. She felt it scrape a rib and shuddered, but the thrust was good and went deep.

Hugh's glass fell to the floor, splashing the deep red wine across it. Seconds later it was joined by an even darker red liquid. Beatrice saw the look of shock turn to surprise then betrayal on Hugh's face. She tried to pull out the knife; she didn't know why, it just seemed like the right thing to do. She tugged but the blade was caught between two ribs. She tried again but still could not shift it.

She had, however, opened the wound and snagged a blood vessel. A spurt of warmth pulsed onto her face, followed a moment later by another. It was running down her blouse. She was covered in it.

Hugh tried to speak. 'What have you done ... I ...' A trickle formed at the corner of his mouth and drowned his words.

The idea of killing had seemed so easy to Beatrice, but now the reality was proving overwhelming. She looked down at her hands and saw the warm sticky liquid snaking between her fingers, rivers of guilt through which she now swam. She tried to rub it off but her blouse was covered in Hugh's blood and her hand became a bloody smear of accusation.

Hugh slid down the wall and sat on the floor of the kitchen clutching his chest, feebly trying to stem the flow. His eyes went from his wound to Beatrice and back and, as they did so, Oliver could see the life fading from them. His mother backed away from the bloody sculpture she had created.

This was not the first time she had killed and this new murder released memories she had tried to repress for so many years. She had reopened Pandora's box and she could never close it. As she backed away, sliding across the floor on her bottom, she left a trail of blood. Hugh Pitt's blood. She was whimpering like a wounded animal.

It had all happened so quickly. Oliver hadn't time to react before she plunged the knife into Hugh's chest and by then it was too late. Everything he had worked so hard to achieve lay in ruins. 'Why did you do that? You've ruined everything.'

Beatrice didn't look at him, her eyes were transfixed on Hugh. His eyes fluttered and closed. The blood still flowed from his body but the spurts had slowed to a trickle. The life force was leaving him and lay across the floor of the kitchen, a sea of dreams that would never be realised.

Oliver stood there in shock. Soon there would be knocking

and if he didn't answer, the door would be forced open. The police and the rescue service would ensure everybody was evacuated before the town became cut off.

Hugh's limp body slumped over as the final trickle of blood fell from his open mouth.

Beatrice looked up in panic. 'Help him, you have to help him.'

'It's too late for that. You've killed him.'

Beatrice tried to stand but her feet slipped on the bloodied floor and she fell down, face first, into the pool that she had created. In a panic, she struggled to get up but her hands slipped on the warm, sticky tiles. She looked like she was trying to swim her way out of a nightmare. She struggled onto her back and began to scream.

Oliver bent down and slapped her hard across the face; it had the desired effect. He sat her up and held her by the shoulders, her face just inches from his. 'Look what you've done. I told you not to, I can't make this right.'

Beatrice wanted to explain but she could taste Hugh's blood on her lips, warm and metallic; the tang of murder. She had tasted it before but never like this.

'Why did you do it?'

'I had to. I did it for us.'

'You did it for you, Mother. It's always been about you.'

Beatrice wanted to argue but she couldn't. Killing Hugh had breached a dam of memories she had built years ago and the guilt ran over and around her. She was drowning in her secrets and now her son would see them. Her dream was over. She had thought this was a stepping stone towards it, but no, this was the stepping stone from which she would fall and drown in the waters of her guilt.

Oliver squeezed her arms harder. He wanted to hurt her, rouse her from the shock, but she was too far gone. 'You have ruined everything. All my plans, my future. Wasn't once enough for you?'

276   Sleep No More

The accusation cut deep and Beatrice looked up at him. 'I did it for you. I tried to give you a future.'

'What,' he looked over at Hugh's body. 'This?'

Beatrice shook her head. 'No, not this. Before, when you were young.'

'What does that mean? It makes no sense.'

'Your father ... He wasn't an easy man ...' she said, desperately rubbing her hands. 'Out, damned spot, out, I say! Who would have thought the old man had so much blood in him.'

'He wasn't old.'

Beatrice locked her glazed eyes with his, uncomprehending. The words had tumbled from her memory, unbidden. She continued to writhe, rubbing her hands and legs, trying to wipe away the blood but only succeeding in spreading it further.

'So much blood.'

'Forget the blood, what about my father? What did you mean?' demanded Oliver.

'He was a difficult man, I did it for you. To give you a future.'

'Did what?'

Beatrice was distracted, lost in the horror that lay before her and the memories it had set free.

Oliver shook her hard. 'What did you do to my father?'

'He was depressed, lost in a well of self-pity. He was no good for you.'

'That's not true, he was a great dad.'

'He was hopeless, he couldn't cope with life. If it wasn't for me we would have been homeless.' There was anger in her words.

'He was a great actor.'

'He was, but he was terrible at life, everything became too much. He was dragging us down with him. If he hadn't died ...' Her eyes filled with tears at the memories filling her brain, consuming her.

'You can't blame yourself. Nobody made him jump in front of

that train. He took himself out there and did it. Chose to die alone.'

Beatrice began to shiver. She was barely keeping it together. He could see in her eyes that she wanted to say more. 'What is it you're not telling me?'

The shiver became a shaking and Beatrice began to weep. The weight of the secrets was crushing her, she had held it for too long. 'The day he died, he wasn't alone.'

Oliver studied her face. He knew what was to come would be terrible, but he had to hear it. He gave her a gentle nod, permission to unburden herself.

'I was there.'

The words hit him like a blow but, somehow, he remained silent.

'I followed Richard in Morris' car. He had walked up to the old bridge and, when I got there, he was sitting on the edge.'

'I know. That's where he jumped from,' said Oliver, choking back a sob.

Beatrice shook her head. 'No, it wasn't like that.' She looked back down at the pool of blood in which she sat. 'So much blood.'

'Forget the damn blood! What about my dad?'

She looked up and there was guilt in her eyes, a guilt that no amount of tears would ever wash away. 'He was sitting on the parapet and he was going to jump.'

'He did.'

She gave an almost imperceptible shake of her head. 'No, he didn't.'

'But—'

Beatrice held up a bloody hand to silence him. 'I walked over to where he sat. He was going to jump, I knew it. I stood quietly behind him, waiting. If he jumped it would be over, we would be free.'

His mother's words shattered everything he had believed since childhood. He didn't speak, he couldn't.

'I waited. And then I heard it. The train was coming. A few moments later I saw steam bellowing from its funnel. Surely, now he would jump.' Beatrice was struggling to get the words out, why wouldn't she. She had held the truth inside her like a stolen memory for so long. Every secret she held was escaping from her. Every word was agony.

'I called out his name. "Richard." He turned to me and I saw it in his eyes.'

'What did you see, Mother?'

Beatrice crumpled. 'Hope.'

Oliver didn't understand. *Why would his father have hope in his eyes? He killed himself.*

'I saw it, Oliver. I saw it and ...' she paused as uncontrolled sobs shuddered through her body. He waited as she gathered herself. 'I saw hope. He wasn't going to jump.' Another round of sobs. 'I reached out to him and—'

Oliver softened a little. 'You tried to save him?'

Beatrice slowly shook her head. 'I pushed him!'

The room swam and Oliver thought he was going to fall. He gripped the table and held himself steady as he tried to comprehend what she had said. He looked down at where she sat on the floor, bathed in the blood of Hugh Pitt, drowning in a sea of her own blind ambition. He now knew where his madness had its origin: he was his mother's son. 'You pushed him?'

His words hung in the warm, deadly air of the room. He watched his question permeate his mother's consciousness. She turned slowly and looked up at him. She tilted, her eyes unfocused, lost in a memory she had tried to suppress for so long.

'Pushed?' This time his tone was firmer, edged with anger.

'Pushed.' She nodded, her voice barely audible.

'You killed my father.'

'He wasn't going to jump. I just ...' she trailed off into an incoherent ramble, rubbing and rubbing her hands on her clothing. But this much blood could never be wiped away.

'Just what? Just wanted to make sure?'

She nodded. 'Yes. I saw it in his eyes, he'd changed his mind. I couldn't face it.'

And now Oliver fully understood. His mind had fought against believing what his mother had told him but now it was horrifyingly clear. His mother had killed his father. All these years, all those lies. Everything he had ever believed had been built on sand. He slumped down next to his mother and surveyed the carnage of the room. All this blood could never be washed away before the knock on the door came.

The police had been knocking on doors in College Lane. In just a few minutes they would be knocking on his. If he didn't answer, they would force their way in. It was over.

'Why?'

It was a simple question and yet the reason was so deeply rooted and complex that he didn't expect an answer.

Beatrice slowly shook her head. 'We needed our lives back. Richard was drowning and taking us with him. It was for the best.'

Perhaps it was the way in which she said it, dismissing the killing of his father as an expedient act. Whatever it was, he found himself leaning forward and pulling the knife from Hugh's chest. The blade ground against a rib but Oliver was strong and forced it free.

Beatrice gave a frightened shriek as Oliver turned quickly towards her and swept the blade across her throat. For a moment there was a look of surprise on her face that seemed oddly comical but then a red line appeared. She tried to speak but her vocal chords had been severed. The line became a waterfall, filled with hope for a life she would never attain.

He held her in his arms and watched the woman that had given him life fade from this world. All his plans had come to nothing.

He was now truly alone, a self-made orphan. He felt his mother shudder and knew it was over.

He sat there for several minutes watching as her blood spread slowly across the floor and mingled with Hugh's. A confluence of two lives; rivers that would never reach the sea.

How had it come to this? He leaned his head back against the cupboard and allowed his mother to slip down onto his lap. Her head flopped back at an unnatural angle that life would never have permitted.

The words came floating from his lips, like a memory that had waited a lifetime to be spoken. He had said them before, many times, but they weren't real then; the meaning was all part of an act. Now they were real and, for the first time, he properly understood them.

'She should have died hereafter.
There would have been a time for such a word.
Tomorrow and tomorrow and tomorrow
Creeps in this petty pace from day to day
To the last syllable of recorded time,
And all our yesterdays have lighted fools
The way to dusty death. Out, out brief candle!
Life's but a walking shadow, a poor player
That struts and frets his hour upon the stage
And then is heard no more. It is a tale
Told by an idiot, full sound and fury,
Signifying nothing.'

The dream was ended. There would be no final curtain, no encore. There was nothing that could ever make this right. He shoved his mother from his lap and watched her slide onto the floor. He was done with her, done with everything. He began to cry.

His self-pity was disturbed by a firm knock on the door.

'Police. You need to leave the premises. Imminent flood danger.'

Oliver scrambled to his feet, slipping on the sticky, blood-drenched floor as he did so.

The knock came again. 'Police. Is anyone in there?'

Oliver walked down the hallway and saw himself in the mirror, covered in his mother's blood. He couldn't open the door looking like this. 'Sorry, I'm in the bath. What do you want?'

'You have to leave, sir. Imminent danger of flooding.'

Oliver knew that was a lie; this part of Old Town was way too high above the river to flood. 'OK, I'll dry off and come down in about ten minutes.'

There was a momentary hesitation as the policeman considered his answer. 'Very well, sir. Make your way to the Shakespeare Memorial Fountain at the end of Rother Street. Give your name to the authorities there.'

'OK,' said Oliver. He waited to make sure that the policeman had moved away. He had one thing left to do before he … before he what? He hadn't considered that. Died … Escaped? He had no answer. All he knew was that he wanted to save Felix, to try and rescue one good thing from this terrible night.

When the knocking receded, he quietly opened the door and peeked out. The police were at the far end of trinity Street. He slipped out into the night. He could see residents being escorted from their houses on College Lane by the fire brigade.

Hugging the fence, he made his way into the graveyard of Holy Trinity and crept down the left-hand side of the church until he could see the river. He heard it long before he saw it. The Avon he knew was gone, replaced by an angry surging monster that was no longer confined by the riverbanks.

The recreation ground had long since disappeared beneath an inland sea that surged up the banks of the old tramway in the distance. The water roaring through the weir sounding like a wounded animal. The island that stood between the Witter Lock and the weir was now just a small dot surrounded by raging water. Felix was beyond his help.

He slumped back against the nearest grave and slid down it, suddenly wearier than he had ever felt before. For once he was helpless, unable to control the series of events his mother had unleashed. He started to cry. Tears for his father, tears for his stolen childhood, but more tears of frustration. All he had done had been for nothing. There would be no return to the stage and his name would never be uttered in the same breath as Sir Morris Oxford or Sir Miles Tennyson. He wouldn't even be a footnote in the history of the RSC.

Less than a hundred yards from where Oliver sat sobbing, Whomper was standing in the gateway to the churchyard of Holy Trinity. As he approached the wall, he could hear the roaring of the river as it cascaded over the weir by Lucy's Mill.

The water was higher than he had ever seen it, and he had lived in Stratford all his life. The steps that led up from the hollow were half covered by the inky black water; it was no longer a hollow but an inlet. Anything below the tin shed rehearsal theatre would be underwater.

In the distance he could see the boathouse had become an island too. He turned back and walked along the path through the graveyard that ran alongside the river. He would circle around Holy Trinity and head down towards Lucy's Mill Bridge. He knew he wouldn't be able to get across but he wanted to see just how high the water was.

As he approached the wall at the south end of the graveyard, he saw someone sitting against a gravestone, sobbing. He stepped closer. In the dark, he could see the figure was covered in something; as he got nearer, he realised what it was. His senses were begging him to turn and run but Whomper ignored them. 'You OK?'

The crying man did not look up.

'Are you OK?'

The crying man slowly raised his head and Whomper recognised him instantly. He said nothing and waited as Oliver wiped his bloody hand across his face.

'Not really.'

'Can I help?'

Oliver laughed. 'I doubt it.'

'Do you need a doctor?'

Oliver looked down at his bloody clothes. 'It looks like it, doesn't it.'

'Not your blood then?' Whomper cursed inwardly at the stupidity of his own comment.

'No,' he shook his head. 'Not my blood.'

There was an awkward silence; how could he respond to that? 'Do you want me to get help? You could be injured.'

'Not me, I'm unkillable.'

'No man that's born of woman?' The words were out of his mouth before he could stop them and he saw a flicker of recognition in Oliver's eyes.

'You're not Macduff, are you?'

Whomper wasn't but now he knew who was. He started to back away. 'I'm going for help.'

Oliver watched him turn and begin to jog towards Old Town. For a big man he moved well. He considered leaving but what was the point? The dream was ended. He would wait and see how the night played out. The final curtain would soon fall.

Chapter 53
The Final Curtain

Whomper's jog had turned into a sprint as he charged down Chapel Street. He had to get to Guild Street, to the station. As he crossed the road at the end of Ely Street he saw Toby walking towards him. 'Toby.'

Toby looked up and smiled. 'Running. Are you OK, Whomper?'

Whomper grabbed him by the shoulders. 'It's Oliver Lawrence, he's by the church.'

The smile vanished from Toby's face. 'Are you sure?'

'Yes. It's him.'

'Where?'

'Back of Holy Trinity. He's leaning on a grave, near the wall by the weir.'

'OK. Go and get Fred and tell him where I'm going.'

Toby started to move away but Whomper grabbed his arm. 'You can't go alone, Toby. He's covered in blood. Something terrible has happened.'

'Is it his?'

'No.'

'Get Fred, I'm going.'

Whomper held him firmly. 'Sorrento. It's you!'

Toby looked confused. 'I haven't got time for this, Whomper. Go and get Fred.' He broke from Whomper's grip and sprinted off down Chapel Street towards Holy Trinity.

Whomper watched him go, then turned and ran as hard as he could towards Guild Street.

Toby turned the corner of Chapel Street onto Old Town to be

confronted by lots of residents that had been displaced by the rising waters. The fire brigade were taking names and addresses in the Memorial Gardens.

As he ran past, a fire officer called out to him. 'You can't go down there, sir.'

'Police,' shouted Toby without breaking stride. He was soon out of sight as the road curved into Trinity Close. He realised his heart was beating far faster than the running justified. This was the moment.

For a second, he questioned whether he should be confronting a serial killer on his own. Thank God he'd taken his waders off. He knew he couldn't wait for reinforcements; it was now or never.

As he rounded the corner of Holy Trinity he saw a man sitting down, slumped against a gravestone. He slowed to a walk and only stopped when he was a few yards away. He stood for a moment in silence, unsure of what to say.

Oliver raised his bloodstained face and smiled. 'Ah, DC Toby Marlowe.'

'You know me?'

'I have a TV. You've been on it quite a lot lately.'

'And you're Oliver Lawrence.' It seemed a stupid thing to say. The man in front of him was covered in blood, none of it his. Who else would he be?

'You'll go far with deductive skills like that.' A weak smile tickled the corner of Oliver's mouth. 'Is this the bit where you tell me I'm under arrest?'

'I suppose it is.'

'Seems a bit underwhelming, doesn't it. I was hoping for a rooftop chase or a shoot-out.' Oliver looked genuinely disappointed.

'Oliver Lawrence, I arrest you under ...'

Oliver held up his hand which was smeared with the blood of his mother and Hugh Pitt. Toby wasn't to know that though, not yet.

'I'm afraid I can't come quietly, it's not in my nature.' He looked Toby up and down. 'I don't suppose you've even got any cuffs, have you?'

Toby winced; he hadn't. 'I have reinforcements on the way.'

'Ah, Birnam Wood has come to Dunsinane.'

'It has.' Toby took another step closer.

'Hold it there, DC Marlowe. I have no wish to hurt you, it would be pointless now.'

'Then come quietly.'

Oliver shook his head. 'I'm afraid I can't do that, I'm not cut out for prison.'

Toby looked closely at Oliver. He was a powerfully built man and he doubted he could take him in a struggle. He knew he didn't want to find out. He had to play for time, hope that Whomper would get Fred. 'We can't just stay here all night.'

Oliver laughed. 'No, that wouldn't work, would it.'

'Whose blood is that?'

Oliver looked down at his stained clothes. 'Good question.' He pointed at his chest. 'This is probably my mother's. This bit on my trousers, that's Hugh Pitt's. I slipped in it when I pulled the knife out of his chest.'

'I see. And did you put the knife there?'

Oliver grinned. 'What a quaint way to describe a stabbing,' he chuckled. 'No, DC Marlowe, I didn't put it there. My mother did.'

'Lady Beatrice Oxford?'

'I know, took me by surprise as well. You just don't expect your mother to do a thing like that, do you?'

'Why would she kill Hugh Pitt?'

'You know, I've asked myself that question. I've a horrible feeling she was going to blame it on me.'

'But why would she kill Hugh, why not kill you? They were going to head up the new season.'

Oliver shrugged. 'Loose ends. I was a loose end. Kill Hugh and blame me, job done.'

'Where are the bodies?'

'You're the detective, work it out.'

Toby made a decision. He wasn't certain it was the right one but he moved to a gravestone a few yards from Oliver and sat down. 'Why?'

Oliver looked out across the raging waters of the Avon. 'Why do you think?'

'Revenge.'

Oliver nodded. 'Go on.'

'You tried to only kill those that ruined your career but then you got careless.'

'Yes, the policeman's wife was unfortunate. Still, accidents happen.'

'And the hospital. Can you imagine what could have happened?'

'It was only a wing, it's not like I set the whole place on fire. If there hadn't been so much police protection, I could have just popped in and killed him.'

'So it's our fault, is it?'

'No, I think that one's on me.' Oliver looked out at the raging torrent. 'Would you do me a favour, DC Marlowe?'

'No.'

'At least consider it.'

Toby eyed Oliver coldly. 'What is it?'

'See that little island over there by the Witter Lock?'

'Yes.'

'There's a culvert in the middle of it and Felix Richards is in there, tied up.'

Toby looked across the river at what remained of the island. 'You can't be serious.'

'Afraid so. I didn't expect the flooding to be so bad. I didn't really want to kill Felix, just put him out of harm's way while I finished my little project. Now ...' He looked towards the island and shook his head. 'I fear it may be too late.'

'So, he's not your accomplice?'

'God, no. He only found out what was going on yesterday. I've been using his house without him knowing.' Oliver had decided to clear Felix's name. Now the game was up, there didn't seem any point in taking him down with him.

'You want us to try and save him?'

'If it's not too late. Him drowning would be pointless now.'

'I'll see if the fire service has a rescue boat.'

Oliver rose wearily to his feet. 'Well, DC Marlowe, it's been lovely meeting you.'

Toby stood up too. 'You're not going anywhere, Lawrence.'

Oliver looked him up and down. 'You don't seriously believe you can bring me in on your own, do you?'

Toby didn't but he was certainly going to give it a try. 'Oliver Lawrence, I arrest you under—'

'Whatever,' said Oliver, slowly backing away towards the wall as he did so.

Fred and Whomper came charging around the corner of Holy Trinity with Mel behind them.

Oliver looked up and chuckled. 'Ah, the cavalry, just in time.'

Fred stepped past Toby. 'Oliver Lawrence, finally.'

'Nice to meet you, DS Williams. You're not as fat as you look on TV.'

Fred moved menacingly towards Oliver.

'Aren't you going to read me my rights?'

'Scumbags don't have any.'

'Fred!'

The warning came from Mel Townsend. 'We do this by the numbers, Fred.'

'You count all the numbers you want, Mel, this bastard is

having some.'

Oliver drew himself up to his full height and faced Fred.

'Remember Sorrento, Toby,' said Whomper.

Oliver looked at Toby. 'Does that mean something to you?'

'I'm not sure.'

Without warning, Toby sprang forward but Oliver was ready. He spun on his heel and, in two strides, jumped up and over the wall and landed in the meadow on the other side.

'Get after him,' shouted Fred.

Toby sprinted towards the wall and followed Oliver over. As he landed, he saw him running towards the weir by Lucy's Lock and realised, to his horror, that there was a rope strung between two posts above it. It had been left by a maintenance crew that worked there a month back. Oliver was going to try and get over to the island using the rope.

'Stop, you'll never make it,' he cried.

Oliver looked back, a crazed smile on his moonlit face. 'Course I will. I'm unkillable.'

By now, both Fred and Whomper were over the wall and running down the sloping grass bank.

Oliver reached the edge and, without breaking stride, leapt out into the raging floodwaters and caught the rope. He swung there for a moment.

If his plan had been to get across the weir, the power of the current had soon disabused him of it. He desperately tried to pull himself across but it was all he could do to hang on. He had put himself in a terrible position.

Toby approached the edge of the weir. 'Come back!'

Oliver smiled at him. 'Don't think I can.'

'Try,' screamed Toby.

Oliver edged his hands across the rope, moved to within four feet of Toby and then stopped. He was breathing heavily.

Toby leaned out, arm outstretched. 'Grab my hand.'

Oliver just hung there, staring at him.

'Grab my hand.'

Oliver shook his head.

As Toby reached out he could feel the cold frothing waters of the Avonpulling at him and soaking his clothes. It felt like the river was angry with him, trying to drag him in and over the weir. He tried to pull back but realised with a sickening jolt that he was slipping towards the river. He let out a little yelp of fear. He was going in.

A pair of hands grabbed his ankles and started pulling him back from the water's grasp.

'What the hell do you think you're doing,' snarled Fred. 'Let him drown.'

Back on the bank, Toby scrambled to his feet. 'No, I want to take him in.'

'It's too dangerous.'

'You'd better grab my ankles properly then.'

'Jesus,' cried Fred. He dropped down onto the bank and grabbed one of Toby's legs.

Toby reached out to Oliver. 'Take my hand, I'll get you out.'

Oliver looked back at him dispassionately.

'Take my hand,' Toby repeated.

Oliver shook his head. 'It's too late for that.' He looked down at his shirt, now washed clean of the blood of his mother and Hugh Pitt, and began to laugh.

'Seems great Neptune's ocean can wash this blood from my hands.'

Toby lunged further into the river and grabbed Oliver's left arm. 'Take my hand. I'll get you out.'

Oliver let go of the rope with his left hand and grabbed Toby.

His grip was so strong it made Toby wince. He tried to call out to Fred but the boiling waters filled his mouth. He turned his head back to Oliver and spat the water out downstream. 'Pull us out,

Fred, for Christ's sake.'

Fred began to pull but Oliver still held tightly to the rope with his right hand.

'Let go,' screamed Toby. 'Let go of the rope.'

Slowly Oliver began to shake his head. 'No.'

'If I let go, you'll drown.'

'No, you can't kill me. No man that's born of woman can kill me.'

Whomper, who was holding on to Toby's other ankle, looked at Fred and then called out, 'Sorrento, Toby. Sorrento.'

Toby heard Whomper's call over the roar of the river and for a moment didn't understand it.

'Sorrento.'

Toby looked at Oliver. What had he said? *No man that's born of woman can kill me.* As he clung to Oliver's hand, he saw the look in his eyes; he wasn't afraid.

He gasped as it all became clear. He realised that everything in this case had brought him to this moment; placed Oliver's life in his hands. Oliver really believed he was Macbeth.

'If I let you go, you'll die. I'm not born of woman.'

A moment of confusion passed across Oliver's face. 'We are all born of woman,' he cried.

'Not me. I was born by C-section at the Sorrento Maternity Hospital.'

Fred turned his head and looked at Whomper. 'I don't believe it, you were right. How did you know?'

Whomper shrugged. 'The man's crazy.'

Oliver was now staring at Toby with resignation; he forced a smile. 'Macduff?'

Toby nodded.

Oliver let go of the rope.

Toby felt his full weight wrench at his arm, threatening to dislocate it. He gripped Oliver's left hand as hard as he could but they had been in the brutally cold waters for nearly two minutes now and their strength was ebbing.

'Get us out,' he screamed.

Whomper and Fred started to pull them from the raging torrent.

As they did, Toby felt Oliver's grip begin to loosen. Toby gripped harder.

'What are you doing, I can save you.'

Oliver shook his head. 'Lay on, Macduff, and damned be him that first cries "Hold! Enough!"' With that he wriggled his hand free of Toby's and was sucked backwards over the weir. He stared into Toby's eyes as he disappeared beneath the boiling waters.

Toby felt the strong arms of Fred and Whomper dragging him out of the river and onto dry land. He slumped there for a moment in disbelief. Oliver was gone.

Chapter 54
The Curtain Call

As the sun illuminated the inland sea that passed for Waterside and the recreation ground, Felix Richards was rescued. He had managed to step through his bonds and pull himself up the ladder to a point where his head was pressed against the underside of the culvert cover. Climbing the ladder had saved his life; the water was up to his chest. He was seriously hypothermic but, apart from that, he was fine; only the mental scars would take time to heal.

Felix was never charged with anything connected to the deaths. On the night he died, Oliver had told Toby that Felix knew nothing about his murders. Fred didn't completely believe it and nor did Toby, but with Oliver gone there would be no trial. And to be honest they all just wanted to forget about the last few terrible weeks. It was finally over.

It had taken four days for the river to subside enough for the police to send in divers. They searched the Avon past Welford and on down to Barton and Bidford but no sign of Oliver's body was found. With a surge like that it could be floating down the Severn, headed for the Bristol Channel, and from there to the sea.

Like a bad memory, Oliver had been washed clean away but he had left a mark that would always remain. So much blood that time could never erase the memory of those terrible weeks of late spring and early summer in 1972. Not the Avon in full flood nor all Neptune's seas.

Three weeks after his rescue, Felix Richards visited the Post Office in Old Town and retrieved his journal from Ting Hu's safe. He took it home to Trinity Street where he burned it in the fireplace, believing his memory was the only witness to Oliver

Lawrence's revenge.

There was also the copy that Ting had made because ... well, you never know!

The End

Acknowledgements

I've gone even darker in this book than I did in Put Out the Light, so, once again, a big thanks to my wonderful editor Samantha Brownley for going there with me. We made a few changes along the way and I think we walked the line well, balancing the darker elements whilst still retaining the humour.

As always, a big thank you to Will Templeton. He's an asset to The Bullington Press team, and his proofreading and setting out are immaculate.

We've got another great cover from the legend that is Pete Adlington. I'm sure you'll agree that Pete has really captured the essence of Oliver Lawrence!

A great big thank you to the lovely Laura Lees for her endless charm and PR support.

Thanks again to Dave Brownley for promoting the books and always being on hand when I need him.

And, finally, to the boss. Lou is my first reader and biggest champion, even though my writing gets in the way of other things. What a woman!